T0273586

KARAOKE
QUEEN

ALSO BY DOMINIC LIM

All the Right Notes

KARAOKE QUEEN

DOMINIC LIM

FOREVER

NEW YORK BOSTON

Forever
Hachette Book Group
1290 Avenue of the Americas, New York, NY 10104
read-forever.com
@readforeverpub

First Edition: September 2024

Forever is an imprint of Grand Central Publishing. The Forever name and logo are registered trademarks of Hachette Book Group, Inc.

The publisher is not responsible for websites (or their content) that are not owned by the publisher.

The Hachette Speakers Bureau provides a wide range of authors for speaking events. To find out more, go to hachettespeakersbureau.com or email HachetteSpeakers@hbgusa.com.

Forever books may be purchased in bulk for business, educational, or promotional use. For information, please contact your local bookseller or the Hachette Book Group Special Markets Department at special.markets@hbgusa.com.

Library of Congress Cataloging-in-Publication Data

Names: Lim, Dominic, 1974- author.
Title: Karaoke queen / Dominic Lim.
Description: First edition. | New York : Forever, 2024.
Identifiers: LCCN 2024008266 | ISBN 9781538725405 (trade paperback) |
    ISBN 9781538725412 (ebook)
Subjects: LCGFT: Gay fiction. | Romance fiction. | Novels.
Classification: LCC PS3612.I457 K37 2024 | DDC 813/.6—dc23/eng/20240223
LC record available at https://lccn.loc.gov/2024008266

ISBNs: 9781538725405 (trade paperback), 9781538725412 (ebook)

Printed in the United States of America

LSC-C

Printing 1, 2024

To Mom,
Thank you for always believing in me.

AUTHOR'S NOTE

Karaoke Queen is a celebration of drag and queer love, but it also contains some sensitive subject matter. Please take care of yourself if any of the following topics are difficult for you.

Content Warnings: alcohol usage; homophobic language; anti-LGBTQ+ violence.

DO NOT OPEN.

That means you, Rex.

Dear Rex,

I know you miss everything that's in here. And I know you want to take it all out again because it used to make you happy.

But before you do, just remember why you hid it all away.

Your father was right. This stuff will only get you into trouble. It already did. You got hurt—badly.

It's better to keep it all inside. Where it will always be safe.

—R

CHAPTER 1

I USED TO LOVE GOING TO KARAOKE BARS.

I'm Filipino, after all. And when you're Filipino, singing is just a basic fact of life. In the shower, in the car, at church. And at some point during every party, the karaoke machine gets dragged out of storage, and everyone sings—from the oldest lolas all the way down to the youngest kids.

I was that kid once: the one who started singing as soon as I could start forming sentences. Even before I could say anything that made sense, I was babbling along to any songs I heard on TV. As I got older, if there was a microphone anywhere in sight, you can bet I was grasping for it, wanting to pour all my young heart into the thing. My mom attributed that to being her child. She was on a teleserye—a Filipino soap opera—for two whole episodes. So, of course, I was destined to be a star in the making.

Every now and then, I still feel that pull to perform. In fact, as I watch the person currently taking his turn during Pink Unicorn's karaoke night, all I want to do is take the mic away from him.

Although the main reason for that is because he's absolutely terrible.

"He does know that 'Hips Don't Lie' has more than one note in it, right?" Kat Sniegowski, my co-worker and best friend, asks as she leans in to be heard over the music. Her curly hair, smelling of apples and honey, tickles my cheek.

I laugh. "And if his hips are supposed to be talking, they're not saying much."

"Hmm." Kat focuses on the singer. "It's too bad he's just standing there like a rock. He's got a pretty sweet ass."

"He's, like, twenty years older than you are, Kat."

"Don't be so judgy. You're supposed to be encouraging me to get out there again. I'm nursing a broken heart."

Kat's just gotten dumped by her most current boyfriend, a slam poet named Sal. And unlike most of the other guys she's dated, this one lasted a long time, at least for her. They dated for almost three whole months before they broke up.

"I'm here to listen to you sing," I say. "Not help you find another boyfriend."

"I thought you were going to sing with me."

"I said I'd *come* with you, not *sing* with you. I'm just here for moral support. I told you, I don't do karaoke." I look down at the table and mumble to myself, "Not anymore, at least."

"What was that?"

"Nothing." My eyes close as I try to block the Shakira-drone out for a bit.

I'm surprised I let Kat convince me to go out with her. I generally tend not to set foot in karaoke bars anymore. Not since high school, when a really bad experience made me wary of ever finding myself in any sort of performance-like venue again. Places like this just bring back all the memories I'd rather forget.

Not that I have anything against the Pink Unicorn itself, which is actually a cultural landmark. It's been around since the 1940s, making it the oldest gay bar not only in Oakland, but in the entire Bay Area. A metal sculpture of the eponymous unicorn hangs outside the front door. It's so old now that the pink color has faded and the horn has fallen off, so it's basically just an off-white horse.

Inside, the décor has stayed unchanged for decades. Posters touting old bands from the eighties and nineties hang on the walls, a scuffed-up pool table and vintage *Pac-Man* arcade game show years of use, and a jukebox in the corner still carries classics like Wham! and Nirvana. Adjoining the bar area is a room with a floor large enough for dancing. On karaoke nights, tables and chairs are set out for people to sit and watch others step onto the raised platform stage to sing. Just like we're doing now, along with the few other people with us in the bar.

Hips-Are-Not-Fly-Guy finally finishes the Shakira selection and, for some reason, decides to end his performance with one massive pelvic thrust before getting offstage.

"There it is," Kat says. "Hot."

I snort and take another sip of my beer.

She flips through the threadbare binder on our table. "What should I do for my song? No Jefferson Starship in here. I could sing some Fleetwood Mac, maybe. Or Janis Joplin? What do you think?"

"You really want to know what I think? That we should ditch this place soon and get pie at Denny's."

A microphone whines as it's turned back on by the karaoke host. "Okay, next up is Jenny. Is Jenny here? Singing Nicki Minaj?"

Jenny, a tiny East Asian woman wearing a purple hoodie, goes up to the stage. She struggles for what seems like a very long time to get the mic down to her height. I keep expecting the karaoke host to help her, but it looks like he's not paying attention to what's going on. I can't tell because I can't see him very well. The multicolored strobe lights keep shining into my eyes anytime I look toward that part of the room. It's making me a little dizzy.

The mic stand finally plunges down to its lowest level with a *thunk*. Just the right height for Jenny. A familiar double-time bass line in the karaoke track sounds through the speakers, Jenny pulls back her hood, and—*WHACK!*

"Whoa!" Kat and I say simultaneously as Jenny slaps her own butt before rapping the lyrics to "Anaconda."

Kat scribbles something onto one of the request slips from the plastic cup on our table. "Okay, I think I know what I want to sing. Could you bring this up to the KJ?"

"The what?"

"The karaoke jockey," she says, pointing to the guy operating the equipment.

Behind a rectangular table up at the front and to the side, equipped with a laptop, a mixing console, and a microphone, sits the guy I can barely see. The KJ, apparently. I strain to look closer at him. He's got medium-length, wavy black hair, glasses, and light brown skin. I can't tell for sure, but if I had to bet on it, I'd say he's Filipino, too.

"Do I have to?" I say. I'm already too close to the stage. My whole body resists any suggestion of getting closer, even if just to hand in a request slip.

Kat pushes me up and out of the banquette. "Just go give it to him."

Her eyes widen as Jenny turns around on the stage, bends over, and continues the song from between her legs.

"And ask him how soon I can sing."

Among Kat's many impressive qualities—effortlessly lustrous hair, impeccable fashion sense, and a general lack of fear of anything or anyone—she's also a bona fide pro vocalist, having graduated from the Berklee College of Music. She even fronted a popular local all-girl rock band for a while. It's the main reason I allowed her to convince me to go out with her. I'm eager to watch her (or really anyone else besides Jenny) perform.

So I force myself to go up. If I make it fast, I won't have to spend too much time on the stage.

At the table, the KJ looks oddly lost, indiscriminately

poking at some keys on his laptop, pausing, scrunching up his face, and then doing it all over again.

"Hey. My friend over there would like to go next." I nod my head in Kat's direction.

The KJ looks up at me, flipping back a bang of black hair. "What?" He reminds me a little of Henry Golding. Particularly when he sees my face and smiles. I'm a bit dazzled by his pearly white teeth. Or maybe it's just the whackadoodle lights shining in my eyes again.

"She wants to sing this." I hand him the request slip.

He takes it from me and stares at it for a second, as if he has no idea what to do with it. Even though it's literally his entire job.

My request slip isn't the only thing that seems to be throwing him. I can see now that he's working in some sort of DJ software platform that runs the music, sound, and lights, and I don't think he's quite gotten a handle yet on how to operate it. No wonder things seem a little out of control.

He looks at me for longer than I expect. Why, I don't know. Whatever it is, it's making me feel all tingly in the neck. I reach underneath my shirt collar and scratch haphazardly.

"I like your outfit," he finally says, which catches me off guard. Even for me, these clothes are frumpy. I wanted to be as comfortable as I could be in what I knew was going to be an uncomfortable environment, so I've got on sweatpants, dirty sneakers, a yellow T-shirt, and a fleece jacket they gave to me for free at work.

"Company pride," the KJ says, pointing to the sewed-on logo on my chest. "I love it." I can't sense a trace of sarcasm anywhere. No one ever compliments me on my clothes. Kat likes to call my style "helpless hetero meets rodeo clown." It's why I always needed assistance with my performance outfits, back in the day.

But that was years ago.

"Thank you?" I say. If it weren't for the fact that the KJ himself is dressed quite nicely—designer skinny jeans and a navy-blue oxford with the sleeves rolled up—I might think that I've actually met someone with worse fashion sense than me.

"You're welcome," he replies. "Are you Pinoy?"

"I am."

"Thought so. I'm Filipino, too." He reaches out his hand to me. "Paolo."

I grip his hand and shake. It feels nice. Not hot or sweaty, just pleasingly warm. My hands are always freezing, and his hold on mine makes the cold instantly evaporate. I hold on probably longer than I should. "I'm Rex."

WHACK!

Both Paolo and I turn toward Jenny on the stage. Wow. She sure is getting a lot of mileage out of that song.

We force our gaze away from her and look at each other, mouths rigid from trying not to laugh.

"So what do you want to sing?" Paolo asks me.

A tightness in my chest pulls everything inward. "Me? Nothing. This is just for Kat. I don't sing in public." My heart feels hemmed in, making my pulse beat faster.

Paolo's eyes dim. "Oh. That's too bad."

"I mean, I used to. 'All By Myself' was my go-to back in the day."

I have no idea why I tell him this. It's strictly part of my past, never to be resurrected. I just met the guy. Why am I suddenly not wanting to disappoint him?

"I love that song!" Paolo clicks some keys on the laptop, searching through the database. "I know it's in here somewhere..."

"Hey," I say, "I don't actually want to sing. My friend does, though. Like, really badly. So can she go up next?"

"Oh." Paolo picks up Kat's request slip and glances at it. "It's supposed to be first come, first served," he says, setting it down and scooting it over to a small pile of other request slips. "There are other people ahead of her who've been waiting for a while."

I take out my wallet and root around. Twenty? Too much. But a single dollar bill isn't enough.

My fingers take out a crisp five-dollar bill. "How about I grease the wheels a bit?"

"You don't have to—"

"Too late!" I throw the bill down, aiming to get it on top of the request slips, but the bill is flat and I have horrible aim and it ends up floating off to the side and down onto the floor.

"Oops, let me—" I reach down to pick it up off the floor.

When I look up, I find myself staring straight at Jenny's tiny, purple derriere.

She's decided to end the song by throwing one of her legs on top of the karaoke console table and slaps her own behind several more times in beat with the last cracks of the whip— *whack, whack, whipACKK!*

"Let's hear it for Jenny!" Paolo says into his mic. "Next up...is..." He looks down to where I am on the floor, still gripping the five-dollar bill and unable to move after having experienced Jenny's fanny finale up close and personal.

"Next up is Kat!" he says, smiling at me. "Come on up, Kat."

I mouth *thank you* to him and then decide the best thing to do is just reach up, place the five-dollar bill on the table, and gracefully slide away.

Except I'm in a painful crouched position and end up half-crawling, half-slithering across the now super-wide expanse of the stage, aware that things have ground to a halt as everyone watches my awkward exit. Kat just stands there and sighs, waiting as I slowly make my way back to our table.

She takes her place onstage confidently, like she's lived forever in that very spot. The plunky synth intro to "Girls Just Want to Have Fun" begins to bop, and I smile. Early eighties pop is not really Kat's thing. I expected her to do one of her classic rock faves. But once she starts singing, I realize that it doesn't matter that she hasn't chosen something in

9

her wheelhouse. Kat could sing the phone book and make it sound amazing.

As she sings, she stretches out the last syllables of the words *want* and *fun*—not with Cyndi Lauper's poppy melismas but with her own rock growl, making the song seem less whiny and more like a power anthem. Somehow, Kat does the unthinkable. She makes me forget how an iconic song was originally performed.

When she's done, the few people in the room applaud enthusiastically, especially me. Kat's brought me back to happier days, when karaoke used to fill me with so much joy. For the first time tonight, I don't regret agreeing to come with her.

"Fantastic!" Paolo says. "Great job, Kat!"

She throws a fist up in the air.

"Next up is a surprise singer," Paolo announces. In a rare moment when the strobe lights aren't piercing my sight, I lock eyes with him. He's staring straight at me.

My stomach drops. I know what's coming next.

"Rex?" he says. "Can I have Rex up onstage? Singing 'All By Myself.'"

Paolo repositions the spotlight and shines it on me. My face burns with heat. An ember in my stomach, one that's never truly gone out over all these years, flares up. The edges of its flames rip into the sides of my stomach, sizzling.

I'm only vaguely aware that Kat has come back to sit down at our table. She grabs on to one of my cold hands. "Rex, are you okay?"

I'm unable to look back at her. "I . . ."

The light shines so brightly.

I pull my hand away from Kat and stand up from my seat. Beyond the glare of the spotlight, Paolo sits and waits, watching me. They're all watching me.

I hurry toward the front door and exit into the night.

CHAPTER 2

I GOT LOST IN THE MALL ONCE.

Every parent's worst nightmare. Except in my case, it was one of the best things that ever happened to me and my mom.

As a kid, I was what people would now call a bit "extra." My dad used to call me OA, the Filipino slang for "over-acting."

Basically, I was a dramatic kid.

I didn't like typical boy things. Didn't play with trucks or action figures. At recess, I was the one boy dancing around on the school's asphalt playground with all the girls. At lunch, they sought me out to gossip and giggle. I couldn't help it. I was their gay bestie.

Was I teased? Absolutely. Lots of the other boys would laugh at me and my flamboyant ways. But I tried to never let it get to me. I stood my ground, chin held high, and ignored their taunts. I was only ever able to do that because I had someone important on my side: someone who gave me the courage to be myself. I had a mother who loved me unconditionally, with no judgments about my theatrical tendencies. In fact, she supported them.

She sang along with me to all my favorite Disney movie songs. When I tried to learn the choreography to boy band music videos, she'd help direct me. And most of all, she encouraged my love of flashy fashion. No utilitarian outfits for me, thank you, Dora the Explorer! I craved T-shirts with weird designs, socks with colorful prints, sweater vests, oversize bow ties, even scarves. My actual sense of style was atrocious—nothing I wore ever went together or made sense. But I didn't care, and neither did my mom. She'd let me wear whatever I wanted, much to my dad's chagrin.

Toward the end of every summer break, we would go on a shopping trip to the mall to buy school clothes. I looked forward to it the way other kids looked forward to Christmas. And during the summer before sixth grade, I ended up getting lost.

Well, I didn't so much get lost as I lost track of my mom while looking at the boys' shirts. I went into the women's section of the store to look for her and stopped dead in my tracks, stunned at what I saw.

I'd never been in that part of the store before. My eyes grew larger than they'd ever been, barely able to take in all the various colors of the new dresses on display. Fabrics glistened, and embellishments glowed in the overhead lights. Why were the women's clothes so much more exciting than the men's?

I ran my hands over one of the dresses. A satin off-the-shoulder wrap. A thrill of recognition ran up and down my spine, as if it were whispering to me, *Hello, my friend. I've been waiting so long to meet you. Please take me home.*

When my mother finally found me, I was frozen in place, as still as the mannequins I was staring at, imagining my own little grade-school body in the clothes I saw before me.

I turned to her with a smile so huge it eclipsed my face. She simply said to me, "You really are my child."

From then on, my mother and I grew even closer, united in our love of colorful women's clothing.

But now, the closest I'm getting to that kind of colorfulness is the box of doughnuts Kat's currently picking through in one of the small conference rooms at work.

"We should go back to the Pink Unicorn sometime," Kat says to me.

I sip coffee from my mug. "Hard pass."

Kat continues to pick through the doughnuts. "One of these days, you're going to have to tell me why getting up onstage freaks you out so much."

"I told you, it's nothing. Just stage fright."

"All I'm saying is, if you ever want to talk about it—"

"You know these are only for the people who sign up for the doughnut club, right?" I ask.

Kat sighs. "I did sign up. I just kind of always forget to bring in doughnuts when it's my turn."

I give her side-eye.

"What? Leave me alone. I've had a stressful morning. I need some sugar support."

The sound of a door slamming down the hallway makes us both whip our heads up. She hones in on the last strawberry glazed with sprinkles, snatches it, and motions for us both to hightail it out of there before we get caught. I double-check for any potential witnesses in the hallway and signal an all-clear to Kat before we meander back to our desks.

Kat and I work at Symria, a biotech in Berkeley specializing in sustainably made products. The office is quiet today. On some mornings, it almost seems back to normal, the way it was before the pandemic, with scientists bustling in and out of the labs and the other employees working at their desks. But on Mondays, most non–R&D folks work from home. Kat and I would be, too, except the executive team is on-site today. So Kat's boss, the CEO, and mine, the general counsel, expect us to be here.

"Why the rough morning?" I ask her. "Another blowout with Susan?"

"No. Maybe. It was more of a misunderstanding."

"About what?"

"My job performance." She purses her lips upward and stress-exhales quickly, making a lock of her bangs jump. "I say I'm doing fine, and she says I'm not."

We arrive at Kat's desk. She plops down in her seat and chomps on her doughnut with glee but only manages to take a few bites before Susan comes out of her office to ramble off a long list of tasks. As Kat scrambles to write them down, I tactfully excuse myself and go to my desk.

Kat's boss, Susan Axt, is one of the most successful women executives in the Bay Area. She's a great CEO but a demanding boss. As the general counsel's executive assistant, I'm busy, too, though nowhere near as stressed as Kat. I work for Danielle, a social-worker-turned-lawyer who is the quintessential Northern Cal biotech attorney: smart as hell and more into craft beers and surfing than stressing out at work. Everyone loves her, especially me.

Two hours later, Kat comes strolling by my desk. "Let's get ramen for lunch."

"But we get free lunch on Mondays." Symria, like every other biotech in the Bay Area, shares certain characteristics. The office is styled in a blend of college dorm room and West Elm enviro-rustic chic, the workspaces are open, the kitchens are stocked with snacks, and lunches are free Mondays through Thursdays.

Kat sticks her tongue out. "I'm tired of soup and salad."

"But you just said you wanted ramen."

"Japanese soup is better. It has more carbs and pork."

"Okay, fine," I say. "But I can't be late coming back. One of the scientists is coming by my desk at one p.m. to sign a document."

Kat raises an eyebrow. "Which scientist? You're not

usually this eager to get a signature. Is it that new strain engineering dude? Kenneth?"

"Maybe."

Kenneth is one of my many office crushes. He's captain of the company softball team, plays guitar, and has a PhD in biology from Stanford. All of which fills me with lust.

"Wouldn't want to be keeping Sexy Scientist waiting," Kat says. "So let's go."

"Now? It's not even eleven-thirty."

Susan yells out from her office, "Where are you off to, Kat? You know the whole point of the company shelling out half a million dollars a year for catered food is so you don't have to spend hours taking a break for lunch, don't you?"

"And you know that breaks are mandated in California, right? So get off my back!"

My eyes bulge. "Want to get fired much?"

"It's fine," Kat says as she pulls me toward the exit stairwell.

We walk in silence until we get to the Japanese restaurant down the block. After sitting at a table, skimming the menu, and then ordering what we always get, I ask her, "Are you sure you should be talking to Susan like that?"

Kat looks at me over her cup of tea. "Like what?"

"Like you're on the *Jerry Springer Show* and you just found out she cheated on you?"

"First of all, update the refs—Jerry Springer was like fifty years ago. Second, I'd be the one cheating on *her*. And third, don't worry about it. We talk to each other like that all the time."

"Please don't tell me you're quitting anytime soon."

"Why would I quit? I love my job!"

"You just argue so much with her."

She laughs. "I'm not quitting. Trust me."

Kat's relationship with Susan has always baffled me. How can they be screaming at each other one minute and then hugging it out the next?

We gossip about other office mates, and a few minutes later, our waiter brings our food. Shoyu ramen with extra meat for Kat, and chirashi for me. I pick up my utensils and begin to decimate my meal, secretly glad that Kat's made me go out for lunch.

Kat slurps up her noodles. "I thought all Asians loved karaoke. Especially Filipinos."

I know what she's doing. She's trying to get me to explain my little episode at the Pink Unicorn on Saturday. I keep my head bowed and pretend to be too involved in my food to respond.

"It wasn't the place itself, right?" she asks. "I know it's a dive, but we've been to plenty of run-down places and it's never bothered you before."

I keep eating.

"Was it that KJ guy? Did he do something to make you upset?"

Yes. He called me up to sing when I expressly told him that I didn't want to, and it made me want to run and hide and forget the whole night.

"No," I reply. I chew sullenly while trying not to notice

that Kat is peering at me, probably trying to figure out if I'm lying.

Right when it looks like she's about to say something else, she shrugs and goes back to slurping up her soup.

I use my fork as a mini-trident and skewer the last chunk of raw fish in my bowl. "Why did you ask about the KJ?"

"When I was watching you up there with him, it seemed like there was some interesting energy between you two. At first I thought it was a little spark, but maybe I misread the situation."

A spark? Of nerves, maybe, from trying not to get too worked up about being that close to a stage and microphone. But a spark? I have no idea what she's talking about.

"The only reason I was there is because I wanted to listen to you. But I didn't want to sing myself, so I left. And I don't really have any need to go back. For karaoke or any other night."

"Okay." Kat looks at me in that funny way she sometimes does, with a mix of support and melancholy. Like she knows I'm upset for some reason and is trying to communicate that she's there for me with her smile and sad eyes.

I ignore her and finish the last bite of my food.

The check arrives. I pull out my wallet to pay for my half of the lunch. "Wait, where is my . . . ?"

"Rex, did you leave your credit card somewhere again? Honestly, I swear you'd lose your head if it weren't screwed onto your pretty little shoulders."

Kat's right. Not about my shoulders—I have big, broad

manly ones, thank you very much. But I do lose things all the time.

I search my wallet and my pants pockets. "Where the heck is it?"

"When's the last time you used it?"

Staring out into space, I comb through the events of the last few days. "Damn. I never closed out my tab at the Pink Unicorn. I left before I could pay."

"Looks like you're going back there after all." Kat's phone vibrates and brightens on the table. She glances down and reads the message. "And it looks like I have to get back to work, too. Her Majesty's wondering where I am." Kat groans. "I'm replenishing the energy you sucked out of me with some hot Asian yumminess!" she says to her phone.

"Are you talking about the ramen or me?"

She makes a kissy face at me. "Take your pick."

"Uh, Kat, could you...?" I nod at the bill.

"I got it." She places her credit card onto the tray. "But you're definitely paying next time."

BACK AT WORK, after a frustratingly non-flirty signing appointment with Kenneth, I check the Pink Unicorn's website. Closed on Mondays, so I can't go tonight. It's open every other weekday at two p.m., however.

The next evening, I stop by on the way home from our office, keeping my fingers crossed that my card is indeed there and not in some other random place that I can't remember.

The place is empty except for an older white guy seated at the bar watching the news on the wall-mounted TV and drinking what looks like either a large glass of ketchup or a really thick Bloody Mary. He looks familiar. It's possible he was there last Saturday, though I didn't notice him then. He's probably in his late fifties, has wavy salt-and-pepper hair, and though he has somewhat of a dad bod, he's in pretty decent shape for an older guy.

I see the top of the head of a bartender stooped behind the bar, sorting through the shelves underneath.

I clear my throat. "Excuse me? I think I left my credit card here on Saturday?"

The bartender, still hunched down, says, "Hold on, buddy. Loretta worked last Saturday. I'll see if she left it in lost and found or—" *BUMP* goes the wooden counter as the man hits his head. "Ow!"

"Whoa. Are you okay?"

He rubs the back of his head and stands. "Yeah. I'm fine. I've got kind of a hard head."

I stare, blink, and wonder how the man hitting his head made *my* vision blurry, because I am definitely the one seeing things.

"Rex?" the bartender says.

Or maybe I'm not seeing things.

What the heck is my ex-boyfriend from Indiana doing in California?

CHAPTER 3

I USED TO BE A HOOSIER.

Meaning, I went to college at Indiana University Bloomington.

My parents wanted me to go to a school in California, preferably starting at a community college and transferring to a state school to save money. But at the time, I needed to get away. Not from my family. From what happened to me the summer before my senior year of high school. I wanted a fresh start, someplace to redefine myself.

So I secretly applied to a few out-of-state schools, including IU. When I got in, I told my parents that it had a great political science department and a top-notch law school, and didn't they want the best for me and my budding young attorney dreams? But the truth was that I wanted to go there because it was the farthest school from California that I got into.

Now, ten years later, a part of my Indiana past is standing right in front of me in an Oakland bar. My ex. The one I never really got over. Aaron Berry.

"Aaron?" I say, gaping.

He reaches over the counter for me. "Rex! Holy crud," he says. His voice is as deep and rich as I remember, a gravelly baritone that sounds exactly how a grizzly bear probably would if it could talk. He wraps an arm around my upper torso, and his boulder-biceps digs into my shoulder. The bristles of his beard stubble rub against my cheek, making it burn in the most amazing way. And his scent—scotch, denim, bath soap, and a hint of exertion—is so delicious I nearly swoon.

I pull back and sit down on the barstool to steady myself for a few moments and make sure I've identified him correctly.

"What are you doing here?" I ask.

"What am I— Dude, I live here!"

Over the years, as I'd drift off to sleep, I'd inevitably fantasize about running into Aaron again. I didn't think it would actually ever happen. I never planned on going back to Bloomington, and Aaron was too much of an Indiana boy to ever leave.

But now he's here. The hottest guy I've ever met in my life. Six feet tall, chestnut hair, blue eyes, a boyish face with a devilish grin, and the body of a man that could shepherd farm animals by carrying them on his shoulders. Aaron's always reminded me of a cross between Chris Evans and Kristoff from *Frozen*. Roguish and boyish. As if you can never be sure whether he'll smack you on the butt and laugh or grab you by the back of the neck and pull you in for a kiss. My preference would be for both, one right after the other.

"You actually left Indiana?" I ask him.

Aaron blushes, turning pink. An easy thing for him to do with his light complexion. "I followed someone out here."

"Oh?" I say as neutrally as possible. "A guy?"

"My boyfriend, Russell. It didn't turn out well. We broke up a month ago."

"I'm sorry to hear that," I say, not sorry at all.

When Aaron and I dated, he was still firmly in the closet. In fact, we didn't really date so much as have a secret sexual relationship. He didn't want anyone to know he was dating a guy, so we never actually called ourselves *boyfriends*. I pushed him on it a couple of times because I wanted people to see that we were going out, to show him off. That ended up being a mistake. I was only thinking of myself, and he ended up breaking up with me.

But now he's comfortable saying "my boyfriend" out loud and is working at a gay bar. It's fantastic to see that he's evolved.

And even better to hear that he's single.

"Thanks, man," he says. "Russell took a software job out

here, and I came with him. He hated living here, though. He went back to Indiana. I stayed."

"Why didn't you go back with him?"

"Something about this place made me want to stay." He rubs the back of his neck with one of his beefy hands. "It's funny, I thought he was the adventurous one. Wanting to uproot ourselves and move out to California. But after living here for a month, he was the one who wanted to go back home. While I realized there's so much more to the world than just Bloomington, Indiana. Heck, I thought Indianapolis was cosmopolitan, but it's nothing compared to Frisco."

I flinch at the word. No real Bay Area resident ever utters it. But I let it slide and make a mental note to teach him the acceptable nicknames—the City, SF, or possibly even San Fran—later. Preferably while we make out back at his place.

"And besides," he says, "I owed it to myself to see if I could make it on my own. I'd just gotten promoted to manager by the owner." Aaron nods his head over to the man sitting at the bar, now deeply involved in an episode of *Designing Women*. "Bryan."

So the older guy's not just some random patron.

"That's great, Aaron. I know you've always dreamed of managing your own place. But it's so different from where you used to work. Is Kilpatrick's still around?"

"Still around and still the same old," he says. "Back home, I didn't have the guts to work at an actual gay bar. Now— well, you know how it is here. More open. And something

25

about this place in particular makes me feel, I dunno, kinda like home, but more so? Not exactly sure why. Whatever it is, the Pink Unicorn helped me be more comfortable with who I am."

A safe space can do wonders for a person. I know that from firsthand experience. In a place where you've been given the permission to truly be yourself, you have the freedom to explore and grow. And hopefully, that place will always be somewhere you can feel secure.

We're not always that lucky, though.

"It's amazing luck that you got a job here, then," I say.

"It wasn't exactly luck."

"What do you mean?"

"My mom and Bryan are old friends. He's from Indiana, too. When I told her I was moving out here with Russell, she let Bryan know, and he offered me a bartending job right away. So I've been working here since the day I arrived. About two years ago."

Two years. Aaron's been at a bar just ten minutes from my office for two whole years, and I had no idea. Why the heck didn't I come here sooner?

"So," he says, leaning back against the counter, "what are you doing here on a Tuesday evening all by yourself?"

"Funny thing," I say. "I forgot to close out my tab when I was here on Saturday."

"Ha," Aaron chuckles. "So you haven't changed."

He crosses his arms over his chest, and I can't help but

watch as his biceps grow even bigger. A whisper of excitement winds its way through me.

"Neither have you," I say.

Aaron grins and holds my gaze for a few endless moments. My throat goes dry.

"Oh, your card," he says, finally breaking off eye contact. He walks to the far side of the bar and sorts through a metallic box. "Yep, here it is."

When Aaron hands it to me, I feel his fingers brush mine. He smiles at me, maybe implying the touch wasn't accidental.

"Uh...maybe I should just leave it here to keep open a permanent tab. Now that I know you're here, I'll have to start coming on a regular basis. To *catch up*," I say with as much innuendo as possible.

"Perfect idea. I'd love to see you come back often," he says.

"Heh." I feel my face get hot. "Just maybe not on karaoke nights."

"So you're not a fan of it, either," Aaron says.

"You don't like karaoke?"

"It's fine. But you know me. I don't really know a lot of popular songs. I've got my favorites, and they're good enough."

True. One of the things about Aaron that I couldn't quite understand: he didn't really listen to a lot of music. His music collection was a whopping three CDs: Garth Brooks's *No Fences*, Shania Twain's *Come On Over*, and a compilation of vintage TV theme songs. I usually like to have music on when I hook up, but I learned not to ever listen to his after completely losing my erection while listening to the theme song from *The Golden Girls*.

"And our karaoke night isn't very popular," Aaron adds. "It's part of the reason I don't work Saturdays anymore. That, and I have this regular thing now."

"Oh?" I hope he's not referring to some new guy he's seeing.

"Yeah. Joey."

"Oh."

He smiles. "Joey's a twelve-year-old kid from Oakland I volunteer to hang out with once a week while his mom works the evening shift at a hospital. I'm his Big Brother."

"Nice," I say, both relieved and impressed by his volunteer work.

"It's too bad, though. No one hardly ever comes on Saturdays anymore. We hired a new host, but he hasn't gotten up to speed yet."

"Paolo seemed okay to me." Except for the fact that he didn't really know what he was doing with any of the controls. Or that he tried to get me to sing even after I said no. Actually, maybe he wasn't so great.

Aaron picks up one of the bar towels and starts drying off some of the glasses from the dish rack. "He's a nice guy but doesn't really have the kind of personality you need for the stage. Back at Kilpatrick's a few years ago, when we started doing karaoke, they'd hire one of the IU theater majors to come beef up the night. It helps when you've got someone who's a good performer to host. It gets the crowd going. Those kids were always so amazing. I don't always know the music, but I know a good show. That's the kind of karaoke I could get behind."

My fingers begin to quiver. The same way they used to right before I'd reach for the microphone.

Aaron appreciates good performers. I used to be one. A really good one. I know all about karaoke. I know how to be on the stage. How to entertain a crowd. I used to...

"You know, I might be able to get more people in here," I blurt out.

Oh, no. I can't believe I just said that.

"Oh, yeah? Are you volunteering to host?"

"Me? No." Dammit. "I just mean, I..." I look around, grasping for some alternative ideas. The Pink Unicorn has definitely seen better days, but there's obviously more to this place than meets the eye, if it helped Aaron to come out. This old bar is important enough to him that he ended up staying here instead of going back home.

What if I could help improve the Pink Unicorn?

What if I could be a part of something that makes him happy?

"The décor could use a little brushing up. I'm pretty handy with interior decoration." Nope. No one should allow me to come near any sort of designing challenge. "And I could help out with social media for the bar. I'm pretty good with TikTok." All my social media accounts are defunct or barely attended to, and I've never once used TikTok.

No, Rex. Don't say it. Don't offer it. "And..." My tummy begins to ache, and my forehead goes hot.

But then I look at Aaron, his chiseled jaw tensing slightly in anticipation of my suggestion, something that might help his bar out.

"I know someone who could host your karaoke night."

Crap. My stomach tenses up into a ball of wires. What am I thinking? I can't put myself out there again. It's a bad idea.

I'm about to take back what I said, but Bryan swivels his head around to us and says, "Well, don't keep us hanging, young man. What do you have in mind?" As involved as he was with his bowl of peanuts and TV, I didn't think he was paying the slightest bit of attention to anything we were saying.

Aaron puts down the glass, throws the drying towel over his shoulder, and leans in so close that I can smell his breath, hot and soothing like a eucalyptus shower. "Yeah. Tell me what you got."

Back in Indiana, Aaron wasn't ready to be serious with me. Maybe he is now. I've got another chance with him. A real chance at a real relationship. And right now, I've got his full attention.

But I don't have the slightest clue about how to remodel or create better publicity for the bar. And most of all, I don't know if I'm ready to put myself out there again, performing and hosting a show. In public. Making myself vulnerable. It would take one heck of a reason.

Though Aaron is one pretty damn good reason.

I just need more time to think about it all.

"Sure," I say. "But I've got another commitment right now." Not a lie, at least, since I'm having dinner with my family. "Are you free later this week?"

"My Friday's open," he says. "Loretta, the other bartender, asked to trade with me. I can do it this week since Joey's visiting his grandparents on Saturday. Means I have to work karaoke night, though. Yahoo."

Good. That gives me a few days to think about what I'm going to say. And when we meet again, it might as well be in a more romantic environment. "How about dinner Friday? I can tell you all my big ideas then."

"I'd like that." He smiles his incredible *aw shucks* smile at me.

"Perfect."

Now I just have to figure out what the heck my actual plan for the Pink Unicorn is going to be.

CHAPTER 4

LOST IN THE AFTERGLOW of running into Aaron (and the anxiety of trying to come up with good ideas for him), I almost miss an incoming call from my sister, Eva, while driving to my parents' house for dinner. I patch it in through the car's Bluetooth.

"What's up?" I say.

"When are you getting here?" Eva says. "Mom is making me watch that campy Filipino soap opera of hers on TFC. Hurry."

Eva, though twenty-four years old and almost finished with her master's degree in social work at San Francisco State University, still lives at home. So she's vulnerable to our mother's utter devotion to teleserye.

Mom was a local beauty queen as a young woman and

won a contest to be on the Filipino TV show *Anna Clara*. It's not hard to see why Mom had a brush with stardom. At fifty-six, she doesn't look a day over forty. It's almost embarrassing to be seen with her in public. Most people can see her family relationship to us—the dramatic cheekbones, the button nose, the strong shoulders—but they always think she's our older sister instead. I take some comfort in knowing that we'll probably inherit some of Mom's youthfulness. Hopefully, it will balance out Dad's unfortunate head of hair, which began graying at thirty-five and is now almost completely white at sixty.

"I'm fifteen minutes away," I say to my sister. The traffic from the Pink Unicorn to San Leandro is heavier with commuting traffic than I'd expected. "Just get Dad to overrule her and switch the channel to something else."

"Like I'd want to watch the National Geographic Channel instead. No thanks. I'll stick to Mom's soap opera. Even though I can't understand anything they're saying."

Neither Eva nor I have the ability to speak Tagalog, though I can somewhat understand it. I was three years old when we left the Philippines to move to the States. Eva was born here. Our parents tried to encourage me to stick with it, but I resisted, wanting to fully acclimate to English like all my new school friends. After months of trying to convince me otherwise, our mom dropped it and switched to more passive-aggressive means of keeping Tagalog alive. Like blasting The Filipino Channel whenever we're home.

"It's always the same thing anyway," I say. "Someone's cheating on someone else. Someone's maid steals money to pay for her kids' education. The son has a secret girlfriend."

"Or is gay," Eva says.

"I'd actually watch that."

"You would. So how far—"

"Hoy!" my mom yells in the background so loudly that I can hear her through the speakers of my car. "Go set the table, Eva. And why aren't you paying attention to the show? Learn more about life in the Philippines."

"Whatever, Mom! If everyone in the Philippines was actually that rich and ridiculously good-looking, I'd move there in a second. Rex, hurry up."

Eva clicks off, and I settle back into the slow stream of traffic.

Half an hour later, I hear the familiar mix of TV and conversation between my mother and sister as I enter the house. Whether it's gossiping, bickering, or just catching up on the day's activities, they always have some nonstop discussion or another going on. Meanwhile, my dad is nowhere to be found. Which means he's in the garage working on a project in his workshop.

I inhale the familiar scent of rice steaming away at the counter. "I brought some cheesecake from Berkeley Bowl. What'd you make, Mom?"

Eva throws a kitchen towel at me. "What did *I* make, you mean."

"You cooked tonight? I'll just have the cheesecake for dinner then."

"Hey!"

"Don't make fun of your sister," Mom says, chopping away at some lettuce for a salad. "You know I've been teaching her how to cook. It's a useful skill. One that I'd be happy to teach you, if you're interested, Rex?"

Mom has been asking me a lot lately if I want to help her prepare meals for her church parties. I always assumed it was just a way to get free labor.

"Maybe at some point."

She harrumphs and keeps chopping. "Fine. Keep eating your takeout. What happens when I die? You'll never have Filipino food again."

"Mom, this is the Bay Area. There are lots of Filipino restaurants around."

"And none of them can cook like me. Now go make yourself useful and get your dad."

Just off the kitchen is the entrance to the garage. Though it's only a few steps away, I considered it a completely different world growing up. It was off-limits for most of my youth. Too many dangerous objects lying around—sharp-edged saws, nails, and unfinished wood.

When I turned eleven (the same year I discovered my love of women's clothing at Macy's), my dad sat me down on a fold-out metal chair next to his woodworking bench and invited me to watch him while he worked. After I felt comfortable, he said, I could help him with household projects. And then, maybe, I could join him on weekends on-site at some of the jobs for his cousin's woodworking business.

I gently refused, saying it wasn't really my thing. He wasn't surprised, of course. But to his credit, he did manage to show me a few useful DIY things around the house, which I became incredibly thankful for years later when I bought my first condo.

"Hey, Dad. Dinner's ready."

"Sige, sige. Coming." He sands away at a small box. I can't be sure from where I'm standing, but it looks like a birdhouse.

"That looks neat. Is it for the garden?"

"I haven't decided yet." He looks up, and, as he so often does, scans my face. As if doing that will tell him what he needs to say next. "It depends on how good I make it."

"Oh, so if it sucks, you'll give it to me?"

He stares, blinks, and laughs. "Yes. Probably," he says, wiping his hands on his dirty sweatshirt.

My relationship with my dad has been good for years now. Since I came back home from college, we've reached a place where I don't feel uncomfortable around him anymore or sense that he feels any uneasiness around me. But it's taken us years to get here, and I try not to take it for granted. Whenever I begin to second-guess my decision to leave the old me behind, I try to remember how much has gone into protecting myself from the harm my dad warned me about when I was a kid.

AFTER WITNESSING ME falling in love with a dress display at the mall, my mom knew that I wanted to learn more. She began to teach me things surreptitiously, away from my dad's disapproving gaze, by allowing me to sit by her side as she got ready to go out.

She showed me what the basic pieces of a woman's wardrobe were, the benefits of specific silhouettes and the downsides of certain fabrics.

And she introduced me to the wonderful world of women's shoes. Ohmigod, the shoes! I was entranced by them. Especially any with high heels. I loved how they made my mom taller and more regal, like a queen.

Even more than the clothes and shoes, though, it was the makeup that truly fascinated me. I'd been aware of makeup before, but only in terms of what actors wore on TV. How they used it to transform themselves into superheroes or mythical creatures, making them into things they were not. What thrilled me about my mother's makeup was that it didn't make her into something she wasn't—it made her into more of herself, accentuating the woman that was already there.

I wanted all of that for myself. The chance to make me even more than I already was.

And I was already a lot.

After a few weeks of watching Mom prepare herself, I thought it was only natural that I'd go from learning how she did it to doing it myself.

She refused.

"You're far too young, anak. Maybe when you're older."

I wasn't disappointed, though. How I decided to interpret what she said was: *I've taught you all you need to know. Now you figure it out on your own.* I was certain of this because of the big wink she gave me as she walked out of the bedroom, leaving me alone with her riches. It was definitely more than just a tender punctuation point. It was tacit permission.

Afterward, whenever she was busy preparing food for dinner or on the weekends when she was off running errands, I'd sneak into my parents' bedroom, ears attuned to Dad's hammering in the garage to make sure he was busy, and sort through my mom's things. I learned what she used daily and what she wouldn't miss for a few hours or even a few days. The special things I knew she kept the farthest back in the closet. Hidden. Shiny dresses for when she wanted to look as radiant as she possibly could. There were shoes back there, too, with heels higher than the everyday ones. I'd pilfer a few things from my mother's makeup collection in the bathroom as well, sneaking them into my bedroom and trying to recall my mother's detailed instructions on how everything worked.

The first time I tried putting everything on, what I saw in the mirror was not quite a princess in a ballgown. Nowhere close, to be honest. But I still felt as if I were on my way to being a more extraordinary version of myself. I knew I'd get better with practice.

Over the next few weeks, even as careful as I was with

putting everything away, I had a feeling that Mom knew what was going on.

Once, at dinner, she stared at my lips, and then, with widened eyes, she grabbed her napkin and wiped my mouth with it. My father's gaze went to me, and I went rigid, knowing that she'd just wiped away traces of her lipstick on my mouth.

She *tsk*ed as she tucked the napkin away discreetly, out of my dad's view. "Rex, you need to be a more conscientious eater. Close your mouth when you chew."

I breathed a sigh of relief as the concern in my father's face dissipated and his focus went back to eating.

Now, knowing that my mother was in on my secret self-transformations, I decided I didn't need to be as careful as I'd been.

That was a huge mistake.

One afternoon, I'd taken a few of my mom's more colorful things—a short cocktail dress, iridescent green pumps, and a pre-packaged collection of makeup in a color palette called "Carnivale."

After weeks of experimentation, I'd finally gotten to the point where everything seemed to fit right, with makeup that wasn't a complete disaster. Things were still far from perfect, but for the first time, I felt truly transformed. I was finally pretty. And I wanted to celebrate.

I put Britney Spears's *In the Zone* into my CD player, navigated to the last track, and pumped it up. The synthetic strings of "Toxic" took over my room.

In front of the full-length mirror hanging on my wall, I

sang along in my naturally high voice, proud of being able to match Britney's vocal range. I waved my arms, shook my hips, and pretended I was one of the sexy flight attendants from her video.

My lipstick was blotchy and my eyes were overly lined, but I felt fabulous. The singing, dancing person on the inside finally matched the appearance on the outside. My heart soared. I danced faster. Sang louder.

Until my dad appeared in my room.

I froze in terror.

I'd let my guard down and had left my bedroom door open a crack. Maybe he'd heard me while coming into the kitchen to get a snack. Maybe I was so loud he'd actually heard me from the garage. All I know is that the look on his face was something I'd never seen before.

Before I could even react, he reached out and turned off my CD player.

"Why are you dressed like this, Rex?" He was shaking, but not from anger, it seemed. The look on his face was the same as when we'd almost gotten T-boned by an SUV while driving to church the week before.

He was afraid.

"Take all that off right now, Rex. I won't allow this in my home. You will not go down this path in life. You are opening yourself up to bad things."

I couldn't move. I just stood there as he stared at me, his face full of dread.

After what seemed like a lifetime, he finally left my room.

I wiped the lipstick off my face with the back of my hand and sank down to my knees on the floor.

But as shaken as I was, I didn't fully obey him. Not at first. I didn't quit when he told me to. I couldn't.

That didn't happen until years later.

Since then, though, my dad and I have been great. Of the few benefits bestowed on me for turning my back on my drag, my improved relationship with my dad is undoubtedly the best.

AT THE DINNER TABLE, we chew our food in silence. Eva made, or tried to make, Mom's chicken and pork adobo. But the pork is tough, the chicken is stringy, and the sauce is so acidic it makes my eyes burn.

I force down a mouthful of food and take a long sip of my water. "Great job, Eva."

"Shut up, Rex."

"Kids," Dad warns.

Mom swallows so hard her eyes bulge. "Adobo is not so easy to make, you know. The ratio of ingredients must be just right." She pats Eva's hand. "It's fine for a first try. You'll get it right next time."

"I don't even know why I have to keep trying," Eva says, frowning.

"How else are you going to land a husband?"

My father and I burst out laughing. Eva says nothing, chewing with a wrinkled brow.

"And how about you, Rex?" my mother asks. "Are you dating anyone special these days? When will you be bringing someone nice over for us to meet?"

Over the years, I've dated a bunch of guys. Many, actually. None have lasted. And "dated" might be too generous a term. But things might be changing. If I play my cards right, there might be a chance for me to be with Aaron. This time, officially and out in the open.

"There *could* be someone," I say, getting excited. So excited, that I accidentally scoop too big a spoonful of Eva's super-sour adobo into my mouth. My mouth curls into a snarl as I chew, trying my hardest to eat it all.

Mom asks, "Oh? Did you meet him at work? Is he one of the lawyers there?"

"No. That would be super-awkward if I dated one of them."

"He's one of the scientists then?" my dad asks.

"Someone I knew from IU. Well, not IU exactly. He was a bartender at Kilpatrick's in Bloomington."

"Bartender? You better make sure to go back to school and get your law degree, Rex." My dad pushes his plate away, which, admirably, has been finished. "You'll have to support him."

"Bartending is a valid job, Dad. Don't be so snobby," Eva says.

"And so is being an EA," I say quietly.

"Ano yun, Rex?" my dad asks.

"Nothing," I say.

"So where does he work?" Eva asks.

"The Pink Unicorn. In Oakland."

"That place has the best drink specials!" Mom and Dad look up at this. Eva stammers, "I mean, that's what I've heard, at least."

Eva, the successful, straitlaced student, has always been their golden child. Especially compared to me, the one who disappointed them by not going to law school, which I said I'd do after a break from college and then again after becoming the legal team's EA at Symria. Meanwhile, Eva is about to graduate at the top of her class and already has interviews lined up with a few hospitals and clinics. The last thing my parents want to hear is that she's out boozing it up at local bars.

"Honestly, it's a bit worn down," I say. "I told Aaron I might have some ideas about how to spruce things up a bit."

"Really, Rex? Are you going to help them redecorate?" my mom says, her smile strained. She knows me all too well. "I can always help if you'd like."

Mom's always had a keen eye for design. "That'd be great, actually. And they need better publicity. A better presence on social media would help."

"You know I can help you with that, big bro," Eva says.

Perfect. As the event coordinator for one of the Filipino student organizations at SFSU, Eva's got plenty of experience with creating social media posts.

"And...I was thinking of maybe also revitalizing their karaoke night," I say.

"What's this?" Dad says.

"Karaoke?" Eva says.

"Oh! You need my help with that for sure, diba, anak?" Mom asks.

Did I mention that my entire family *loves* karaoke?

"Okay, calm down. I still have to figure out all the details." And I'm not one hundred percent sure that I want to go through with the whole thing, anyway.

"Rex, that would be so nice if you could be involved in performing again!" my mom says, practically dewy with delight.

"I didn't actually say that *I'd* be performing, just that—"

"I'll help by singing, too." She takes a big inhalation of breath. We all know what's coming next.

Eva groans. "Mom."

Dad juts his hand out to grab my mother's. "Hon, not at the dinner—"

My mom, her hands up like Eva Perón, lets loose, " 'I came in like a racquetball! I never hit someone I love! All I wanted was to break your walk! All you ever did was, wreck knees! Wre-e-eck knees!' "

"Wreck knees? Mom! Do you even listen to the words you're singing?" Eva says, exasperated.

"*Che!*" Mom says. "It's not my fault all these pop songs don't make sense. I don't understand why Miley Cyrus is singing about having bad legs. Don't hate me because I'm such a good singer."

My mom is definitely not a good singer. But she doesn't let that stop her.

"Eva, is there any more adobo?" my dad asks. "Maybe you can give some more to your mom. To fill her mouth with."

As my family continues to make fun of each other, I keep second-guessing my karaoke idea for the Pink Unicorn. Even what little singing my mom does creates a tiny ache in my stomach, and not just because of her malaprop lyrics. Is it too late to back out of saying I'll help Aaron and his bar?

As if answering me directly, my phone buzzes. It's a text from Aaron. **Dinner Friday at 7 still ok?**

I respond immediately. **Oh yeah. Let's do it.**

The words stare at me, and I realize I've said something slightly inappropriate. Too late to delete it. Maybe if I follow up with—

For sure. But dinner first? ;-) Aaron replies.

CHAPTER 5

THE PLACE I PICK for my dinner with Aaron, AquaMarine, is one of the best new restaurants in the city.

It's gorgeous, although in a slightly rough part of San Francisco's SoMa district. The front door is the color of topaz flanked by walls of rough-hewn concrete, like a precious jewel amidst stones. As you step inside, you're greeted by low lighting, which makes the turquoise glass fixtures glow seductively. And inside the main dining room, the tables are covered in lapis linens and flickering faux candles.

I fidget with my watch, check (for the fourth time) that I have my credit card, and brush stray pieces of lint off my pants. Eva helped me put together my outfit of chinos and a red merino sweater, so I know my normal lack of fashion sense hasn't sabotaged me. Though Aaron isn't here yet, he's not late. I'm just anxious and fifteen minutes ahead of schedule.

Since our table isn't ready, I sit in the impressive lobby area, big enough to house its own restaurant, and go over the ideas I'll present to Aaron. The redecoration and publicity suggestions that my mom and Eva have helped me come up with will be an easy sell. What will be more difficult is pitching the idea for the new karaoke host. Me.

I'm not sure what will be harder, though: convincing Aaron that it's a good idea or convincing myself.

You'd think my dad discovering me prancing around in my Britney Spears getup in middle school would be enough to scare me away from drag forever. And though the fear of him finding out and becoming disappointed in me again made me stop for a while, I began to wither away inside after a few weeks of going without it. I wanted— needed—to see the makeup back on my face. To feel the fancy dresses on my body. To express on the outside what I felt inside.

I started acting out at school. Wore flashier clothes. Grew my hair out. Even dared a tiny bit of eyeliner under my eyes, hurrying out before my dad could see it and making sure to wipe it off before I came back home from school. It helped a little.

But it hurt, too. I was already the most flamboyant boy in school, and the uptick in my femininity made it even harder. My friends from drama class had my back, and I'd spent years cultivating a thick skin to tolerate the taunting. But even I had my limits.

Some of the seniors from the football team started to do this thing where they'd yell out "Sexy Rexie alert!" whenever I entered the cafeteria at lunchtime, whistling at me. When that started happening, I knew I wouldn't be able to take much more.

I needed my drag back. I needed to be able to explore my femme side at home and in private. Safe from the bullies in the outside world.

And I'd need an ally. One whom I'd stupidly decided not to confide in before.

I needed my mom.

One Saturday morning, as we stood side by side at the washer and dryer folding clothes, I told her everything: that after she'd given me the insider view of her world, I'd kept learning on my own, practicing with her borrowed things. And that I'd eventually gotten caught in a dress and full makeup by Dad.

"Oh, Rex!" she said. "I had a feeling you were trying a few things on your own, but I didn't know for sure. You should have told me everything you were doing! I could have helped make sure your dad didn't find out about it. Hay naku, I'm not surprised he acted like that."

"Because I'm . . . gay?" I said, without even realizing it. It was the first time I'd ever actually said it out loud, though there was no way my mom, or anyone else on the planet, would've been surprised by my coming out.

My mother cupped my face and gazed at me. "My sweet child." She threw her arms around me and hugged me tight. "No, anak. It's not because of that. We have always suspected that you were gay, and it makes no difference to us at all. That part would not be a surprise to your dad."

A small, stubborn weight inside me that I didn't know I'd had came loose and began to float away. I wouldn't have thought that I'd have any fears about coming out to my mom. Like she said, it's not as if me being gay would have been a surprise to anyone. Still, you never know for sure how someone will react when you tell them your truth. And to hear those words of support from my mom, to feel it in the way that she held me, meant the world.

"Then why was he so mad, Mom?" I muttered.

She kissed me lightly on the forehead. "It has to do with your uncle Melboy."

My parents had only ever mentioned Tito Melboy in passing. I knew that he was Dad's eldest brother, the oldest of three boys. Melboy was gay and had acted mostly as a surrogate mother to Dad and their youngest brother. Their mother, my lola, had died when my dad was just in grade school.

But no one ever told me why they never talked about Tito Melboy like they did my other uncle, Tito Reg. I'd assumed it had something to do with Tito Melboy being bakla. *Yes and no*, my mom had said, not elaborating. She wouldn't tell me more than that. And I knew better than to ask my dad, who bristled at the sound of his brother's name.

"What does Tito Melboy have to do with it?" I asked.

"Let's not go into that now. I want to focus on you," she said, unsurprisingly avoiding the subject again. "Are you so set on continuing this?"

On top of the dryer was a pile of her summer dresses. I reached for the strap of one of them. The fabric was silky smooth between my fingers, like a soft caress on my skin.

I nodded silently.

"Sige. Now that you're in high school, maybe it's okay now. But first things first." She eyed the dress in my hands. "No more stealing my clothes. You need your own things. Which means—time to go shopping!" she said, clapping her hands.

Later that afternoon, we drove into San Francisco. The Castro was our first destination. I'd been wanting to visit the neighborhood for a long time, to see what it was like to be around so many other LGBTQ people. As we parked in front of the majestic Castro Theatre, with its crimson and cream marquee announcing the Frameline Film Festival, my whole body shook with excitement. I saw men walking hand in hand, rainbow flags fluttering free, and people wearing whatever they wanted. Leather chaps, sparkly spandex, and rainbow-colored dresses.

We headed straight for the wig shop. It sat next to an adult entertainment store whose window displays for gay adult videos caught my attention.

"You're definitely much too young for that, Rex," my mom said, turning my head away. My cheeks flushed with embarrassment. But once we entered the wig shop, I completely forgot about the displays next door. What I saw inside was exhilarating.

The walls on every side were lined with rows of mannequin heads sporting all sorts of wigs. Short and straight, curly and poofy. Black, blue, pink, and white. My head swam with the many possibilities of what I would look like with them on.

The salesperson, an older Black woman with close-shaved blond hair, looked at my mother. And then me. She smiled conspiratorially and asked, "First time, sweetie?"

"Yes, his first time!" my mother said as I blushed.

The woman launched into a tutorial about wigs, teaching us about the different types. How to wear, care for, and style them. And, most importantly, which ones would be best for a budding young drag queen.

We walked out of that shop with two pussycat wigs (one white, one pink), a shoulder-length black one, and a long blond lace front. I'd gotten an education along with the goods, and in every store we went to afterward, we were met with similar enthusiasm and advice. Something about seeing a mother support her son in his pursuit of drag seemed to bring it out in the people we encountered. Probably because it wasn't something they saw every day, even in San Francisco.

At Victoria's Closet on 17th Street, two young women helped us find dresses and skirts. At Tooty's in the Haight, a kind older man attended to me patiently as I tried on almost a dozen pairs of women's shoes, eventually settling on four different pairs of high heels. And at Kryolan, almost the entire staff wanted to walk me through the basics of drag makeup, pointing out all the essentials for concealing and priming. All the things that my mother hadn't known or ever even heard of.

My mother and I lugged several bags full of purchases into our house that evening, which she helped me sneak into my bedroom. In an old leather suitcase in my closet, I safely tucked away my new treasures underneath winter clothes and blankets. I needed to wait until my dad would be away at work before I could take them out again. It took everything I had not to dig into the trunk and look through it all, though. I wanted to revel in the colors, scents, and textures.

When Dad finally left to help his cousin build bookshelves for a school in Pleasanton the following weekend, I reopened the trunk and took out everything. That week I'd spent each day trying to recall the lessons I'd learned from all the people who'd sold us my things. I combined that with what I'd learned from my mom, *America's Next Top Model*, and the makeup tutorials I watched on YouTube. I was ready to pick up where I'd left off, before my dad had caught me. But this time, I'd be much better at everything.

I took out a pleated miniskirt, a white crop top, a cardigan, and high heels, intending to do Britney's "...Baby One More Time" look. But because the skirt and cardigan were pink, my outfit reminded me of another blond bombshell. Regina George from *Mean Girls*.

I picked up my blond wig, spread the elastic rim wide with my fingers, and slipped it carefully onto my head. The lace front worked like magic, making it seem as if the hair was actually growing out of my scalp. I stared at myself in the mirror. For the first time, even without any makeup on, I saw a real queen.

And then I realized. I knew what my drag name should be.

I'd known for a long time that Rex meant *king* in Latin. That's partly why my dad gave me the name. And Rex mundi meant *king of the world*.

But *queen of the world* was *Regina* mundi.

Regina Moon Dee. Queen of the world. That's who I was when I put on that wig.

Every weekend after that, I'd wait for Dad to leave the house, and then I'd hole up in my room and work on my makeup and outfits.

My odd sense of style meant my colors and pieces never quite matched. My mom would help when she could—nixing certain combinations and suggesting others. But after a while, she left me to my own devices. "It's okay to have your own style, Rex. And...there's only so much I can do to help you," she said, meaning she'd taught me everything she knew, though she might have implied more than that.

So I pulled Eva into my world. She didn't have any advice

to give me. She was only in grade school. But she always motivated me, her face rapt as she'd watch me get ready. She was fascinated by my process. And in particular, she loved what she would call my "bedroom music concerts."

I started doing this thing where, in full drag, I'd turn on my favorite song and sing with a hairbrush in front of her. My preternaturally high voice meant that I had no difficulty at all hitting the high notes, allowing me to belt to a high C before needing to flip over to head voice. I was thankful to be able to sing exactly like my favorite divas.

But my enthusiastic audience of one (sometimes two, when Mom wasn't too busy with errands) made me realize that I was getting to the point where I didn't want to do drag for just my family. I wanted to share it with others.

But how? I couldn't do it in public. My dad would find out about it if I did.

And then, after watching an episode of *American Idol*, I had an idea.

I searched online for downloadable karaoke tracks and found Britney Spears's "I'm Not a Girl, Not Yet a Woman." While it was downloading, I took out my makeup kit and went to work. My skills had gotten marginally better. The blocking of my eyebrows was solid, and my contouring wasn't half bad. My eyeliner was still slightly crooked, and I had a feeling my eye shadow color combination of pink and yellow didn't match my outfit, but who cared? I felt gorgeous.

I took out a dress Mom had gotten for me from a thrift

store in Berkeley, a seventies A-line with a blue floral pattern. I put that on, plus a pair of platform heels.

For the final touch, I slipped my blond lace-front on and applied concealer and powder foundation, blending it across the lace.

I poked my head out my bedroom door. "Mom? Eva? Can you guys come up here?"

My mother's face lit up when she saw me. "Wow! Very good job this time!"

"You're soooo pretty!" Eva said, cooing with her hands clasped together.

My scalp began to heat up. I was glowing with pride. (But also, that wig was damn hot.) "Thanks!" I said. "Now, can one of you film me with the digital camera? I want to record myself."

Eva rushed down to grab the family camcorder, which we barely ever used. I instructed my mom on where to sit and film me from. I clicked on the karaoke track and sang, adding my own flair instead of sticking strictly to melody, improvising new harmonies and even some entirely new lines like the singers on *American Idol* would do.

When the song was over, Eva jumped to her feet, clapping loudly.

"Beautiful, Rex!" my mom said.

"*Regina*, Mom. Regina Moon Dee."

"Ay yes. Regina," she said. "So what will you do with this?" She handed the camcorder back to me.

"Upload it to YouTube," I said. "No one will watch it, but

I don't care. I just want to share my singing and drag with other people."

I posted it online, hoping that a few people would stumble upon it and enjoy it.

I never would have expected what happened next.

Back then, going viral was still relatively rare. But it happened to me with that video. Regina Moon Dee, bedroom drag queen, was an overnight sensation. My karaoke-style music video racked up hundreds of views in one day. Thousands in a week. And though a few people commented on my basic makeup skills, people were entranced with my uncanny ability to sing a woman's song in the original key.

They asked for more. And I gave it to them. I made other videos, posting almost a dozen videos online and amassing almost 50,000 followers by the time I was a junior in high school. It was a thrill, sharing my talents with the world. And maybe I could've just gone on like that, being a semi-famous bedroom drag queen, safe with my little online music videos.

But then Tito Melboy came into my life and encouraged me to take Regina Moon Dee public. Which was a total dream come true.

Until it wasn't.

As I sit in the lobby of AquaMarine glumly recalling what shattered that dream, I notice the heavy front door swinging wide open as if it were nothing. Aaron enters the lobby and looks around, improving my mood instantly. He doesn't see me at first. A look of confusion grows on his face, and he begins to backtrack out of the restaurant.

"Aaron! Over here." I stand up and wave at him from the lounge sofa where I've been waiting.

"Oh, hey. I thought I was in the wrong place." He looks around at our surroundings. "Am I dressed nice enough?"

"You're fine."

He is. Very fine. Even in black slacks and a gray polo shirt he looks like a designer cologne ad come to life. His hair is freshly cut, his beard is newly trimmed, and he smells of sandalwood and spring water.

After sitting down in his plush, velvet seat, Aaron visibly relaxes until our hostess hands us our leather-bound menus.

"Holy crud. This place is expensive," he says.

He's not wrong. Dinner tonight will take a considerable chunk of my money. How do they get away with charging nearly a hundred dollars for seafood?

The descriptions sound interesting, though. One of the main course offerings, sea bass with two sauces (maple soy reduction and white balsamic glaze) is described as *adobo*. Another, the *pakbet*, is kabocha squash, haricot verts, and bitter melon with Berkshire pork belly and caviar. It's Filipino-based, which is a pleasant surprise. Most high-end Asian places rely on the typical Chinese or Japanese flavors.

The prices are extremely high, though, and I don't want there to be any stress or anxiety on Aaron's side. I want this night to be perfect.

"Don't worry. It's my treat," I offer.

"Nah, don't do that. I'll pay my portion," he responds.

I know he's just being a typical guy, but I can't help but feel that he's also pushing back against the true nature of what we're doing. Which is having a date that I asked him on.

"Actually, I have this half-off coupon," I lie. "It's almost like you're paying, right? I'll get this dinner. You can get the next one."

"Yeah? Okay, then. That's a deal I can't refuse." He holds my stare for a moment and smiles, and my insides melt. "So, tell me more about your ideas for the Pink Unicorn," he says.

After dinner with my family earlier in the week, Eva and Mom brainstormed with me. Their redecoration and social media plans both sound great to Aaron, which I expected. There's still the most important change, though, the one that I know will bring in the most business right away.

"A total rehaul of karaoke night," I say. "We'd do away with the old plastic song binders and take advantage of the KJ software program. When I was there last week, I noticed your KJ was working in something called SYNGX. I did some research, and there are a bunch of functions in it that could really modernize the evening. Make it easier and more fun for guests to request and sing songs via an app on their phones."

Aaron nods. "Yeah, I sort of knew about that. Bryan has been trying to get Paolo to work out the controls for the new system, but he hasn't figured it all out yet. It doesn't help that he cancels on us half the time. He has some other job that calls on him to fill in for other people a lot, or something like that."

"Where?" I ask.

"Not sure. He's never told us."

"Well, that brings me to the second part."

My knees start shaking underneath the table. I place my hands on top of them to make them still. "It might be good to split the host duties. Have one person, like Paolo, do the technical stuff while another person hosts the show. Like you mentioned to me before, it'd be great if that main host were a good performer. And I have someone special in mind."

"Oh, yeah?"

It's been years since I've been Regina Moon Dee. But I used to be so happy in drag. And I had loads of fans, hopefully some of whom would gladly come to a karaoke night hosted by me. As I look into Aaron's eyes, almost seeming to glow from all the many shades of blues around us, a familiar heat blooms in my chest, and I know that he'll absolutely love my plan.

I take a deep breath to slow down my racing heart. "Yes, I—"

Aaron snorts, startling me. His focus has shifted to something behind me.

"What?" I ask, twisting my body to look.

"Sorry. It's just, that waiter over there seems really lost."

At the far end of the dining room in the dimly lit section, one of the servers holding a tray tries to deliver the food to one of the tables, but when he sets the food down, the people crinkle up their faces, so he scoops the food back onto his tray and approaches another table, where they also shake their heads *no* at him.

I turn back to face Aaron.

My knees have finally stopped shaking. My heartbeat has calmed down. "Her name is—"

"Did you guys order the crispy kare kare and pandan waffles with sweet chili fried chicken?"

Dammit. The clueless waiter is now trying to give us the food. "No, that's not our order," I huff. "If you could just—"

"Paolo?" Aaron says to the hovering presence behind me.

Paolo steps to the side of our table with his lost tray of food. He's dressed in the AquaMarine uniform of navy slacks, white tuxedo shirt, and checkered bow tie.

"So this is where you work," Aaron says.

"Hey, nice to see you, Aaron!" Paolo says. "And—"

"Rex," I say.

"I know. I remember," Paolo says. I notice for the first time how awkwardly he's carrying the tray of food, with two hands on the sides instead of balanced on the palm of one, as if delivering a meal to a patient at a hospital instead of to diners at an upscale restaurant. "You really did not want to sing at karaoke last Saturday," he says to me.

"I tried to tell you," I say.

"What's this?" Aaron asks.

"Nothing," I respond quickly.

"You're welcome to come back to karaoke night any-time," Paolo says. "To sing or not."

He looks genuinely hopeful that I might actually go back to the Pink Unicorn. More than hopeful, in fact.

Well, whatever it is, he's about to get his wish. If I could just finish telling Aaron the plan.

"Paolo?" Another server, an older Latino gentleman with an impressive mustache, comes up to our table. "Those go to table four, by the window," he says, pointing and then mim-ing the correct way to carry the tray.

"Oh," Paolo says, startled out of whatever he was think-ing. "Right." He swivels the tray up onto his right hand and steadies it with his left. "Sorry to disturb you guys."

"No problem," Aaron says amiably as Paolo heads over to his correct destination.

The older server gently clasps his hands. "Would you two like some more time, or can I get you started with some drinks?"

"Actually, yeah," Aaron says. "Could we have two glasses of prosecco to start? We'll be ready to order food after that. Rex, let me get the drinks."

Before I can say anything to protest, Aaron places his hand on mine.

I don't say anything for a few moments, though I'm not sure why. And then I realize it's because I've stopped breath-ing completely. During the time we were together, Aaron never once touched me in public, though I always wished he would. Now his hand is on mine, and in full view of everyone in the restaurant.

"Yes. Please do," I finally say.

"Very good," the server says. "I'll get those out to you and will be back to take your order."

"You've got some great ideas," Aaron says to me as the server heads back to the kitchen. "I'm glad we're doing this. And I'm really glad we ran into each other again." He squeezes my hand, and a golden warmth spreads across my entire body.

"Me, too," I say, still somewhat breathless.

"So. The new host?" he asks.

"Host?"

"For karaoke night? You were about to tell me her name."

"Right! Regina Moon Dee," I say.

"Nice name. Sounds interesting. Is that a stage name, or—"

"It's a drag name."

"Oh." Aaron pulls his hand back. "Okay."

I see it on his face. Apprehension. And something more. Like distaste.

My heart starts pumping all the blood away from my extremities and into a tiny space in my forehead, making it pulsate. All that lovely warmth in the rest of my body dissipates.

"I...uh, I mean, *she's* a great performer," I say. "She's, um, she's..."

"I just don't get the appeal of all that drag stuff. It's like, why would a guy want to get dressed up in women's clothing? It's too much for me."

My hands have gone completely cold. All the blue colors around us seem like signs of an impending winter.

"She's got a big fan base," I manage to say. "Although she hasn't been performing for a while. But a lot of people would love to see her come back. I'm pretty sure she'd bring in a lot of new customers." I'm babbling at this point, not really sure of what I'm saying because I don't think there's any way I can salvage this.

While Aaron stares at me, I try to think of some other idea for karaoke night. "Maybe instead we could—"

"Hold on." Aaron's brow furrows. "If you think it'll bring in more business, I can try to roll with it."

My heart stops hammering away at my head.

Okay. He might be open to Regina Moon Dee. But only as the host of karaoke night. Not as someone he'd date. And definitely not as his boyfriend. It's written in all the tension lines on his face.

"Uh, great," I say, not really sure how to proceed. It's probably best to stall until I can come up with some better idea. "Why don't I talk to her and see what she says?"

The server returns with two filled champagne flutes. They're filled to the top, bubbles fizzing through the crystal-clear glass like a million tiny pinpricks.

Aaron holds a glass high, and I copy him.

"To a new and improved karaoke night," Aaron says.

"Cheers." I force a smile and clink my glass against his.

"Starting tomorrow," he says, sipping.

I'm glad I haven't started drinking the prosecco yet or else Aaron would be covered by one colossal spit-take right now. "I'm sorry, what?"

"No time like the present, right? Have your friend come tomorrow night and do a trial run hosting karaoke," he says. "Before I say yes, I want to see what she's got to offer."

CHAPTER 6

"SO YOU TOLD HIM *NO*, RIGHT?" EVA ASKS.

Lucky for me, Eva gets up early, even on the weekends. It's why I've called her first thing in the morning for advice instead of Kat, who doesn't get up until eleven a.m. on Saturdays at the earliest.

"Not exactly," I say, pushing the last bits of soggy cereal around in my bowl.

"I know *I've* been ready for Regina Moon Dee to make a comeback for years now. But are you?"

Even if I am able to muster the courage to take my drag out of mothballs, it doesn't solve the bigger issue. "Maybe?" I reply. "But even if Aaron's open to hiring Regina, he's definitely not interested in dating her. So if he finds out I'm Regina, there goes my shot at being with him again."

"Okay, not to question your taste in men, but do you even want to be with someone who doesn't like drag?"

I pause. Is Aaron really the dream guy I've made him out to be if he's not interested in something that used to be such a big part of me?

That's the thing, though. Drag was a big part of my life, but it isn't anymore. I've learned to live without it. What I'm considering now is just a temporary fix. Something to pump up business at the Pink Unicorn and get it going again. At some point, I can find someone else to take over. Maybe even have a rotating roster of karaoke hosts. And then my life as Regina Moon Dee can be put to rest once again.

"To some people, drag can be a little...confusing, I guess." I flash back to my last day performing. "Besides, I wouldn't do it forever. I'd stop before he ever finds out my true identity."

"And how exactly are you going to do that?"

"That's what I was hoping you'd tell me!"

"Okay, okay. Let me just think about this for a second," she says, her voice getting louder. She's struggling to be heard over someone screaming for help in the background.

No, not screaming. Or crying, which was my second guess. I eventually realize it's Mom, singing a Beatles song in the living room. At eight in the morning.

"Why is Mom doing karaoke this early?" I ask.

"She just joined the church choir. It's her way of warming up before Saturday rehearsals."

I hear "Is that Rex?" in the background, the sudden

absence of the karaoke track, a mic being dropped, and, "Rex!" my mother yells into the phone. "Why don't you come to church with us tomorrow? And come hear me sing in the choir!"

I massage my brow. "I might have a conflict tomorrow, Mom. I'll try," I say, knowing full well that I won't.

"Rex," my dad's voice booms in the background. "Too busy to come to church, ha? I'm sure it's because you're studying for your law school test. Right?"

For whatever reason, my father has been under the impression that I've been preparing for the LSAT for the past few weeks to apply to law schools.

Maybe because I lied and said that I was.

"Yes, exactly," I say. "I'm studying."

"Good. You need a top score to get into a good program, anak. Make me proud, okay? But take a break and come and support your mom tomorrow at church. Don't let us be the only ones to suffer."

"What?" Mom shrieks.

"I mean the only ones to enjoy!" Dad says. "Ai! Aray ko!"

Even from over the phone, I can tell that Mom is pinching one of his love handles. My ear fills with screaming and laughter.

"Hold on," Eva says. "Let me go into a different room and spare you." The sounds of our parents' roughhousing recedes into the background.

"Much better," I say.

"Agreed," Eva says. "Hey, do you want me to tell Mom

tomorrow that you actually showed up at church but sat in the back pew so she didn't see you? I can just text you what Father Jim says for his homily, in case she tests you on it."

I snap my fingers. "That's it, Eva. You're a genius."

"Tell me more."

"You've always been the smartest one, the best student—"

"About the plan that you obviously just thought about, dummy. What is it?"

"I can be in two places at once. With your help. So you'll have to come with me to the Pink Unicorn tonight. I'm going to hand my phone over to you for the evening."

"Uh, okay?"

"Just don't go through my photos."

"Ick. I definitely will not," Eva says. "But speaking of photos, you should send me a few pics of you in drag. Even if they're old. We don't have enough time to take updated ones. I'll just figure out a way to doctor them up somehow."

"What do you need pics for?"

"Duh. For publicity."

My heart skips a beat. "Publicity? For tonight?"

"You want to prove you can pull in people, right?"

"Well, I was going to invite Kat."

"That's not enough, Rex. I'll get the word out on socials this morning. It's not a ton of time, but we can try to get at least a few diehard Regina Moon Dee fans to come."

Eva's right. If I want to prove to Aaron that I can bring about a karaoke renaissance for the Pink Unicorn, we need to attempt to bring in a bigger audience tonight. And advertising Regina Moon Dee's comeback would definitely help.

Still, when I think of putting my image back out publicly, I can't help but feel everyone's eyes on me, and my face gets hot, as if someone's focused a spotlight and turned up the intensity to maximum.

"Okay." My throat is suddenly parched. I go to the sink to pour myself a glass of water. "I'll send you what I have. Thanks for handling that. You'd think a bedroom drag queen would be better at social media, but I haven't had an online presence in years. It's progressed way past me."

"You'll catch up," Eva says. "I'll post something on Instagram and Facebook, maybe do a quick teaser on TikTok. Wait, does Regina Moon Dee even have a TikTok account?"

"Nope."

"A virgin TikToker! Love it. People are going to be so excited to hear you're going to be back in drag and performing in public again. Especially Mom. Have you told her yet?" she asks.

"I haven't," I say, taking a sip of water. "Could you tell her for me?"

Feedback from the karaoke system in the living room squeals in the background. I hear our mother, now joined by our dad, singing, *I want to hold your haaaaam! I want to hold your ham!*

"Just be sure not to let Dad hear about it," I say. "I'll already have my hands full tonight making sure Aaron doesn't figure out that I'm Regina. If Dad came, too, it'd be a disaster."

"I'll be careful," Eva says. She lets out a tiny squeak. "We're going to have so much fun! It'll be like old times. I just wish Tito Melboy was here, too."

"Yeah," I say simply.

"One of these days you should talk to him again. Don't you miss him?"

I don't say anything for a while and just listen to my parents singing loudly in the background.

"Be sure you're at my place at seven p.m., okay?" I say.

She sighs, says, "Yeah, yeah," and hangs up.

Don't I miss Tito Melboy? Of course I do. I miss his throaty laugh, his chubby cheeks, and his hugs that last for days. I miss the smell of his floral perfume, the swish of his hips, and the way his hair comes all the way down to his waist when he lets it down. And most of all, I miss having someone else around who knows exactly what it's like to have been feminine their whole life. To love wearing women's clothes. To walk in heels as if they were born in them. Yes, I miss Tito Melboy. I miss my drag mother.

My own mom was always such a big champion of mine that I never thought I'd need another one. But the summer before my senior year in high school, I discovered what a gift it was to have a second mother. When Tito Melboy came into our lives.

I'd known that my dad and my uncle Melboy hadn't talked in years, but I didn't know why. Tito Melboy was my dad's favorite brother, until he wasn't. And though Tito Melboy also lived in California, he might as well have lived on Mars, because we'd never met him. Dad was content to avoid his brother by pretending he didn't exist. All we knew of our uncle were half-told stories and angrily cut-off conversations.

When my uncle asked us for help, though, my dad couldn't ignore him any longer. Tito Melboy was moving to the Bay Area from Los Angeles and needed a place to stay. And family always comes first when it comes to Filipinos, especially those in need. My mom gently reminded my dad that he needed to put aside whatever disagreement he had with his kuya and help him.

And by reminded, I mean harangued until he finally caved in and let Tito Melboy come stay with us for however long he needed.

When he and my dad arrived home from the airport, Tito Melboy threw himself into our house, leaving my dad to struggle with the four large suitcases he'd brought with him.

"Sharon, diyos ko!" he said, his voice as loud as a police siren. They hugged like long-lost friends. He had on men's clothing, but only by strict definition. Jeans (skin-tight), a button-up silk shirt (in a festive pattern), and a pashmina scarf (definitely not men's). He had a big torso with impressive cleavage, thick, hairless arms, and ample hips and thighs. A purple scrunchie held his long hair in a ponytail, which swung around his head like an elephant's trunk as he moved through the house. And though he didn't have on any obvious makeup, he must have been wearing something. His skin was too glowing to not have been enhanced in some way.

After finally loosening himself from my mom's embrace, he examined Eva and me. "Look how big you both are now! Eva, how old are you?"

"I just turned ten!"

"Practically an adult. And you, Rex. Naku, gwapo talaga! You know, the last time I saw you, you were just a baby. You don't remember me, do you?"

He gave me a hug. A cloud of women's perfume engulfed me. My eyes watered, though I wasn't sure if it was because of the scent, the hug so tight that it momentarily stopped my lungs from working, or the fact that in that one fragrant instant, it felt as if I'd found someone I'd always needed. Right then and there, I wanted to tell him everything about my secret life as Regina Moon Dee.

Just because he was feminine, though, didn't necessarily mean he knew anything about drag. I had to make sure. That night after dinner, as Mom talked to a friend on the phone and Dad excused himself to work in the garage, I tried to find out.

Eva and I took Tito Melboy up to my room for our favorite summer night activity, watching *RuPaul's Drag Race* on my little TV. I wanted to see how he responded to it, to see if he was drag-friendly.

Within a minute, I had my answer.

"Ay! You record this? This is my favorite show!" Tito

Melboy squealed. "Raven is the best. She's my makeup inspiration. Do you want to see?"

He whipped out his phone, and on the screen was a picture of a gorgeous plus-size queen with pageant-style hair piled high on her head and a ball gown draped around her. She looked like a goddess come down from the heavens.

"Is that you, Uncle?" Eva asked, astonished.

"Yes! Beaucoup Buko. The Empress of Manila."

While Eva *ooh*ed and *ahh*ed over Tito Melboy's pics, I took my phone out and shyly returned the gesture by showing him pictures of me as Regina Moon Dee.

He looked at the screen and then looked at me. His big brown eyes widened as he brought an open hand to his chest. "Is this you? Ang galing naman ng pamangkin ko! And wow, your color combinations are so very, ah…creative. Who taught you how to do this?"

"Mom, mostly. But a lot of it's just me experimenting."

"Ah. Of course your mom would encourage you," he said, smiling. "Can I see what kinds of things you have?" he asked me.

I pulled out my stash of clothes, shoes, wigs, and makeup from the secret suitcase at the back of my closet. Tito Melboy sifted through everything. "How long have you been collecting all of this?" he asked.

"Ever since Mom started taking me shopping. Three years now."

"You've been doing drag for three years?"

"Longer. Before that, I was just stealing stuff from Mom."

"Since you were just a child! I guess talent must really run in the family, then? Although I think it skipped your dad."

"He's good at making other kinds of things, I guess."

"Does he know about this?"

"No."

"Good." He picked up one of my wigs, a fluffy, blond piece, and poked his fingers through the large curls. "He wouldn't approve."

Here was that connection Mom had been talking about.

"Is that why Dad and you don't get along?" I asked quietly. "He found out about my drag and got super-mad. Mom says it has something to do with you. Is it because you're... bakla?"

I was afraid of Tito Melboy's answer. I didn't want to hear that my father disliked me for the same reason he had stopped talking to his kuya. Because he was gay.

Melboy sat on my small bed, making it groan under his weight. "Not because of that, Rex. Well, not exactly because of that. You should understand, when I was growing up in the Philippines, being bakla was not exactly the same as being gay here. In the States, if you are gay, you can be a lot of different ways, diba? You can be macho. In fact, the more straight-acting you are here, the more desirable. I learned this when I came here. But when I was a boy in the Philippines, if a bakla person was masculine, people would get confused. They would think he was being dishonest, trying to be someone he was not. That's because people expected us mga bakla to be feminine. And since I always acted more like a woman, well...I was not always understood, but I was more tolerated. And sometimes even loved."

"Even by my dad?"

"Oh, yes, especially your dad! He never cared that I was bakla. No one in our family did. Your lola died when we were little, so I helped your lolo around the house. I took care of your dad and your tito Reg. I cooked, I cleaned, I mended their clothes. They considered me their big sister, their *ate*. Actually, your dad? He was my biggest protector. He would always stand up for me against the neighborhood bullies."

"So why did he get so mad at you?"

Tito Melboy reached up, pulled off the elastic tie that held up his long hair, and let it cascade down. As he talked, he pulled his fingers through the long, black strands. "We didn't have enough money growing up, Rex. What we were making selling food at carts on the streets was not enough. So I began to look for ways to earn extra cash. I began to dress fully in women's clothing and perform at bars. I was making a lot of money. But I was also getting into things I should not have. Drinking. Staying out late. And I had so many suitors. Some of them were not such good guys. I sometimes got attracted to the rough types, the ones who were bad news. It got to the point where I was barely home anymore. I fought with your lolo about it. And then I left home. Your dad was maybe around your age at the time, and he blamed me for abandoning him. Which I guess is true."

Something on Tito's face closed off, becoming hard. He stayed quiet for so long that I assumed he was done telling his story.

Eva cracked up at one of the *Drag Race* contestants' jokes, which startled Tito Melboy.

He blinked a few times and turned to me. "Why don't we have a little tutoring session tomorrow when your parents are at work, ha? Just don't tell your dad."

I couldn't believe someone I was related to was so much like me. I had been convinced—and afraid—that my love of drag destined me to be the black sheep of the family. I should have known from Dad's cryptic warning that my uncle had beaten me to it.

I nodded and smiled wide at Tito Melboy. He pulled me into his arms and gave me one of his everlasting hugs.

Our first drag lesson was on a scorcher of a summer day, the kind where there was so much heat it became visible, coming off the pavement in waves. It was so hot that my parents gave us permission to turn on the air-conditioning before they left for work, instead of just using the fans to save money. "Trust me, Rex, you'll be glad we get to use the air con today. Drag is a mix of adding and subtracting, but mostly adding. You will have to get used to performing in hot circumstances—in many layers under heavy lights or outdoors in summer events. But for now, we stay comfy."

He retrieved a large aluminum carrying case from one of his suitcases and flipped the latch open with a *clack*. I gasped when he opened it, revealing multiple levels that spread out, like a butterfly unfurling its wings. "One day I'll buy you your own case," he said, winking.

We sat at my desk with our respective makeup sets and lighted mirrors. As Tito Melboy went through his routine, I followed and copied him. I asked questions when I didn't understand something he was doing, but mostly, I watched and listened as he told his stories. He'd learned a lot in his many years working the gay nightclubs in Manila and had even established his own house of queens. Since his drag persona was Beaucoup Buko, he called it the House of Buko.

"Back then, I was like a baby coconut," he explained as he blended in his concealer. "Young, juicy, and sweet. Trust me, those men couldn't get enough of me!"

I giggled. "You did say you had a lot of boyfriends."

"Yes," Tito Melboy said, his contour brush hovering over his cheekbone. "And not all of them were bad news. Some were actually very kind to me. Do you have a nobyo yet, Rex?"

I frowned, forcing wrinkles into the streaks of foundation around my eyes. "No. And I probably won't ever. Not looking like this."

"No, don't say that, pamangkin."

"It's true. Maybe in the Philippines it's different. People appreciate baklas there."

"Ha!" Tito Melboy guffawed, a sound so abrupt that I almost dropped my blender sponge.

"What?" I was confused. "I thought you said no one cared that you were bakla?"

"No one *in our family*, Rex. I had my...what do you call them here? Haters?" he said. "Actually, did you know that people in the Philippines used to be more open-minded when it came to us mga bakla? Many years ago, before the Americans came, before even the Spanish came, people like us were respected. Even revered. Some say that the word *bakla* is a mixture of *babae*, meaning 'woman,' and *lalaki*, meaning 'man'—because we were the best of both, as well as something beyond—a mix of masculine and feminine. Something like a third gender. A lot of people who were bakla were part of the babaylan, or spiritual leaders.

"And in that way, I think that we still carry on that tradition. We are performers, but we don't just entertain, diba? We uplift. We inspire. We are special, you and I, Rex. And one day, I know with all my heart, you will find someone who sees that about you as much as I do."

I forced myself to smile, wanting—needing—to believe that my uncle's prediction would someday come true. But no matter how much I loved the femme parts of myself, I just couldn't see another guy liking them, too.

Tito Melboy continued teaching me all throughout the summer. Not just about makeup and clothes or padding and tucking. He educated me about drag culture and Filipino history, too.

But I also managed to show my uncle a thing or two.

One afternoon, while chowing down on some bistek tagalog that he'd cooked for Eva and me for lunch, Lady

Gaga's "Poker Face" began to play on the TV we'd left on in the living room.

"Rex made his own video of that song, Uncle Melboy," Eva said, her mouth full of beef and onions. "He's better than Lady Gaga is."

"What is this?" Tito Melboy asked.

I sheepishly retrieved my laptop from my bedroom and showed him the video Eva mentioned. Dressed in a black latex bodysuit and long blond wig, I sang "Poker Face" as I danced around our backyard. It had almost 10,000 views.

"Wow, Rex! Ang galing naman! You can sing so high!"

"He's the best singer ever!" Eva said.

Tito Melboy tousled Eva's hair. "Yes, I agree, my darling. Do you just make home videos? Or do you also perform outside?" he asked me.

"I'm too young to go out on my own. And there's no way I could hide it from Dad."

"But you have such a talent! Not only are you beautiful, but you can also sing. Not everyone can do that." He chewed thoughtfully for a few moments. "Rex," he said, swallowing, "I think I have an idea."

He had a way to get me to perform in public. A wonderful, perfect place called Dreamland.

I remember how happy I felt when I first saw it. And then when I first performed there.

I try to hold on to that feeling and try not to fast-forward past it, to the events that happened after. I need to stay positive. To not be afraid. Not if I'm actually going to go through with being in drag again.

My plan for a new karaoke night will work with me at the helm. It's going to give the Pink Unicorn, and Aaron, the boost they so desperately need.

I can do this. I can perform as Regina Moon Dee again. And I can make sure that Aaron doesn't realize that she's me.

At least, I hope I can.

CHAPTER 7

STANDING ON THE PINK UNICORN'S STAGE as Regina Moon Dee belting "Bohemian Rhapsody" with Kat, I can't help but feel like a star reborn.

Aaron looks happy. He'd been hesitant about the idea of a drag queen hosting karaoke night, but now the satisfaction on his face is unmistakable. Just like every other person's in the bar.

A familiar energy rushes through me. I feel powerful. Confident. And drop-dead gorgeous.

FOUR HOURS EARLIER

"Sweet cheeses! Why does your face look like that?" Eva says while standing at my front door.

"Like what?" I say.

"Like a circus elephant sat on a clown car."

I groan and pull her into my condo. "I thought I did an okay enough job. You know I always needed Tito Melboy or Mom's help to get things just right. And it's been years since I've put on makeup. I'm totally out of practice."

"That's an understatement. It's a good thing I came early. Here." She hands me a plastic container of food. "I tried making Mom's adobo again."

I cautiously open the lid and take a sniff. "It smells pretty decent, actually."

"You'll have to wait to eat it because I need to fix all this first," she says, circling her hand over my face.

I know that all the prep and foundation work I've done on my face is fine. It's just the colors and shapes that have eluded me, as usual. Styling and makeup are not my forte. The stage is where I'm most at ease.

Where I used to be most at ease, at least.

Eva and I head to my desk, where I've laid out all my cosmetics. I sit and try to relax as she starts readjusting my makeup.

"Is everything else ready to go, at least?" she asks.

I nod.

After Eva had given me the idea this morning on how to be in two places at once, I texted Aaron.

Just talked to Regina Moon Dee. It took some convincing, but she said yes!

He responded back right away. Sounds good. Bring her over a little before karaoke starts at 8 so we can introduce her to Paolo.

About that . . . I texted back. Something came up and I have to accompany my dad to something. But my sister Eva will be there to help out.

No response. Not even three dots. A minute passed. Two.

Finally, Aw, too bad. No worries, I'll let you know how your friend does.

I let out a sigh of relief. Great. I'll check in with you during the night to see how it's going—which was all part of my plan.

Sounds good. Talk soon. xo

XO. A kiss and a hug. Only two little letters. But good enough for me.

About an hour later, when I knew she'd be awake, I called Kat.

"Hello?" she rasped.

"You're getting your wish. I'm going back to the Pink Unicorn for more karaoke."

"I knew you'd come around eventually," she said, coughing.

"Yuck. What were you up to last night?"

"A little reunion with the band. You know how those Nine Tails girls can party."

"I remember," I said.

When they were still together, Kat and Nine Tails not only knew how to rock a stage, but they also knew how to throw epic parties. Copious amounts of alcohol and several packs of cigarettes would inevitably be consumed. A fight or two would always break out, and sometimes a hookup. They weren't very good with boundaries. Part of the reason why they eventually disbanded.

"So, you want to come join me tonight?" I asked.

"Of course, bestie. Wouldn't miss it."

"Awesome," I said. "I want it to be a good time. Do you remember how I told you I ran into my ex at the bar?"

"Yep. Cornfed Chris, the shuckable hunk from Indiana. You had dinner with him last night, right? You said you were going to give him some ideas for updating the place, but you never actually told me what. Is this part of it?"

"Yes. And...I have a few things I need to explain. Are you sitting down?"

"Hell, no. I'm flat on my back with a pack of frozen lima beans on my head. But I'm as prepared as I'll ever be. Hit me."

I proceeded to tell Kat everything. My life as a teenage bedroom drag queen. My short career as Regina Moon Dee, karaoke hostess extraordinaire. The event that led to my falling out with Tito Melboy and to me putting my drag away. And my plan to bring it back for karaoke night at the Pink Unicorn.

"I was wrong," Kat said after I finished. "I wasn't ready for that."

"I'm sorry I never told you anything about my drag past. I knew you could tell last weekend's freakout was more than stage fright. I just wasn't ready to explain it all to you. It doesn't change anything between us, does it?"

Kat laughs, her voice still hoarse. "Are you kidding? If anything, it makes me love you more. I'm so proud of you for doing this."

"You are?"

"I mean, don't get me wrong, not the biggest fan of you needing to hide your identity from Midwest Muscleboy—"

"Let's start calling Aaron by his real name, please."

"—but the fact that you're getting back into drag in public makes you a damn superhero in my eyes. So hell yes, I'm going to be there. And I'm bringing my girls. Party part two! We're gonna have an awesome time."

Telling Kat my story ended up being the boost that I needed. Knowing she'd be there to support me was the final thing to get me over any last remaining bits of hesitation I had about being Regina Moon Dee again.

I went to my closet and dragged out my chest. The one that my father had given me as a gift years ago.

After I came back home from IU, my dad brought me out to his workshop, unveiling his present to me from underneath a cloth tarp—a wooden chest patterned in seventeenth-century Spanish-Colonial style. He'd made it himself, crafting it in his spare time out of mahogany with iron mounts and ivory inlay. It had taken him years. A symbol of his love for me.

And then, inside of that chest, I placed a piece of myself.

Before I closed it for good, I wrote a letter, in case I was ever tempted to reach for Regina's things. To remind myself of why I hid it all away. I locked the chest and even put a DO NOT OPEN sign on it. It's been hidden away in the back of my closet like that for almost a decade now.

I burrowed to the back of my closet and pulled out the sealed chest, the sign still on top. I wiped my hand over it.

The dust scattered, making me sneeze. My eyes watered as I unlocked the chest and took out the sealed envelope with my final warning to myself. I tore it open and read it.

Dear Rex,

I know you miss everything that's in here. And I know you want to take it all out again because it used to make you happy.

But before you do, just remember why you hid it all away.

Your father was right. This stuff will only get you into trouble. It already did. You got hurt—badly.

It's better to keep it all inside. Where it will always be safe.

—R

I stare at the letter for a few moments, my eyes still teary from the lingering dust and the memory of how hurt I was when I wrote those words to myself.

And then I set it aside.

My favorite dress lay on top—a ruby-red sequined pageant dress. A thrill ran through me from feeling its fabric. My hands dug through the other clothes, fingers brushing spandex and silk, velvet and velour. Underneath were my shoes, makeup boxes, and wigs in their silk cases. The smell of everything, powdery and perfumy, filled my lungs.

I set out everything I needed and proceeded to get ready.

Some of the makeup was old, a few of the bottles crusted shut. But I made use of what I could and took my time getting into the rhythm of it again.

After two hours of work, I was certain that I'd done a decent job preparing my makeup, until Eva came over and told me I'd blown it.

After half an hour of rectifying my mistakes, she pulls her face back from mine and squints at me. "Much better. Take a look."

I turn to the mirror and am instantly relieved. Only my two mothers—my mom and my drag mom—were ever able to rein in my tacky tendencies. Eva's never done my makeup before. It's good to know she hasn't followed me down the road of bad taste. "You're very talented, sis."

"I know," Eva says. "Now, where's your dress?"

I point to the red dress lying on my bed, and Eva smiles. "Oh wow. I remember when Tito Melboy made that for you. Your first original piece. You were so happy that night, you started to cry. Which made us all cry, of course."

He'd given it to me in a big box with a fancy bow before my first appearance at Dreamland.

My eyes start to get misty. "It was the best gift anyone had ever given me. And I'd already been given a lot," I say, thinking back to all the many things my mom had purchased for me. Things that I couldn't imagine any other mother getting for their son. I was so lucky to have them both in my life.

Eva sighs. "Now let's just hope it still fits. Come on," she says, looking at her watch. "We don't have much time before we need to head over."

At 7:20 p.m., we drive over to the Pink Unicorn. It's just ten minutes away from my condo, so I was expecting to have plenty of time to settle in, quietly set up, and relax before people started to trickle in for karaoke night.

I couldn't have been more wrong.

When we arrive, there are no parking spaces in front. Instead, the street on both sides is lined with cars, and right outside the bar there are people waiting to get in. A line stretches down the length of the building. It takes me almost ten minutes to find a place to park, something that's usually quick and easy.

"Did you see all those people?" Eva says to me.

I haven't gotten out. I haven't even turned the car off yet. I'm holding on to the steering wheel and staring out the windshield, immobile. The car seat holds on to me, sucking me deeper into its cushion. My stomach churns, and my head begins to feel leaden underneath my wig. For a moment, I want to just put the car back into drive, go home, and put my Regina Moon Dee drag back in my storage chest.

Eva grips my shoulder. "Don't be nervous, big bro."

"I'm not nervous," I say, turning to her and trying not to blink, afraid that the pooling tears will ruin my makeup. "I'm scared."

"Hey," Eva says softly. She reaches around me and pulls me into her. I breathe in her familiar jasmine shampoo scent. It saves me from my sunken place.

After I turn off the engine, Eva gets out, walks over to my side, and opens my door. She looks super-cute. She's worn a ruby-red silk blouse that I've loaned her and is even wearing a bit of my makeup to match me. And I'm not sure exactly what it is, but there's something else about her that feels even more comforting than usual.

"You are going to slay," Eva says. She pulls me up out of my seat and closes the car door behind me. I slip my arm in hers. As she accompanies me to the Pink Unicorn, she rubs my forearm to comfort me.

A woman in line turns toward the sound my heels make as they *click-clack* on the sidewalk. "Regina!" she screams.

"You got this," Eva says to me. "I'm right here."

I peck her on the cheek and then throw my arms wide to the people. "Hiiiiiiiiiiii!" I say. The word floats out onto them, sparking them into a fire-like frenzy. They tear loose from the line and flock around me, forming a stopgap that forces me to pause every few steps to say hello, grasp an elbow, or allow someone to reach in and hug me or take a selfie.

It takes a while for Eva and me to make our way to the entrance. Once inside, we see that it's already full of people. Never in my wildest dreams would I have thought we'd get such a huge response with just a few hours of notice, that there would be this many people out there wanting to come spend an evening with me.

Bryan meets us at the door. "You must be Regina Moon Dee! First of all, jeez Louise, you're gorgeous. Second, holy shit, we are mobbed. Why didn't Rex tell me you had this many fans?" he gushes.

I wink. "A lady never tells all her secrets."

"Where is Rex, by the way?" Bryan asks sincerely and absent of any innuendo. I'm pretty sure he doesn't know that I'm the person he's asking about.

"Family emergency," Eva says, smiling big at Bryan. "Hi, I'm Eva. Rex's sister. I'm here to help out in his place."

"Well, we're happy to have you. Both of you," Bryan says. "Go get some drinks. On the house, of course!" he says, before going back to managing the line of people waiting to get in.

At the bar, Eva sits on one of the stools and waves at Aaron down at the other end, currently pouring a line of green apple-colored cocktails. "Hello? We'd like to order drinks," she says.

"Just a sec, buddy," Aaron says, his deep voice rumbling. His red flannel shirt is unbuttoned at the top, showing hints of his chest hair and making me remember all my childhood fantasies about being ravaged by the Brawny paper towel man.

He scoots the drinks over to a group of people who are not-so-secretly looking our way, pointing and smiling at me. "Now, what can I get ya—" His smile slowly fades as he stares at my face.

It feels as if my corset has suddenly squeezed all the breath out of me.

He knows who I am. It's all over before it's even begun. I

should just turn around and run back out the door before the situation gets any worse.

"Sorry," Aaron says, brightening up again. "Don't mean to stare. I've just never seen one of you up close before."

Air finds its way back into my lungs. "I find that hard to believe," I say. "This is the Bay Area. There are Filipinos all over the place."

Aaron stammers, "No, uh, I mean..."

"Just giving you a hard time, handsome," I say, smirking. "I know what you mean. I'm Regina Moon Dee." I gesture to Eva. "And this is Eva, my—"

"Friend," she says. "Rex's sister."

"Pleased to meet you both. Thank you for coming on such short notice, and for being responsible for all this," he says, waving his arm over the crowded bar. "It's too bad Rex isn't here to see it."

"You'll just have to tell him all about it the next time you see him. And make sure to thank him generously," I say, trying to load that last word with as much meaning as possible.

"You bet I will," Aaron says, and winks at me, making my heart swell. "It's already a party in here, and you haven't even started the show yet."

As if on cue, Kat and her friends walk in through the door. Kat's always put together, but tonight she looks even hotter than usual, rocking her favorite leather pants, a gold sequin top, and high-heeled boots. Her ex-bandmates are dressed similarly to Kat, all in denim and leather and sexy, sparkly things that I'd wear in a heartbeat.

While they head into the main room, Kat comes straight toward us. I'm overjoyed to see her, but worry nips at me. Will she remember not to let on that she knows me? Kat's a great singer, but how good an actor is she?

Looking right past me, she says to Aaron, "Can we get a round of four vodka shots?"

As he walks to the back shelf to grab more shot glasses, Kat shrieks, "Ohmigod! Sorry, I totally did not see you," and goes in for a hug.

I freeze. I'm about to say something to remind her not to say anything when she embraces Eva instead. "How have you been? It's been too long," Kat says to her.

"I know!" Eva says.

Kat looks back at me and says, "Hi. I'm Kat."

Good. She won't give anything away. She—

"Rex?" she says suddenly.

"Shhhhh!" Eva and I shush. I look over at Aaron pouring shots, and thankfully, it doesn't seem as if he's heard her.

"Holy flaming nuts! I never would've guessed it was you!"

"And we have to make sure no one else does either, okay?" I whisper at her.

"Yes. Got it." Kat seals her lips shut with her finger. "Mm lpss mmm sld," she mumbles.

Aaron brings Kat her drinks, and a new group of thirsty patrons approach, trying to get Aaron's attention. They swarm around us and converge, closing in around me. They're animated, friendly, but still—I'm starting to feel a little claustrophobic. My eyes dart around, looking for some-place else to move to.

"Ladies, please come back this way," Bryan says, to the rescue. "You can catch a breath in the office before the show starts."

"Thank you so much," I say.

"I'll stay out here and wait for Mom to arrive," Eva says.

I nod and allow Bryan to escort me through the throng of people, past Aaron at the far end, who's now so busy try-ing to keep up with drink orders that he's only a red-flannel blur.

The office is much roomier than I imagined. There's an en-suite bathroom, a desk with an ancient PC, a large filing cabinet, and a futon sofa. Someone's also been thoughtful enough to set up a makeup mirror on the desk with a bright lamp, a small electric fan, a bottle of water, and a granola bar for me.

Still in slight shock over how crowded the Pink Unicorn is, I plop down at the desk. "Is the fire code going to let you have that many people inside?" I ask Bryan.

"Fire code? Sweetheart, back in the day we used to break all sorts of laws here, and fire codes were the least of them. Remind me to tell you about the time Boy George and his entourage dropped by."

"So it's okay if we just crowd them in?"

"It's not, really. But tonight, I don't care. We'll manage to get all your fans inside somehow."

"Thank you, Bryan."

"No. Thank *you*. For doing this for us. And for Aaron. Especially for Aaron." Bryan's eyes begin to water. I'm surprised to see him get so emotional.

Before I can say anything, he stoops down and gives me a bear hug before disappearing out into the noise of the crowded bar.

As he leaves, Eva enters, holding the door open for someone. "Look who's here!" she says as our mom slips into the office. I leap up to hug her.

She kisses me, leaving a candy-apple-red mark on my cheek. "My Regina! Wow, ang ganda ganda ng anak ko!"

Speaking of beautiful, Mom's just as gorgeous in her red satin dress, high heels, and long, dangling earrings.

"I'm so glad you're here," I say.

"You know I would never miss such an important night."

"Thanks, Mom. I know how much you missed me doing—"

"A night of karaoke! One where you control all the songs! Naku, I can sing so many. What will I sing? How about Taylor Swift? I'm sure you will have many Swiffers in the audience who would appreciate my superior rendition."

"Swif*ties*, Mom," I say, laughing. "And you know I can't just let you sing whenever and whatever you want tonight. I have to be fair."

"Please, anak. Show business is never fair." My mom takes out a small pad of paper and a pen from her purse. "Now, let me just start making a list of songs for you..."

I give Eva a pleading look.

"Okayyyyy, Mom," Eva says, pushing her gently toward the door. "Give Regina her space so she can get finished preparing."

Our mother pays absolutely no attention to her and continues scribbling song titles as Eva scooches her out of the office.

"Eva," I say, "Dad doesn't know, right?"

She leans back against the door, closing Mom outside of it with a click. "Mom told him she's chaperoning my night out dancing with friends. He definitely had no interest in being a part of that."

"Thank you. And thanks for helping me."

"Of course!" Eva says. "Now give me your phone so I can pretend to be you."

I pull my phone out of my purse and hand it to her. "Nothing vulgar, please. Unless Aaron likes it."

"Blech," she says, sticking out her tongue. She gives me a side hug and says, "Break a leg," before heading back out into the bar.

I do some last touch-ups, brushing a little more powder onto the nose, blotting out some of the excess lip gloss, and moistening the ends of my wig with a few spritzes of spray conditioner. As a final touch, I spritz on a bit of Princess by Vera Wang, Beaucoup Buko's favorite perfume, my own little way of having her here with us.

It's close to eight o'clock. Nearly time to begin the show.

I creep out of the office and stand at the end of the

hallway, peering out into the main area of the bar. The crowd now fills the entire space, all tables, banquettes, and stools taken with people stuffed into every corner. Thankfully, my mom, Eva, Kat, and her friends have been able to get table space near the front of the stage, where I can see them.

We've got an audience. And me. Now all we need is our karaoke jockey.

I search for Paolo, but he's not at the console table.

When my eyes land on the microphone in its stand onstage, a dull ache thuds in the top corner of my forehead. I resist the urge to rub at it so that I don't disturb my makeup.

I make my way over to Aaron. "Should we get started soon?" I ask him.

"Yep," he says while pouring drinks. "As soon as our tech guy gets here. He's just running a little late. Again."

"I'm here!" Paolo says, rushing into the bar. Straight from the restaurant, it looks like, because he's still wearing his uniform of slacks, shirt, and bow tie. "Sorry, I was working on something and lost track of time."

"Buddy," Aaron says, "you gotta get here earlier. You need to get everything set up."

"I know. I'm sorry."

Aaron pours a bottle of Corona beer into a frosted mug. "At least you have some help tonight."

"Help?" Paolo says. He straightens his glasses and looks at me. And the look on his face is not what I was expecting.

At first, I'm afraid he's identified me. But it's not recognition on his face. Nor is it confusion. Or slight apprehension like Aaron's reaction, or outright shock like Kat's. It's something more like...attraction? He's beaming from ear to ear, as if he very much likes what he sees. I know I'm looking snatched tonight—my makeup is on point, and despite Eva's fears of me not being able to get into my old dress, it fits like a glove over my padding. Still, I'm a bit surprised by his response, making me wonder if he even knows that I'm a drag queen.

"We're going to try mixing it up a little tonight, Paolo," Aaron says. "This is Regina Moon Dee. She's gonna be your co-host."

I throw up one of my hands, palm to the sky. "Surprise."

"Co-host?" Paolo says.

"While you attend to all the impressive technical things, I'll be on the mic. Doing the boring talking stuff."

"I've got a good feeling about this," Aaron says, handing the beer to Paolo. "I think you'll make a good team."

"I guess we'll find out." He sweeps his arm out toward the main room in a gentlemanly gesture. "After you."

I bow my head gracefully at him. "Thank you," I say, squeezing my way through the crowd to the stage area.

"You're welcome," Paolo says, scooting right up next to me. "*Rex.*"

CHAPTER 8

I KEEP MY COOL AND MAINTAIN MY STROLL, smiling tightly and saying nothing until we reach the stage.

Paolo sits down at his KJ table. I say to him, "Whoever you think I am, you're mistaken."

"No, I'm not," he replies. "I can see you, Rex. Plain as day."

I lean over close and hiss into his ear, "I don't know how you figured it out, but if you tell anyone, this microphone of mine is finding a new home." I look down at his behind.

His eyes widen. "Yikes."

Eva runs up to the stage. "What is up with you two?" she says. "Quit flirting!"

"We're not flirting!" Paolo and I say at the same time.

"Then get your act together. People are waiting," Eva

says. I look out at the bar and see Aaron and Bryan watching us curiously.

"We'll talk about this later," I say to Paolo. "Just get things ready. And here." I hand him an already filled-out request slip. "Queue this up for me."

Paolo's eyes light up, reminding me of the first time I talked to him, when I'd told him the title of my favorite karaoke song. He smiles and proceeds to click a series of controls on his laptop screen. The house lights go down to half, and the colored lights above me turn on, swirling in a slow, seductive tempo.

I move to the center of the stage and tap my microphone. The dull thump sounds through the speakers and bounces around inside me. My heart beats faster. Mom, Eva, Kat, and her friends in the front row sit in anticipation with huge smiles. But beyond them, the rest of the crowd melts into a sea of semi-darkness. I can't see the looks on their faces. Can't determine their feelings. Or their intentions.

But I can see Paolo. I look over at him, and he's glowing. Literally. He's messed up the light controls and has aimed the roving spotlight on himself. He's on the edge of his seat, waiting for the night to begin, for me to introduce myself, and to finally sing.

The spotlight wanders off him and inches across the stage, finding me. But unlike the one he'd shone on me our first night, this one is soft and inviting. I take a breath. I tell myself, *Eva and Mom are here. Kat and her friends are, too. And*

Aaron. And Bryan. They're all rooting for you. Just take a deep breath and focus on that old familiar feeling, just like riding a bike. A more glamorous bike with handlebar tassels, and a sequined seat, and lots and lots of padding.

I try to decide what to say. How do I reintroduce myself? Long explanations of where I've been all these years run through my head. Do I tell them all why I've been hiding? And why I've decided to come back by hosting karaoke night at a dive bar in Oakland?

In the end, I address none of these things. I just sing-song into the mic, "I'm baaaaaack!" and my ears fill with the sweet, sustaining sound of the audience's roar.

"Sounds to me like you're ready for the first song of the night!" I say. "So let's start the evening off right."

My mother, for some reason, begins to stand up. I shake my head and smile aggressively at her to make her sit, but she seems oblivious to my warning. Thankfully, Eva pulls her back down into her seat.

I turn to Paolo and mouth, *Hit it.*

"I'm Coming Out" by Diana Ross lights up the video monitors. The guitar riff starts, and I let my voice fly. The voice that always had people mistaking me for being a girl on the phone. The voice I've been trying to force downward into a more masculine range for the past few years. Now I can finally use it to do what it was meant to do: sing in my natural range.

In the now exuberant lights that Paolo's turned on in the rest of the room, I see how stunned Kat and her friends are.

And even from a distance, I can tell from the way that Aaron's and Bryan's mouths have dropped open that they can't quite believe what they're hearing. But the grins on everyone else's faces tell me that they're all fans who know what I'm capable of. So I give the audience what they've been waiting years for. No twirling, or kicking, or over-the-top flourishes. Just me connecting with them. I sing about how much I have to give, about all the things that I want the world to see and hear. That there's no need for me to fear. I'm coming out.

When the song fades, the room erupts. Eva looks as if she's barely able to restrain herself from rushing the stage to hug me. Kat is shaking her head in disbelief. And back at the bar, Bryan and Aaron are clapping heartily.

"Thank you all so much!" I say. "Now let's keep the fun rolling. Next up is a known crowd pleaser—"

My mom stands up again. And my sister pulls her back down.

"Can I get Kat up onstage?" I ask.

Kat runs up, throws her arms around me, and says, "I fucking love you so much."

"My my! What appreciative patrons you have here at the Pink Unicorn," I say into the mic, motioning Kat with my head to tell Paolo what she wants to sing. "Folks, if the powers that be are happy with me tonight, I might be able to extend my hosting residency here. So drink up and be sure to tip that hunky bartender back there, would you?"

Kat rejoins me in the center of the stage.

"So what have you got for us tonight, Ms. Kat?"

"'Get the Party Started'!" she says, grabbing the mic and punching the sky.

The intro to Pink's dance-pop anthem starts up. The lights go wild again, slightly out of control in that Paolo way. The lyrics to a completely different song, "Get Down on It" by Kool & the Gang, pop up on the screen behind Kat. But it doesn't matter. She knows Pink's lyrics by heart. And like I knew she would, Kat kills it from note one, belting her way through every part of the song.

While she sings, I sit next to Paolo at the KJ table, helping him organize the request slips that people have already started to hand to him.

"You were incredible," he says to me as he sorts. I don't know if it's the lights in the room or the massive amounts of electricity running through the speakers near us, but he seems to be vibrating with energy.

I reach out and touch his forearm lightly, almost expecting it to shock me. "Thank you."

He looks down at my hand. I retract it quickly.

"Why are you ashamed of who you are?" Paolo asks.

"I'm not ashamed."

"So why are you keeping your identity a secret?"

"I just don't want people to know who I really am."

"Why?"

"I just don't," I say, starting to get irritated.

"But it looks like your friend Kat already knows."

"She does now. Yes."

"How about that other girl? And the woman next to her? Are they related to you?"

"Yes. My sister, Eva, and my mom. They both know."

"So then, who doesn't?"

Over at the bar, Aaron is busy making drinks for several people who are now standing and waiting. I grab a lock of my wig and start twirling the end of it as I watch him. It quickly tangles into a messy knot.

Paolo follows my line of sight. "I see," he says.

I'm about to say something, make sure he understands how important it is that he not tell Aaron, but Kat is already starting to wind down her song. The music vamps its way to the end, and Kat improvises over it with some scatting, something Pink didn't do in the original version, sealing it at the end with a high, belted note.

"Yass, queen!" I say, jumping up to join Kat center stage. She plants a big, sloppy kiss on my cheek before popping the mic back into its stand and heading back to her table. "My, my. I wish my last boyfriend was that appreciative. We'd still be together if that were the case. Speaking of which, is my next beau just around the corner? José, you're up!"

The people applaud enthusiastically, already with much more energy than last weekend. I've managed to lift up the mood of karaoke night, exactly how I'd hoped.

José is one of the people I recognize from last Saturday as one of the regulars. A cute, heavier-set guy who reminds me of a Latino Jack Black. He begins his rendition of "American Pie," and I realize two things. It's a good choice in terms of audience singalong participation, and it's eight minutes long. Plenty of time for me and Paolo to have a little emergency chat.

I grasp Paolo firmly by the hand and pull him away from the desk.

"Um, what's happening?" he asks.

"Shhhh." I lead him off the stage, down the side of the room to the back where the bathroom is. Bryan raises his eyebrow at us as we pass the bar. "Just need a little help adjusting my outfit, honey," I say, blowing him a kiss.

Once inside the bathroom, I turn the door handle lock. "Please don't tell Aaron."

"Why not?"

"He's not...comfortable with drag queens."

"He seems to like you plenty from what I can see," Paolo says.

One of the last pieces of advice I ever received from Tito Melboy echoes in my ear. *If a man is attracted to you as a man, then he will not love you as a woman.*

"He might appreciate Regina Moon Dee," I say. "But he wouldn't love her."

Paolo's face drops. "Oh."

I don't know why the unmistakable sadness on Paolo's face distresses me so much. I felt the same need to placate him when I refused to sing last weekend, when he looked as if I'd let him down personally. "We have history," I say. "He's my ex. He broke up with me. But I think we might have a real shot this time."

"Not if he knows you're a drag queen, though."

"Yes," I say. "That's right."

"But...that sucks." Paolo looks at me intensely, as if daring me to turn away. "Why be with someone you have to hide yourself from?"

I have a hard time holding his stare, but I force myself to, because it's important that he hear me and understand. "I have the right to keep myself safe. And no one has the right to tell me how or when I come out to people."

Paolo's eyes begin to soften, and his mouth twitches. "I—"

The door swings open. Aaron steps inside the bathroom.

Crap! I thought I'd locked it.

Without hesitating, I pull Paolo into me.

And start kissing him.

"Oh, dang!" I hear Aaron say, though I can't see him because Paolo's face is completely covering mine, his eyes bulging right out of his glasses.

I roam my hands frantically over Paolo's body, embracing him for a few seconds longer before coming up for air. "First peek's for free, handsome," I say to Aaron. "You'll have to pay for the rest."

"I didn't know anyone was in here," Aaron says, blushing. "Word of advice, use the dead bolt next time." He points at the lock before backing slowly out of the bathroom with his hands up.

Paolo and I just stand there looking at each other for a few moments. His lips are smeared red with my lipstick. I grab a paper towel, and without thinking about it, moisten it with my tongue and wipe the lipstick off his face.

My cheeks burn when I realize what I've done.

Paolo just stares at me.

"I'm so sorry, I don't know why I—" I say.

"We should get back," Paolo says, doing a quick heel turn and exiting the bathroom.

I take one last look at myself in the mirror, smooth out my lipstick with the tip of my pinkie, and then close my eyes and sigh before following Paolo back out to the stage.

We're just in time. José is singing the seventh and final refrain of "American Pie." By this time, everyone in the Pink Unicorn is singing along, so I do, too, grabbing the host mic off the karaoke desk and joining in. Paolo's the only one not singing. He's got his head buried in the next request slip and is queuing up the next song. He seems upset. I know what I did in the bathroom was an overstep.

But there's no time to address it right now. The song will be over soon, and I can tell from the look on my mom's face that she won't be able to last another minute without getting her chance to sing.

"Let's hear it for José, everyone!" I say. "We all love a good slice of pie, don't we? Especially ones with a little extra fruit, if you get what I mean. Now I have a special treat for you all. She's the real thrilla from Manila. Giving you soap opera star realness, my...*aunt*. Sharon!"

Mom runs onstage and grabs the mic from my hand. "Thank you, thank you, Regina!" She pinches my cheek. "Okay! This one is for my kids. Hit it!"

The screens light up with the title card, and the song track starts.

Oh, no. It's "Lady Marmalade." Mom's favorite inappropriate family singalong about sex workers. Which she's dedicated to Eva and me.

I try to leave the stage, but Mom grabs me by the wrist and points her lips to the mic in the stand. There's no escaping it. I have to sing a sexy song with my mom in front of a packed house.

To be honest, though, we have a great time singing together. And when we're done, Mom doesn't really ever sit back down. She's either on the side dancing and singing along to whatever song is being sung or mingling around and talking with other people in the bar. I've forgotten how much she's always the life of the party wherever Eva and I go. I haven't been out with either of them in so long. Not since Dreamland, in fact.

While Jenny (Ms. Anaconda from last weekend) sings the Mariah Carey version of "Without You," I sit down next to Eva. It's getting to that point in the night when different parts of my body are starting to complain. My feet are sore, my waist wants to be let out, and my entire head is overheated from the wig cap and my larger-than-life wig.

"How's it going with you-know-who?" I ask, looking down at my phone on the table.

"Check it." She hands it to me, and I scroll through the text conversation she's been having with Aaron as my proxy.

How is it going with Regina? she asks him.

Your friend's really got the crowd going. I'm making more drinks tonight than I have in a long time.

Told you! I just wish I could be there. It would be more fun than this.

Eva's uploaded an old video clip I'd taken of me with Dad at a party at his cousin's house. It's perfect fake proof of me being somewhere else.

Wish you were here, too, Aaron texts back.

(This makes my heart leap.)

So does Regina get the job? Eva asks.

Let's talk. Want to come over to my place tonight after I'm done closing up? Around 2:00. I know that's really late. So no worries if you can't.

My heart starts hammering in my chest.

He's sent me his address, and the text chain stops there.

"What do you want me to say?" Eva asks.

This is it. What I've been dreaming about for the past few years but never believing would ever happen—a second chance with Aaron. I can't imagine he wants to just talk about Regina Moon Dee. He wants to hook up. Meeting him at his place at two in the morning is very late, but at least it gives me plenty of time between now and then to go home, change, and take off all my makeup.

Jenny lets out a screechy high note, and I wince. I look

up at Paolo at the KJ table, who's doing the same thing. We both laugh.

But instead of turning away immediately afterward, we keep looking at each other.

Jenny continues, back on pitch now, sounding centered and sweet. She sings about how she can't forget the look on her loved one's face as he leaves; he's smiling, but in his eyes, his sorrow shows.

At just that moment, a roaming stage light lands on Paolo, illuminating him. My breath catches.

"Hey," Eva says. "What should I say?"

I blink rapidly and look away from Paolo. "Tell Aaron *yes*," I say.

She nods and sends Aaron a thumbs-up emoji. I sneak a look back at the bar and see Aaron pull out his phone. He glances at it, smiles, and continues shaking his cocktail tumbler.

At around 10:55 p.m., as the current singer ends her number, I'm about to announce the last song, when feedback squeals through the sound system, making everyone in the bar cringe.

Tap, tap, tap. "Is this on?" Paolo says into another mic that he's pulled from under the KJ desk. "First off, I want to thank the beautiful Regina Moon Dee for hosting. She's really brought something special to the evening."

The way Paolo says *special* makes me get hot under my corset. I smile awkwardly at him and grab a nearby bar napkin to blot my suddenly sweaty forehead.

"I've had so much fun tonight listening to all the fantastic singing. So I'd like to try a little song of my own, if you don't mind?" He looks at me as if he's asking for my permission specifically. "Because this is one of my favorite songs."

Instrumental music starts. The unmistakable intro to Celine Dion's version of "All By Myself." The song Paolo had queued up for me to sing last weekend by surprise.

I lean back against the bar counter to listen. My interest is piqued. "All By Myself" is not easy. At least not for a woman. For a man, the song sits a bit lower, in the baritone-tenor range. The highest note is hard for a guy but not unattainable. Not like it is for most women attempting to belt it.

The song begins, and Paolo sings.

Except, for some crazy reason, he is, in fact, attempting to sing it in Celine Dion's range. So what are low notes for a female singer are already high notes for him. I shake my head in disbelief. I'm the only man I know who can actually do this. That's why it's one of my go-to songs. People are always gobsmacked by my ability to sing it in the right octave.

Though a bit breathy, Paolo actually starts on pitch. But the notes only go upward. And from the way Paolo's face strains—his nostrils flaring and the veins on the side of his neck hardening into steel—I can tell what comes next is going to be rough. My fingers grip the sides of my barstool. I'm going to need to strap in for this ride.

Paolo squeezes the microphone. His body compacts into a rigid mass. The refrain begins its familiar ascending phrase, and he attempts (*All*) with every note (*by*) to launch them high enough (*myself*) onto the right places on the music staff. And every note falls well short. (*All*) In one case, (*by*) almost by several steps, (*myself*) causing my testicles to tighten and shrink until they're tiny marbles.

Paolo takes a deep breath. Here it comes.

Anymore!! he screams. The entire bar reels backward in their chairs. I see Kat almost fall over in hers. My mom actually sticks her fingers in her ears.

The long-held note of the last syllable of *anymore* goes on and on, getting more flat as it goes.

But the funny thing is, I sort of like it.

Sure, Paolo is so far away from the original key now that he's defied the laws of physics. But he doesn't seem to care at all. It looks like he's enjoying every second he's onstage. He's selling that song, actual notes be damned. It's kind of sexy.

And I'm not the only one who appreciates Paolo's performance. When he's done, people reward him with applause. Kat and the Nine Tails gals even stand up and hoot.

Their response reminds me of why people love karaoke. Not everyone is a trained singer. But anyone, given the right amount of courage (liquid or otherwise), can take their turn at the mic and share what they have with everyone else. It doesn't have to be pretty or perfect. It just has to be them. And I think it was obvious to everyone at the Pink Unicorn that what we saw was truly Paolo. Every last off-pitch bit of him.

He sits back down at the KJ table, and I realize something. The anxiety that I felt at the beginning of the evening has disappeared. Eva, Mom, and Kat being here has helped. And the fact that Aaron and Bryan seem pleased has definitely made me feel a lot better.

But somehow it's Paolo's performance that has wiped away every last trace of the fear that I had. I'm not sure why.

"Ladies and gentlemen, and everyone in between and beyond," I announce onstage, "I'm sorry to say, but it's almost time to say good night."

A huge *awwww* from the crowd.

"Thank you all so much for coming. I'm so happy to have been your karaoke queen tonight. Let's all close out the evening by singing this last one together, shall we?"

The screens light up with the title card to "Bohemian Rhapsody." I invite Kat onstage, pointing at the second microphone. She squeals with glee and hops up next to me.

To say the subsequent group singalong is anything less than a total train wreck would be lying, even with us leading it. Our take on Freddie Mercury's opening slow bars is solid, but as soon as the other people start chiming in with the choral parts, it's all downhill, right from the first "scaramouche." But it doesn't matter at all. Everyone's faces are shiny and happy as they sing their lungs out.

As the final piano chord sounds, Paolo expertly fades the stage lights and turns the house lights back up, gradually transitioning to lo-fi hip-hop. He already seems more at ease behind the table. Maybe it's because it's easier to focus on the controls while I host. Maybe it's because of something else. All I know is, he looks extremely content, which is good.

Because our kiss in the bathroom, even though it was fake, was still something he didn't ask for. And I've been thinking about it all night.

Because of how rude it was of me, of course.

Kat hugs me. "Babe, that was lit! They'd be insane not to hire you permanently."

"Thank you, darling," I say. "I would tend to agree. But I should confirm with the powers that be." I give her two air kisses and let her rejoin her bandmate friends.

Mom leans against Eva at their table, looking tired and a little tipsy.

"Time to get Tita Sharon to bed," I say.

Mom perks up. "Che! I can sing and dance all night!" she says, and begins to sing the soundtrack to *My Fair Lady*.

"Yep, time to go home," Eva says. "I'll drive her. You okay getting home?"

"I'll take a rideshare. You just take care of Mom."

She puts her arm around our mother's waist and pulls her up. I accompany them to the front door. As they walk down the sidewalk, I can hear Mom still singing "I Could Have Danced All Night."

"Your aunt is quite a character," Bryan says, setting a colorful cocktail in front of me as I take a seat at the still-busy bar.

"Yes, she is." I sip the drink, leaving behind a trace of gloss on the glass. "Mm. Extra sweet. Just how I like them."

Bryan winks at me. "Me, too."

I smile. "So, how'd I do, boss?"

113

"You know, I've seen many a celebrity come through here. But not one of them can compare to you."

"Stop it, you're making me blush."

"I'm serious," he insists. "Want to know why? Because with everyone else, you can tell it's all about them. But not with you. You make everyone else feel like they're the star. That's why you're so special."

I look around at the patrons, still enjoying the afterglow of the evening's festivities. "You're too kind," I say.

"Just calling it like I see it. But what do I know? He's the one you have to please," Bryan says, jerking his head toward Aaron at the other end of the bar. He retrieves a bowl of snack mix from under the counter and places it in front of me. "In case you're hungry," he says with a tender pat on my hand, before attending to people waiting for drinks.

Someone taps me on the shoulder. "Regina?"

I turn around. It's Eva. "What are you doing back here?"

"Mom and I—uh, I mean *my* mom and I were about to leave but then realized I forgot to give you back your phone," she says, handing it back to me. "Good thing, too. Check the last text."

"Sure. I just need to talk to Aaron," I say, taking the phone and proceeding to the other end of the bar.

"You should really read it—"

"In a minute. After I've—"

"REGINA," Eva says.

I stop in my tracks and turn around slowly. "Yes?"

"Read. The. Text."

I glance down at my phone. Aaron has sent me another message. Good news. Bryan's closing up for me so I can meet up with you earlier. My place at midnight?

And Eva has responded: Sounds good! See you then. :)

"Why did you say that?" I ask. My scalp goes hot. God, I've got to get this wig off me. And now I have precious little time to do it.

"You seemed pretty raring to go!" Eva says.

"Yeah, but now I only have half an hour tops to get ready!" I whisper. "Crap, crap, crap."

I look around and see that Bryan has already taken over all the bartending duties. Aaron is nowhere in sight.

"Regina and Eva," Aaron says from behind me, making me jump. He's got his jacket on and his keys are in his hand. "Please stay and enjoy. Drinks are on us. And here—your fee for tonight." He hands me an envelope of cash.

"Thank you, darling. Should I plan on coming back next week?"

Aaron looks to Bryan behind the bar, who nods and gives him two big thumbs-up. Aaron smiles at me and says, "Yes."

I smile back. "Wonderful."

"I hate to be rude, but I've got to run," Aaron says.

"Hot date?" I ask, winking slyly.

"Something like that."

Now I've really got to take all this stuff off. For many reasons.

"See you next week," Aaron says.

"I'll be counting the days," I say to myself as Aaron leaves.

I swivel to go say goodbye to Kat and check in with Paolo, but Eva pulls me away before I'm able to do either. "No time, big bro. You have to go!"

As we hurry out the door, the last thing I see is Paolo, now strangely sad, watching me as I leave.

CHAPTER 9

MY HEART RACES AS I SIT ON AARON'S COUCH, staring at him. I've never seen him like this before. What the heck do I do now?

HALF AN HOUR EARLIER

"What's taking so long?" I ask Eva.

I wipe the glue off my eyebrows with cotton balls and oil cleanser while she continues to tug unsuccessfully at my dress. "The zipper's stuck. I think you've gained weight over the last couple of hours."

"No fat-shaming!" I say to her reflection in the mirror. "My body swells up sometimes when I'm stressed, that's all."

The clock is ticking. Eva's gotten me back to my Oakland condo in record time, but that still only leaves me twenty minutes or so to get out of drag. Meanwhile, our mother is sleeping on my sofa, her head elegantly resting on a stack of my throw pillows.

"There we go!" Eva says victoriously.

Air rushes into my lungs, and my newly freed torso expands. "Much better. Thank you."

Eva continues to take my dress off, pulling it down my body like a banana peel. "This brings me back," she says. "Remember how I used to help you take off all your stuff back at Dreamland?"

When Eva and Mom were able to accompany Tito Melboy and me to our shows at Dreamland (they couldn't come every time because Dad would've gotten too suspicious), they'd help us de-drag so that we could hurry home before Dad would start to wonder where we were.

"You were an incredibly helpful ten-year-old," I say.

"I know. That's why Uncle gave me this," she says, caressing the beaded necklace around her neck.

That's why Eva's appearance seemed so comforting to me this evening. She's been wearing the necklace Tito Melboy gave her. I remember watching him construct it out of glass beads and seashells during the summer he spent with us. As he worked, he told me it was a simpler version of a traditional baliog necklace, like the ones his tita from Mindanao used to make.

"Uncle said I needed something special, since I was such a good assistant," Eva says, and laughs. "He also told me I could get him out of his clothes faster than some of his old boyfriends, which I didn't really understand until years later."

"He was so proud of you," I say.

"He may have been proud of me, but he adored you, Rex. Like you were his own kid."

That's because I *was* Tito Melboy's kid. His drag child.

I pluck a makeup remover wipe from the box on my bathroom counter and start cleansing my face. "Thanks for helping," I say. "But I think I got the rest of this handled."

Eva picks up her purse. "Happy to help. I'm just so glad you're doing drag again. And Tito Melboy would be really happy, too," she says, giving me a side hug before waking up Mom to go home.

Yes, Tito Melboy would be happy.

I stare at my reflection in the mirror. My face is red because of the scrubbing, and my hair is flattened from being underneath a wig cap all night. Tito Melboy was the one who showed me the fastest ways to take off the layers of adhesives, foundations, and colors from my face. How to put a wig back into its case properly. How to hem a skirt. How to mend a torn garment. And how to perform in front of a packed room of people. Live. Not just on videos taped in a bedroom. He was the one who taught me everything I know about being a true queen.

That summer before senior year, after I'd told my uncle about my secret life as Regina Moon Dee and shown him all my performance videos, he let me in on his own secret.

"Are things with you and my dad any better now that you're here?" I asked him one day. My dad was sometimes a bit grumpy around Tito Melboy at home, but mostly, he seemed civil and was even outwardly appreciative of his cooking for us.

"Yes," Tito Melboy replied. His brow furrowed as he cut away at a chunk of high-density foam at our kitchen table. "But I feel a little bit guilty about why."

"What do you mean?" I asked, watching with fascination as he sculpted homemade hip and thigh pads for me.

"In order to make peace with him, I told your dad a little lie. I said I had stopped doing drag professionally. That I wanted to focus on family instead."

I fake-pouted. "So you don't actually want to spend time with us?"

"Of course I do, Rex. I love getting to know my beautiful niece and nephew." He pulled me in and placed a quick peck on my forehead. "No, I lied about quitting drag. In fact, the main reason I came here was for a job that I'm starting very soon."

Tito Melboy had come to the Bay Area to manage the shows at Dreamland.

The drag-themed restaurant opened in the nineties, gradually became a must-visit tourist destination over the years. Its hostesses, waitresses, and performers were all drag queens, both cis gay men and trans women, and mostly people of color. As Beaucoup Buko, Tito Melboy would be in charge of planning, promoting, and scheduling the shows. She'd also be the de facto mother to all the queens. The person she would be replacing—her own drag daughter, Baby Buko—was moving to New York at the end of the summer to manage Dreamland's new Hell's Kitchen location.

Dreamland was thrilled that Beaucoup Buko, a top-notch performer, would be taking Baby's place. She had years of experience managing bars in both the Philippines and Los Angeles and was known for her creative and bold event ideas.

My uncle's first idea for Dreamland was to infuse it with new talent. Namely, me.

"You will be perfect for this new weekly show I'm going to add to the schedule," he told me.

"Doing what?" I asked, trembling from both excitement and terror at the idea of performing in public for the first time.

Tito Melboy patted my knee. "You'll see. But first, I will give you an idea of what you're getting into."

He knew I was young and inexperienced, and that he'd have to convince me first. He suggested we go to Dreamland's famous Drag Brunch, the most family friendly of their shows. It was notoriously difficult to get a table for it, especially at the last minute. But with one phone call to Baby Buko, VIP seats were reserved for all of us—my uncle, my mom, Eva, and me. (We told Dad that we'd be going jewelry shopping in San Francisco, which he, of course, had no interest in taking part in.)

Eva and I were thrilled to finally see a professional drag show. And anything as dramatic as a restaurant full of drag queens was right up my mom's alley. "What should I wear, Melboy?" my mom asked as we got ready. "I have so many ideas. But I don't want to attract too much attention and overshadow the other girls!"

"I don't think that will be a problem, Sharon," Tito

Melboy replied, smiling at me and Eva behind her back. Even with Mom's impressive collection of clothes, I had a feeling nothing she wore would come close to the queens' extravagant outfits.

When we got to San Francisco, we couldn't find a street spot. So we ended up parking at a small garage. As my mom and Tito Melboy continued their nonstop gossiping, I went to get the ticket from the office and then promptly lost my ability to talk.

The parking attendant was the most beautiful guy I'd ever seen.

He had a Mediterranean look to him, Italian or Greek perhaps. Dark, curly hair, thick eyebrows, and a prominent, sculpted nose. His uniform (dirty with a few grease stains, making him even more hot) was open down to the top of his pecs. The sight of his wispy chest hair entranced me. He smelled like Axe body spray and axle grease. And though he was older than me, it couldn't have been by much. He looked like he was probably a college student.

"Hi," I said dumbly, my throat suddenly sore.

"Hello," the young man said. His voice was deep and sultry. The accent was hard for me to place, though I was pretty sure he was Eastern European. His name tag said *Ivan.* "How long will you be here?"

"Um, I don't know how long I'll take it. I mean, how long I am. Oh, my god."

Ivan's sexy lips turned up into a smirk. "No worries. See you when I see you," he said, and handed me a parking ticket. When I went to pull it from him, he held on firmly, making me work to get it. He winked and let go.

My family stood waiting by the car.

"All set?" my mom asked.

"Yeah." I looked back to see Ivan still watching me. "I'm ready. And excited."

"I can see that," Tito Melboy said, glancing at the tenting going on in my pants and chuckling to himself. Embarrassment made even more blood rush to my extremities, making it hard to walk out of the garage.

But my embarrassment was forgotten when Baby Buko greeted us with huge hugs at Dreamland's entrance. She was a willowy queen with flowing limbs and a lamé gown that dripped off her like liquid emeralds. "Welcome, welcome!" she said, taking us inside the restaurant.

My mouth dropped as we entered. For some reason, I'd expected the place to be small and dark. But the restaurant was huge, with large windows that let in lots of sun, making the place feel bright and airy. The décor was tropical-themed—lots of bamboo furniture, palm-leaf plants, and a festive wallpaper with a birds-of-paradise print, its repeating pattern of red-orange plumes scaling the length of the walls.

The place was already packed, but the entire staff moved around with ease. It was as if they were choreographed—from the seating of guests to the way the queens weaved around the room to avoid running into one another's massive trays of brunch drinks and appetizers. It was easy to see that Baby Buko ran a tight ship.

"Baby!" Tito Melboy said, grabbing hold of his drag daughter's hand. "Ang ganda naman dito! The pictures online don't do it justice."

"And the girls are just as beautiful as the restaurant!" my mom added. "By the way, is it okay that Eva and Rex are here? They're underage."

"Of course, of course," Baby said, ushering us to our reserved seats at a table right at the front near the stage. "Look around. There's plenty of kids here. Anything before nine p.m. is family friendly. The adult shows are after nine-thirty p.m. only."

The late-night shows were labeled "adults only," but even those weren't risqué, Baby told us. Sure, the queens had more colorful language and maybe slightly more revealing outfits, but Baby's policy was that, if you felt embarrassed to bring your mother, she didn't want it at Dreamland. "This is no Red Light ping-pong ball whorehouse," she once said to one of the performers, scolding her for doing a too-raunchy striptease one night. Her girls knew to keep it clean. And Sunday Drag Brunch was one hundred percent wholesome.

It was one of their busiest events, so there were at least ten girls working the dining room. While my family perused the menu, I watched the queens as they moved around, chatting with the guests as they took their orders. Tito Melboy told me that, while one would perform in the show, the others would seamlessly fill in and attend to her table.

Our waitress, a twenty-something queen from Taiwan named Benta Box, was a whirlwind, carrying multiple trays of food and delivering them all with a gorgeous smile. Baby Buko informed us that Benta, who identified as trans, was a seasoned performer. She had worked three different shows at Dreamland to make enough money to get her top surgery done. I couldn't wait to see what she'd do during her turn onstage.

When our plates of loco moco and huli-huli chicken came (Dreamland's Sunday brunch menu was Hawaiian-themed), we all dug in. As we ate, Tito Melboy leaned over to whisper in my ear.

"Notice how the girls hold themselves, even when just delivering food? They stay poised at all times."

"You'll need to cultivate stamina. See the shoes? They don't take the easy way out by wearing comfortable ones."

"Take a look at her wig, Rex. See the perfect shading she uses to blend in the hairline?"

Baby Buko opened the brunch show with a Tina Turner lip-synch. Afterward, all the girls, including Benta Box, took their turns, and she was indeed spectacular, doing a perfect lip-synch of Taylor Swift's "You Belong With Me."

But while they all did a great job, I could feel that the show was missing something. Something that my uncle knew I could provide.

After the show was over, as the queens went back to their tables to close out everyone's bills, Baby Buko sat down with us. "Tell me, what did you think?" she asked.

"It was amazing," I said. I glanced at my mom, who had clearly enjoyed both the meal and the show, and at Eva, who looked as if she'd just spent the entire day at Disneyland. I'd never seen a kid so happy to be sitting at a restaurant for two hours.

Tito Melboy beamed. "I'm so proud of you, Baby. It's wonderful here."

"The owners take good care of us, Mama," Baby said. "They're especially good to the trans community. We all feel safe here."

I wondered if Baby herself was trans. It was impossible to tell who was and who wasn't. I assumed that's how both the cisgender male drag queens and the trans queens wanted it to be. As far as they were concerned, they were all drag performers. All that mattered was a commitment to the art.

"Rex, your uncle tells me you're a budding young queen yourself and that you should be given the opportunity to perform here," Baby said. "Would you like that?"

"Yes! Would that be okay, Mom?"

She squeezed my hand. "What an opportunity! Of course, anak. I will support you. My little superstar."

"Well," Baby said, sharing a look with my uncle, "how about we start you early? I can give you a spot in next week's show."

My head swirled. I'd actually be performing live. In real time. In front of real people. Except, "What about Dad?" I asked.

"I will take care of that," my mom assured everyone at the table.

"And do you know what you would do for your talent number, Rex?" Tito Melboy asked.

I didn't. Not right then. But I'd have the whole week to think about it and to prepare.

I'd thought that the excitement of that moment would be something I'd never forget, and yet for years I had because I'd forced myself to, pushing it down deep inside me.

Until hosting karaoke on the Pink Unicorn stage, when it all resurfaced.

Actually, it was before that. As soon as I unlocked my chest again to prepare for the evening, euphoria rushed through me—when my makeup, wigs, dresses, and shoes were finally released from their containment.

Now I feel a different kind of thrill as I break speed limits left and right to get to Aaron's on time.

It reminds me of the first time I went home with him in Bloomington, after sitting at the same spot at Kilpatrick's, ordering the same beer over and over for weeks. Talking to him. Flirting with him. Even though—no matter how hard I'd try—he'd never give me any clear confirmation that he was gay, I kept at it, hoping that I had a chance. And when he finally invited me over to his place after one of his shifts one night, that thrill burned inside me. I was excited, but not entirely sure what he wanted. Maybe he just wanted to talk. Maybe we weren't going to have sex.

Thankfully, we did. Back then.

Tonight? Who knows. I'm trying to stay optimistic. But even when we were together, I doubted myself, never sure if he was fully into me. I was always fighting the sneaking suspicion that he didn't think I was good enough for him.

It's fifteen past midnight when I arrive at Aaron's. My T-shirt, snug in all the right places, is slightly damp with nervous perspiration. It doesn't really matter, though. If things go the way I want them to, it won't be on for long.

I feel a little better when Aaron answers the door. He's got on what I used to call his "hookup clothes," the same outfit he'd always wear whenever I'd go over to his place to get busy. Sweatpants, a white T-shirt, and Cincinnati Reds baseball cap on backward.

"Hi," I say. "Sorry it took me so long. I know it's late."

"You know this isn't too late for me. Come on in."

He heads toward his kitchen—to grab us two beers, I already know. A pilsner for him and a hefeweizen for me, like we'd always had at his place.

The state of his apartment is exactly the same as it was in Indiana: neither neat nor disorderly. A distinct man-smell permeates the rooms, unwashed clothes and meat-heavy meals mixed with about-to-expire air freshener. From here, I can see into his bedroom. A single bargain-basement comforter hangs off the edge of his bed, clothes are heaped on the floor, and empty beer bottles lay strewn across his dresser.

Aaron comes back to the living room and hands me my hefeweizen. "Cheers," he says, clinking mine.

"Cheers," I say. "To the success of my karaoke idea, right? And to Regina Moon Dee?"

He nods and takes a sip, smacking his lips. "Your friend's a keeper."

He seems sincere. And he didn't emphasize the word *friend*. I'm pretty sure that he doesn't suspect I'm Regina.

"Just tell her to keep the hanky-panky out of the workplace, okay? If she and Paolo want to get it on, they'll have to do it someplace else."

Something flutters in my stomach when he mentions Paolo's name. "I'll be sure to tell her that." I take a long sip of my beer and focus on Aaron. "So, speaking of hanky-panky, did you just want to talk about Regina tonight, or...?"

"Heh. I've always liked that about you."

"What?" I give him my most flirtatious smile, hoping he means my seductive charm.

"Your straightforwardness. You're not afraid to say what's on your mind. I always know where I'm at with you."

"That's me all right. You can read me like an open book. Nothing to hide here." A sudden wave of warmth rushes to my neck.

His smile falters. I start to panic, wondering if he can see the deceit written in the redness on my skin.

He turns around abruptly. "Want to chill on the couch?"

I follow him and sit. Close, but not too close. I don't want to come on too strong or go too fast. I need to set the mood by doing and saying the right things. Subtlety and sensitivity are paramount right now.

"So," I say, "too bad about you and Russell, huh?"

Shit.

An awkward smile forms on Aaron's face. "Yeah. It was a bummer."

"But you don't miss him, right?"

Ohmigod, Rex.

Aaron coughs into a balled-up fist and takes a very big chug of his beer. "I guess I look at it this way," he says. "If we're not together, then it just wasn't meant to be."

"Yes. Yes, that's right." I pat him enthusiastically on the knee. "He couldn't hack it here. So he's better off back in Indiana."

"Well, I wouldn't say he couldn't handle it, just—"

"Oh no, I mean..." I grip his knee and then feel him pull back slightly. I start massaging it instead, hoping he'll relax. He doesn't seem to. "I mean you made the decision to stay. And there's a reason for that. There's a reason why you're here. If you didn't, we couldn't have run into each other after all these years."

He looks down at my hand. I'm about to stop massaging his knee, but to my surprise, he puts his own hand on top of mine, stilling it. "I am glad to see you again," he says, looking somewhat at ease for the first time since I've arrived at his place.

I turn my hand and interlace it with his thick fingers. "I'm glad to see you, too."

Aaron smiles kindly. He leans in. My heartbeat quickens as my breathing slows to almost nothing. I close my eyes, and—

"What is that?" he asks.

My eyes pop open to see him staring at the back of my

neck. "Oh god, kill it!" I say, thinking an insect has landed on me.

"This." He swipes the tip of his finger on my skin and raises it to his eyes.

I look at his finger. It's foundation. The dress I had on tonight showed a lot of neckline, so I made sure to color and contour everywhere. But in my rush, I'd forgotten to clean it off the back of my neck.

I flinch. "That's just...uh..."

He sniffs his finger. "Smells kinda sweet. Is it chocolate or something?" he asks, placing his fingertip on his tongue.

"No, don't—"

Too late. He sucks his finger. "Ew," he says, scrunching up his face.

"It's not chocolate," I say, cringing. "It's...self-tanning lotion. There's coloring in it."

Aaron wipes at his lips. "Ick. It's gross. It's—" He coughs. Coughs some more. He starts to hack and wheeze.

"Oh, crap," I say, grabbing his beer bottle off the table for him to drink, only to realize that it's empty.

I run to the kitchen, pour a glass of water from the sink, and rush back to Aaron. He chugs the water. His coughing keeps going but with less intensity.

I rub his back as he leans over his knees.

"Are you okay?" I ask.

"Whatever was in that stuff, I think I'm allergic to it," he groans.

"It probably just went down the wrong pipe, that's all," I try to say as encouragingly as I can.

"Yeah, maybe," he says, and sits upright.

I scream.

"What?" Aaron says.

I shake my head dumbly and stare at his mouth, now starting to puff up.

"It's my face, isn't it?"

I nod quietly, trying not to show my utter horror and failing completely.

"Crap," he says, and trudges to his bathroom.

Great job, Rex. A perfect second chance now gone horribly wrong, all because of a lousy little smear of makeup.

The sound of banging fills the apartment as Aaron opens and shuts bathroom cabinets, presumably looking for something to ease the swelling. I fall back on the sofa, silently berating myself for being so careless with my makeup, when I suddenly remember that another stupid smear caused a situation earlier in the evening. The smudge of lipstick I cleaned off Paolo's face. And I was in such a hurry to leave the Pink Unicorn that I never got around to apologizing to him for it. Maybe that's why he seemed so disappointed when I left. I'd crossed a line, and it looked as if I didn't give it a second thought.

But I am thinking about it. Because for some reason, even though my makeup has literally made Aaron sick, it's my lipstick on Paolo's mouth that I now can't get out of my head.

CHAPTER 10

AARON LIES ON HIS BED CURLED ON HIS SIDE. His snore, soft and low, fills the room with its insistent rhythm. I want to say that's what's kept me awake all night, or that I've made myself get up every hour to make sure he hasn't died from anaphylactic shock, but I'd be lying if I did. As I lay next to him with my hands behind my head, staring at the water stains on his apartment ceiling, I'm thinking about the same thing that's been on my mind all night.

Paolo.

Or rather, kissing him without warning him. The scene has replayed itself in my mind for hours, bothering me like an itch I can't scratch. I need to apologize to him so that I can stop thinking about it.

Now that we're working together, I could do it at the next karaoke night. But that seems like an eternity from now. The problem is that I don't know how to contact him. I suppose I could go back to AquaMarine, if I knew his work schedule. But Aaron mentioned it seemed to be erratic at best.

"Hey. You stayed?" Aaron says, his voice gruff. He's looking up at me, sleep wrinkles etched all over his face, though no trace of swelling remains, thankfully.

"I wanted to make sure that you didn't stop breathing during the night. Especially since, you know, it was me who did it."

"You always did take my breath away."

I smile. "Really?"

"Back then? Sure."

"Ah," I say, my smile fading. "But not now."

"That's...not what I meant. Sorry. But look—I'm fine now," Aaron says, sitting up. "The antihistamines I took last night helped."

"I'm so sorry about what happened. Can I make it up to you somehow?" I say, brushing his arm hair softly with my fingertips. Getting sexy is probably the last thing on Aaron's mind now, but it couldn't hurt to try.

He hops out of the bed and stretches. "I need to get going, unfortunately."

"Where are you off to so early?" I glance up at the digital clock on his wall, its numbers glowing red. "It's only seven a.m. On a Sunday."

This reminds me of the first time he and I hooked up back in Bloomington. I was floating on cloud nine after having had sex with the hottest guy I'd ever met, but the next day, he woke me up at six a.m. "Sorry," he said, "but I need you to leave now. I don't want anyone seeing a guy leave my place in the morning." To save face, I lied and said I had an eight o'clock exam and needed to leave anyway. I knew I had to make certain concessions when he was still in the closet. But what was his excuse now?

Aaron smiles apologetically at me, running a hand through his hair and rearranging it into something less mussed up. "I'm sorry, Rex. There's this running club that has a nine a.m. run in Golden Gate Park. I try to go every week."

"Oh," I say. "No worries. I'll get going." That's a better excuse than not wanting to be outed. The disappointment of not being a top priority for him still stings a bit. But to be honest, there's something else that I'd like to take care of soon: putting an end to my incessant thoughts about kissing Paolo.

"Hey, Aaron," I say, "before I go, I was just thinking about logistics for karaoke night. Now that Regina Moon Dee's the host, she'll need to coordinate a few things with Paolo. Do you have his number?"

"Yeah, I'll give it to you," he says, grabbing his phone from the charging station on his bedside table.

"Thanks."

"Or I can just text it to Regina directly," he says. "I should probably have her number anyway."

"No, you can't!" I say. "I mean, uh, Regina doesn't have a phone."

Aaron tilts his head at me. "Then how was she going to talk to Paolo?"

"Well, I mean, she does have a phone. Of course she has a phone. Duh. But she doesn't like handing out her number to just anyone. You know. Fans can get kind of stalkery and stuff."

Aaron squints. "But I'm not a fan. I'm going to be her boss. I should have her number."

"Of course! That makes perfect sense," I say.

"Great. So?"

"So...?"

"Regina's number?"

"Right. Regina's number, Regina's number." I retrieve my phone from my pants pocket and swipe. "Now where did I put that number? Is it under Dee? Nope, nope. Under drag queen? Hmm. Not there, either." I keep going through my contacts, not looking for anything in particular. Just killing time until I can figure out what to do.

I land on Eva's phone number. She's already impersonated one aspect of me, why not the other?

"Found it," I say. "It's 510-555-7611."

Aaron punches it in. "Cool. I'll just send her Paolo's number right now—"

"No, wait!" I say, reaching out with my hand. "She doesn't like to get woken up early in the morning. And she never remembers to turn her notifications off. Just wait a few hours or so. Okay?" I clench my other hand behind me in a tight ball, stress-squeezing.

Aaron looks at me blankly. He shrugs. "Sure. In fact,

while I have it open," he says, showing me his phone, "here's Paolo's number."

"Thank you," I say, trying not to let on how relieved I am as I quickly punch it into my phone.

Aaron, now fully dressed in his running gear, says, "Thanks for watching over me last night. That was really sweet of you."

"Least I could do."

His eyes flicker toward the front door.

"Well, I should get going," I say, catching his hint.

He walks me over and then hugs me with his barrel arms, squeezing roughly. "Let's talk soon, okay?" he says, shutting the door behind me with a click.

Does it bother me that Aaron was more interested in putting an anti-chafing stick between his legs than me? Yes. But Aaron's always been into sports and being athletic. Let him have his hobbies.

And besides, I have something else I want to do today.

After a big pot of coffee back at my condo, I text Eva, warning her that Aaron now thinks her number is Regina Moon Dee's. She responds with a bunch of very impolite emojis.

I start texting a message to Paolo but decide that's too impersonal. I call him instead.

He picks up immediately. "Hello?"

"Hey, this is Rex Araneta. Uh, Regina Moon Dee, from the Pink Unicorn? Is now a good time? Or did I call too early?"

"Rex! No, it's fine. I'm definitely up already." Metal pots

clang, and food sizzles in the background. He must be at AquaMarine early for brunch service.

"Are you at work right now? I don't want to disturb you."

"No, it's okay, I—" I hear a muffled conversation with someone else, as though he's covered his phone with his hand. And then, "Can we talk later this afternoon? It's a little hectic in here right now. I should be done around three p.m."

"You know what," I say, "why don't I swing by when you're done?"

"You don't have to drive all the way here. Are you sure?"

"I'll be in the city this afternoon, anyway," I lie. "No problem at all."

I don't know why I feel the need to go to him just to apologize. It's much easier to say it over the phone, or even just text it. But whatever I saw in his eyes last night, both in the bathroom and when I left abruptly, makes me want to see him in person.

"Looking forward to seeing you," Paolo says, his voice hushed, as if he's telling me something that's only meant for me to hear.

Either way, when he hangs up, I realize that I'm looking forward to seeing him, too.

AQUAMARINE IS NEARLY EMPTY when I get there later that afternoon, except for two women talking quietly over empty plates and half-finished mimosas. A few workers are cleaning up the other tables around them. I stay in the front lobby area near the entrance, looking around for Paolo.

A tap on my shoulder. I turn around, and the scent of leather and smoke fills my nose. Paolo is still in his uniform but wearing a motorcycle jacket on top.

"Sorry, I was just finishing up some things," he says. His face glistens with light perspiration.

My nose crinkles. "You mean you were in the back alley having a cigarette?"

"What?" He laughs. "No, I don't smoke. I was just helping the cooks. They're trying a new dish—smoked crispy pata. I suggested smoking it with applewood chips to give it an extra kick. We were cooking it on a grill out back."

Paolo leans in close to me, and I feel momentarily lost. It's the smell of him. That combination of smoke and leather that's always thrilled me, reminding me of the type of men I've always found attractive. The ones who ride motorcycles and fix cars. Or maybe it's the way he's standing now, legs apart, shoulders broad, back erect, like he's much bigger than me, though I know this isn't the case. We're almost exactly the same height and build. Still, there's something about him today that radiates authority. Strength. Not the scatteredness that sputtered off him the last time I saw him here attempting to serve food.

He nods toward the dining room. "Want to sit?"

"You're sure it's okay for us to just hang out here?"

He smiles. "I'm on good terms with the manager."

We sit across from each other at one of the tables for two,

tucked into the corner next to a window. Cars and people stream by us in the unusually sunny San Francisco day.

Paolo leans back against the chair, one arm draped on the table, looking as relaxed as he would sitting on a sofa at home. "So, what is it you wanted to talk to me about?"

"It's about last night."

"Which was so much fun, by the way. I've never had that great of a time at karaoke. Ever. You were incredible."

My ears prickle and burn. "You mean Regina Moon Dee was."

He stares deeply. Like he's trying to locate something concealed inside me.

"Sure," he says finally.

"I just wanted to apologize," I say. "For what happened in the bathroom. I shouldn't have kissed you like that."

A dozen different emotions register on his face at once. "Thank you," he says. "I accept."

"And I'm sorry for wiping your mouth with my spit," I add, smiling weakly.

"No worries," Paolo says quietly. "I didn't mind. Really."

We both stare at the table for a while in silence.

A young Black couple walks by our window. The man is pushing a stroller, and the woman is holding the hands of a young boy. They stop for a moment for her to stoop down and tie his shoes. Paolo and I watch them. I don't know why, but it's easier for me to focus on them than it is for me to sit here in silence with Paolo. It's not discomfort I'm feeling, exactly. All I know is that something compelled me to come here to apologize, and now that I've done that, I don't want to drive all the way back home. And not just because of the time it's taken to get here.

The woman gives the boy a raspberry on his cheek. He shrieks with laughter. Paolo smiles and, still observing the family outside, says, "I envy you, you know."

"You envy me? Why?"

"Every day, I wake up, and it's the same thing. I come here, do my job, go home. Hope the next day I'll figure out what I really want to do with my life. And I never do. Or maybe I do know, but I'm too chicken-shit to admit it to myself."

The family outside walks away, farther down the street, out of my sight. Paolo's eyes follow. "But you have a talent. A gift that you can share with the world. I wish I could do that, too."

"Why can't you?" I ask. "There must be something you love to do. That you're passionate about."

"I..." He looks around at the interior of the restaurant, his gaze resting at the door that leads into the kitchen. "My dad. He's expecting me to do something. Be something that I'm not sure I want to be."

"You mean, he wants you to be straight?"

My heart leaps into my throat. I make a few rapid mental calculations, trying to remember. Did Paolo ever actually tell me he was queer? He's a karaoke jockey at a gay bar. He must be, right?

Dammit. I don't think he's ever actually said what he was. Why do I keep messing things up with him?

As if sensing my anxiety, Paolo reaches across the table

and squeezes my hand. "No, that's not it. He's okay with me being gay. Or he's okay now. It took him a while."

"I'm glad. That your dad's okay. Not that you're gay. I mean, I'm really glad you're gay. I mean—"

He laughs and squeezes one more time. "Let's just say he and I have different ideas of what I'm supposed to be when I grow up. And it's not karaoke."

When he lets go of me, I have this overwhelming desire to reach back out for his hand. Instead, I clasp my hands together tightly and place them on my lap, afraid they'll wander and do something I'll regret.

"If it makes you feel any better," I say, "my dad doesn't know I'm doing drag."

"Really?"

I shake my head. "He made it clear a long time ago that he didn't want me doing it. And I obeyed him for years. Until last night."

"Is he why you don't want anyone to know?"

"He's the main reason I've never publicly revealed my identity, yeah. Only a few people know who Regina Moon Dee really is."

"Including me," Paolo says, leaning across the table. The pull of his presence increases, drawing me in. "Can I ask why you don't want Aaron to know?"

Tiny fires flare inside my stomach. My cheeks. My forehead. "I don't really want to talk about it," I mumble.

"Of course." His face softens. "Just know that I'm here if you ever want to talk."

He turns his hand over on the table and opens it, as if waiting for me to place my hand in his. A small gesture that feels as big as the ocean. I want to reach out. Interlace my fingers with Paolo's, like I did with Aaron last night. But my heartbeat rings in my ears so loudly that it's hard for me to think.

"I..." I get up abruptly. "I have to go. But thank you for taking the time to talk. And for accepting my apology." I make an embarrassing half-bow, half-curtsy gesture and quickly turn around, ready to rush out.

"Hey," Paolo says, halting me in my tracks. "That song I sang last night, 'All By Myself'? That was *my* apology to you. I'm sorry if I made you feel uncomfortable that first weekend we met, trying to make you do something you weren't ready to do. That wasn't my intention. Karaoke is supposed to be fun. Always."

The tiny fires in my body extinguish. He's done that somehow. Like he did last night by being with me on the stage. Just by being beside me.

I nod and keep going.

CHAPTER 11

MY REVAMP OF THE PINK UNICORN'S KARAOKE NIGHT was only one part of my improvement plan. Now that I've proven it works, Aaron and Bryan want the full details of everything else. We decide to meet at the bar during the week, which I'm looking forward to. Not just because I want to go over my plan, but because I'm also eager to be with Aaron again.

I haven't seen him since Saturday night. We've been texting each other, but the messages have been frustratingly ordinary, as if we were nothing more than acquaintances. Maybe I'd misread Aaron's intentions when he invited me over last weekend. Maybe this isn't the big second chance with him I'd hoped it would be. Did he actually meet up with his running friends on Sunday morning? Or was he just trying to get me out of his place early, like he always used to insist on? Maybe Aaron hasn't changed at all.

Tuesday after work, I stop by, expecting Aaron to be doing his usual shift. Before I head inside, though, I take a quick look at the building's exterior, taking note of what needs to be worked on. The metal unicorn sign should be replaced, and the awning above the door requires a deep cleaning. But a good coat of paint would fix everything else. Next door to the bar is a closed-down cafe. It's been empty for a long time, if the dust on the stray pieces of furniture inside are any indication. Not a great look to be next to an abandoned space, but there's nothing we can really do about that.

Inside the Pink Unicorn, Bryan is tending bar instead of Aaron. Two people play a leisurely game of pool while two others sit chatting at a table. Other than that, the place is empty.

"Hey, Bryan," I say, waving. "I thought Aaron would be here. I can come back some other time if that's better."

"I'm just covering for him while he's running an errand. Won't take long. Have a seat at the bar. I'll make you a drink. What'll it be?"

"A club soda's fine."

"You sure? It's on the house."

"Well, in that case, make it a club soda with a dash of vodka."

"One vodka with a dash of soda, coming right up," he says with a wink.

He moves about the bar casually, confidently, his gray hair bobbing as he whistles something jaunty. "You two doing okay over there?" he says to the men sitting at the table.

One of them turns around. "We're good, Bryan. Thanks," the man says, who I realize is José.

"You just let me know when you want another round of your usual," Bryan says cheerfully. "Two of my best customers," he says to me. "They've been coming here for years."

"How long have you owned this place?" I ask.

His gaze brightens, as if recognizing someone in the distance. "Gosh. About a decade now. But I was the manager before that for fifteen years. And before that I was coming practically every night. This has been my home for almost thirty years. Still the same as it ever was, god bless it."

Unchanged for three decades. Part of the reason it needs a major renovation, I think. But I just nod and take the highball glass from Bryan when he hands it to me. "To places that feel like home," I say, raising the glass.

He grabs an open bottle of beer from the back counter and clinks my glass. "For as long as they last," he says.

He takes a long sip and looks around the bar, sighing sadly. "I don't know how much more life she's got in her. Gay bars are closing all over the Bay Area. This is one of the last ones left in Oakland."

Many establishments all over the San Francisco Bay Area are being forced to close due to a still struggling post-pandemic economy and skyrocketing rents. Not only gay bars but restaurants, shops, and other small businesses. Lumber Janes, the last remaining lesbian bar in San Francisco, shuttered last summer. One of the few gay bookstores left, Reading and Rainbows in the Castro, closed in October. It isn't much better in Oakland and Berkeley.

"The Pink Unicorn's an institution, you know," Bryan says. "Elton John used to stop by here in the seventies whenever he'd be in town. David Bowie, too. Melissa Etheridge, k.d. lang, even Green Day. They've all been in here. Sometimes they'd surprise us with a short set. Just them and their guitars. Hell, if these walls could talk."

"Would they tell me any stories of yours?" I ask, half kidding.

"One or two, maybe." His pale blue eyes twinkle, and for a moment, I see him younger, his hair darker, his back straighter. Bryan's a handsome older gentleman. I wouldn't be surprised to find out he was a big player back in the day. In fact, there's something about him that feels familiar, almost as if I might have run into him in the past—though I've never stepped foot in the Pink Unicorn until this month, and it doesn't seem like he spends much time anywhere else.

"I'd be interested to hear your secrets," I say.

He doesn't seem to have heard me. He looks past me, his eyes clouding over subtly, landing on someone who's just entered.

"Aaron," Bryan says, "Rex is here to go over his ideas for the bar."

"Great," Aaron says to me. He gives me one of his hearty

embraces, warm and reassuring. For a moment, I feel a bit more optimistic about our chances of getting back together. "Show us."

I pull a folder out of my Symria bag and lay it open on the bar. Inside are some documents I've been working on in my spare time at work: a mock-up design of the redecorated bar, a list of renovations with corresponding items and their costs, a proposed calendar of weekly events, a simple social media and advertisement plan, and a guide for more improvements to karaoke night. Having Regina Moon Dee as the main host was only the first step. I did some research on the karaoke software program that Bryan had purchased, SYNGX, and realized it's never been used to its full potential by Paolo. When I took a deeper dive, I realized it has the capability to integrate light shows and music videos, which can easily connect to the video projection unit and the bar's light system. Not only that, but it can be used in conjunction with a song request app that people can download onto their phones, and requestors would have an easy opt-in to sign up for the Pink Unicorn's mailing list. All of which would modernize karaoke night and make it easier for everyone to make requests. And double as added marketing.

Aaron goes behind the bar, pops open a bottle of beer, and stands next to Bryan so that they can look through everything together. Bryan slips on a pair of reading glasses and skims his finger over the various pages while Aaron looks through the others, drinking.

"I forgot to factor in any improvements we'd do to the

outside," I say as they read. "But I checked, and I think the added cost would be minimal."

Bryan looks up at me. "I don't understand the social media stuff, but the rest of it looks good. And using the kara-oke system to its full potential—I've been wanting Paolo to do that for weeks now. I'm just worried about how much everything would cost. What you've got planned here is a little more than we've got in the bank right now."

"How much more?" I ask.

Bryan and Aaron look at each other.

"A lot more," Aaron says.

"We're not exactly flush with cash these days." Bryan points his chin at the nearly empty bar.

"One thing at a time," I say, trying to stay positive. "Regina Moon Dee's already started pulling in a huge crowd. We can implement the publicity and advertisement plan, and that won't take much money at all. That sound okay?"

"Let's do it," Bryan says. "And could you work with Paolo on learning how to use the other features of the karaoke system?"

I feel a tiny flutter inside my chest. "Sure," I say.

"This is great, Rex," Aaron says, drinking more of his beer. "We owe you for all this. Let me thank you by taking you out to dinner next week. You paid for me the first time so it's my turn now."

Another date? Yes, please.

"Sure," I say, trying to keep my cool.

"Great," Aaron says. "And is it okay with you if two of my

running friends join us? I told them about you on Sunday, and they want to meet you. One of them, Miguel, has a Filipino stepmom. I think you'd like him."

So he did go running. And he's already telling other people about me. I was wrong to second-guess him. "Cool with me," I say.

"Okay, back to my *Moonlighting* marathon," Bryan says, excusing himself to sit on his regular stool at the end of the bar. I notice that there's already a bowl of snack mix waiting for him there.

Aaron glances at my empty glass. "Refill?"

I nod. "Vodka soda."

"Oh, and more good news." Aaron pours vodka and spritzes soda into my glass at the same time, making everything fizz fiercely, bubbles violently spilling up and over. "Joey's mom is changing her shift at the hospital to Fridays soon. So in about a week or so, I'll be able to work Saturday nights and join in on the karaoke fun with you and Regina and everyone else. Permanently."

As he hands me my drink, I plaster a smile on my face and try not to freak out.

"Wonderful!" I say, and chug half of my drink in one swallow. "Just wonderful."

AT THE OFFICE THE NEXT DAY, sitting in a chair next to Kat's, I put my forehead on her desk.

"I'm screwed," I groan at the floor.

"Quit stressing. We'll figure something out," Kat says, blowing a bubble that pops with a watermelon-scented snap. She's wearing one of my favorite outfits of hers—a lilac suit jacket over a cute pale blue top that I'd steal in a second. She lifts my head by the chin. "But good ideas come to me better over food. Let's grab some Chinese at Golden Lotus for lunch."

"Kat!" Susan's yell rings from her open office door and straight down my spine.

"What?" Kat shouts.

"Have you done my expense report yet for my business trip to DC?"

"Like you can call a trip to a sorority sister's birthday party a business trip."

"She's a potential investor, Kat!"

"Fine! After lunch," Kat yells back.

"Lunch already?" Susan says. "Do you even work at all?"

"Why, am I fired?"

"Yes!" Susan says.

"Good! I'm leaving!"

"Good!" Susan yells. "And bring me back an order of egg rolls and mu shu pork. Ooh, and some hot and sour soup, please."

"Golden Lotus is her favorite," Kat says to me. "You got it, boss," she says over her shoulder, before tugging me along after her.

She tucks her arm in mine as we walk toward the elevator.

"I don't think I'll ever understand your guys' relationship," I say.

"That's okay," Kat says, leaning her head against mine. "Susan and I get each other. That's all that matters."

From the outside in, some relationships might not make sense to others. Would people see Aaron and me and think we're not good for each other? Maybe we aren't. After all, he doesn't even know a big part of who I really am.

But we withhold things from people we love all the time. Some secrets are all right, especially when they're for the benefit of the relationship. That's how my dad and I are, and we've never been better.

Right?

Outside, the clouds have gathered, threatening rain. Near our office, there's an unfortunate wind tunnel effect that gathers cool air from the San Francisco Bay and funnels it straight through to our street. Kat and I look up at the sky and do the four-block walk to Golden Lotus more briskly than usual.

"Hey, I'm sorry I can't be there this Saturday," Kat says as we walk. "The Nine Tails girls and I are hanging out again."

"You can't do it at the Pink Unicorn?"

"Actually, we're having a jam session. Nothing serious. Just for old times' sake."

Despite Kat's band's interpersonal problems, they really could rock a room. Literally. I know how much she's missed making music with them.

"That's awesome. I guess we'll both be performing this weekend. But..." I sigh. "What am I going to do when Aaron eventually switches his volunteer gig and starts working karaoke nights?"

"Can't you just tell him that you—Rex you, not Regina you—have a conflict and can't come on those nights from now on?" Kat asks.

"We already did that last weekend. That might work one more time. But then he's going to suspect something's up when he starts noticing that Regina Moon Dee and I are never in the same place at the same time."

"That's it!" Kat says, snapping.

"What's it?"

"You just have to both be in the same place when Aaron's around."

"How am I supposed to do that?"

She starts walking faster, getting more animated. "You need a doppelgänger. Someone to pretend they're Regina. Then have Aaron see you and her together, in the same place at the same time."

"At karaoke night?" I ask, trying to keep up with her. "My fans will notice if someone is trying to impersonate me."

"No, not that night. Some isolated situation where it's just you and Aaron together."

"And what situation would that be? Should fake Regina just come over to Aaron's house one night when we're in the middle of man-love time?"

"No. And please don't ever say *man-love time* again," Kat says. "When you're at the bar on a regular night when Aaron's working, just have Regina Number Two stop by to say hi. Bam, problem solved."

My mind starts racing with this improbable scenario. Could it work? It would just take one time for Aaron to see Regina and me together and then he'd always think we're separate people. Even when I conveniently tell him that I'm not able to come to karaoke nights for whatever reason. I'd have to figure that out, too. But one step at a time.

We arrive at Golden Lotus. I open the door for Kat, and we hurry in, just beating the first few spatters of raindrops.

"Okay," I say, a little breathless from our speed-walking. "It's worth a try. But who would I ask? Another drag queen? I haven't really kept in touch with any from before." This is true, unfortunately. I haven't spoken to the girls from Dreamland in years.

Kat makes a gesture for *two* to the host. He pulls two menus from the wooden shelf next to the door, and we follow him into the dining room.

"Doesn't have to be a drag queen," Kat says, sitting at the table and looking through the menu. "They just need to look enough like you. How about Eva?"

Eva's face does look similar to mine because we're siblings. But it wouldn't work. "She's too short. And would Aaron really believe she's a man in drag?"

"What about this uncle you said was your drag mom? Could he do it?"

I pour us glasses of water. "We're not really talking anymore." My heart grows heavy. I miss Beaucoup Buko and would love to see him again. But would he really help me after all this time? "He's also a lot rounder than me. And last I heard he moved to Palm Springs."

"Paolo?"

My hand seizes up, making me almost drop my water glass. "What? No way."

"Come on, you have to admit that he'd be the perfect person, physically."

She's right. We're around the same height and build. And our faces aren't completely dissimilar. Certainly, with enough makeup, I could make him look like Regina Moon Dee.

"He doesn't know the first thing about drag, though."

"He doesn't have to walk the runway, Rex. He's just coming into the bar to say *hi* and *bye* to you and Aaron. It'll be five minutes, tops. You can teach him everything he needs to know."

Something about Kat's idea tickles the back of my neck and makes the hairs there stand up. Probably just because I'm excited by a possible solution to my problem, that's all. Though now the image of Paolo in the bathroom with lipstick on his mouth has come back, morphing into something different. Now I see Paolo with my mascara on. My eye shadow. My wigs. My clothes. I can't stop thinking about how amazing it will all look on him.

"It could work," I say.

"Of course it'll work," Kat says.

Our waitress approaches. "Are you ready to order? Or do you need more time to decide?"

Kat looks at me. "Do you know what you want?"

"Yes," I say. "I do."

CHAPTER 12

I'VE ALWAYS BEEN A SUCKER FOR A GOOD MAKEOVER. From the ugly duckling and Cinderella to *Pretty Woman* and *The Devil Wears Prada*, stories of transformation have always fascinated me. Humble, ordinary people coming into their own and becoming extraordinary. Being seen. It's exactly what I feel when I do drag.

The week before I was set to make my debut at Dreamland, fear and excitement clashed inside me nonstop. Even though I was just seventeen, I'd already amassed thousands of online fans. I knew that I could make good videos.

But would I be any good in front of a live audience?

Tito Melboy went to work prepping me. First, he took me on a shopping trip to consignment stores to search for clothes. He didn't want me to wear something I could find right off the rack, but he didn't have enough time to make me something from scratch. He was looking for the perfect garments to alter into a one-of-a-kind outfit for me. I tried picking pieces for myself, but no matter what I did, I just couldn't figure out how to find things that went together or that complemented my skin tone.

"Rex, tell me truthfully—are you color-blind?" he asked me in the store.

"No, Uncle."

"Ah, sayang. That's a shame. It would have explained a lot. Oh, well, we all have our talents," he said, and put back all the things I'd chosen.

Finally, at a vintage shop in the Haight, Tito Melboy found the perfect red-sequined gown. It was large, extravagant—which didn't really suit me—but it meant that he'd have enough material to work into something more scaled down and suitable for my age.

Over the next three days, as I practiced my debut song in my bedroom, he worked on my dress. When I was finally able to try it on, I'll never forget what happened when I looked in the mirror. Doing drag had always been freeing. Now I felt much more than freedom. Actual power seemed to course through my body. I finally understood why we were called queens. It felt as if I could truly rule a country. Or the world.

Eva screamed from my bedroom door. "You're a princess!"

"Shhhh!" I hushed, even though I knew Mom and Dad were at work.

"Just let her, Rex!" Tito Melboy said. "She's happy for

you. And I am, too! Look at how beautiful you are. Never forget how this feels. Hold on to it forever."

My first live performance finally rolled around. After early morning church, we all told Dad we were going to a potluck lunch at my ninang's house in Daly City (whose constant gossiping he found insufferable), leaving us free to go to Dreamland's Drag Brunch.

All the way there I was a bundle of nerves. Not just because I was excited to finally perform publicly in drag, but also because I was anxious to see if Ivan would be working at the garage again.

When we arrived, I let out a tiny squeak of joy. Ivan was in the parking garage office, leaning so far back in his chair I was afraid he'd tip over. Like before, my voice went raspy when I asked him for the ticket. He seemed to be amused by my shyness, smirking as he prepared it for me.

"You gonna be coming every Sunday now?" he asked.

"Um. Maybe," was all I could manage, trying to clear my throat of endless anxiety phlegm.

"Nice."

"Do you, um, work every Sunday?" I asked.

"Yes. Sunday mornings. And Friday nights," Ivan said, handing the ticket over to me.

I gripped it in both hands and walked to our car to put it on the dashboard, looking back longingly at the office.

"Let's go. We're going to be late," Tito Melboy said, eyeing Ivan as we left the garage.

We had planned to arrive two hours early so we could

get dressed in Dreamland's dressing room. Mom and Eva helped us lug all our things in two rolling suitcases that we had snuck into the car at home, making sure my dad didn't see us. The dressing room, though not large, was generous in its furnishings, decked out with all the essentials for any of the girls who wanted to finish getting ready there instead of arriving in full drag. There were four makeup stations with lighted mirrors, lockers for everyone to keep their belongings, and two racks to hang up outfits.

My uncle and I crammed into one station while Eva played around with a set of starter makeup that Baby Buko gave her. She was older than I was when I started learning about makeup so I knew it wouldn't be a problem with Mom, who was busy chatting with Baby, anyway.

Benta Box, still dressed in jeans and a baseball cap, prepared at the station beside us. She was baking her makeup—laying foundation, concealer, and powder and giving it time to set. "I'm so honored that the legendary Beaucoup Buko will be working with us," Benta said to Tito Melboy. "And you, new girl," Benta said, pointing a brush at me like a knife, "don't dip into my tips or I will cut you."

I snapped my wig cap onto my head and froze. She burst into laughter.

"Don't mind her," Baby said. "She's just kidding. We share everything, including the tips. But most importantly, we share our knowledge and support. You already have a drag mother," she said, winking at Tito Melboy, "but now you have an entire drag family."

The girls around me snapped their fingers.

I looked at Eva and my mom. "Since you're all my family, would you all do me a big favor? Please don't tell other people who I am, okay? My dad, he...he doesn't know. And I don't want him to find out."

The girls nodded, many of them looking as if they knew exactly what it's like to keep their drag a secret from their families.

"So, Regina," Baby said, placing a hand gently on my shoulder, "are you ready to work?"

"Yes! But I've never waited tables before."

"We will train you, don't worry. You can just shadow Benta today. I mean, are you ready to perform your number?"

"Definitely," I replied.

"Good. Because you're up first."

Two hours later, as Baby took to the stage to announce the beginning of the show, I watched from the back of the restaurant, hiding behind a large potted plant and trying not to nervously rub all the sequins off the dress Tito Melboy had made for me. Dreamland was full of people—gay brunchers, young couples, families, and groups of women enjoying bottomless mai tais—and I didn't want to let any of them down.

"Hello!" Baby said into her handheld microphone. "I hope you're enjoying your food. Try the mango dream pancakes, they're a slice of tropical heaven. And speaking of a slice of heaven, for our first act, I want to introduce you all to someone new. A fresh, young face. Damn her! It's okay, though. I'm not jealous. Beauty fades, but talent is forever," Baby said, waving a hand over herself. The restaurant responded with cordial laughter. "Please give a warm welcome to Regina Moon Dee!"

I slinked out from my hiding place and walked up to the stage, worrying about absolutely everything. In the few seconds of silence between the quieting down of the audience's polite welcome applause and the music, I looked out into the crowd. The other girls, usually busy taking orders, delivering food, or socializing with the guests, paused respectfully to watch me start. They all seemed so cool-headed and confident. Not a stray hair or blemish or snag in their tights. How could I possibly compare to them? I wasn't a real queen. I wasn't a pro. I was just some dumb kid who recorded videos of my mediocre looks and karaoke singing.

But when I saw Eva and Mom and especially Tito Melboy in the far back, now decked out in her own hand-stitched beaded ball gown as Beaucoup Buko, I knew I couldn't let them down.

The karaoke track started. A steady quarter note pulse of a familiar piano chord echoed through the speakers. The intro to Celine Dion's version of "All By Myself."

I began to sing.

Someone let out a surprised gasp. It could have been one of the patrons or one of the girls. Maybe even Baby. But it wasn't my family, who knew what my voice could do.

Most girls at Dreamland, Baby had told me, only did

lip-synchs. There were a few over the years who also sang live sometimes, but they had low, male-register voices. If they did women's songs, they were usually re-pitched several keys lower so that they could hit all the right notes.

I didn't need to do any of this. I just needed to sing.

Everything was perfectly still. No food was being delivered. No plates were being scraped by utensils. Everyone gave me their full attention.

When I reached the infamous part of the refrain—the three ascending notes on *"a-ny-more"* that end in a high F, almost impossible for most women to sing, let alone men— the entire restaurant erupted into applause. The queens waved their hands and screamed, and Baby looked at Beaucoup, mouthing, *Oh, my god!*

I'd never experienced anything like it before. Online, I could be avalanched with likes and comments. But the impact of those things hit me obliquely, like having a nice meal one bite at a time. Now I was eating the best dish on the menu and swallowing it whole all at once. I never wanted the feeling to end.

Baby Buko said that I was Dreamland's newest hit.

I don't even remember the rest of the show. All I know is that, after it was all done, I was overwhelmed and exhausted from all the attention I received that day.

As Mom drove us home, she started tossing out ideas for my future performances. "You should do Whitney Houston, anak! And Mariah Carey, and some of Lea Salonga's songs, too. For the next brunch, you should sing 'A Whole New

World' with your uncle. What do you think, kuya?" she said to Tito Melboy.

"Great selections, Sharon. But I have an even better idea than singing at Sunday Drag Brunch," Tito Melboy said.

He had a better—bigger—idea, indeed. Tito Melboy was planning a new weekly event that he'd mentioned to me previously: a happy hour karaoke show in the two hours before Friday's six o'clock dinner service. Hosted by two people.

Him. And me.

I was thrilled. And terrified.

"Uncle, singing in front of an audience is one thing," I said, already sweating at the thought of his proposal. "Being a good host is another skill entirely."

"Yes, that's right. But they are related. They both require awareness and flexibility. And an extra special something you have that most people, even your mother, do not."

"What?" I asked.

"A face prettier than mine."

"Che!" my mom said, slapping Tito Melboy on the shoulder.

His pudgy body bounced as he laughed. "Joke *lang*!"

As my mom and uncle continued to cackle in the front seats, I struggled to wrap my head around this new opportunity. Like my tiny little window into drag had suddenly expanded into an IMAX screen so big I could barely take it all in.

"Mom, would you still be able to cover for us with Dad?"

She wiped her eyes from laughing with Tito Melboy. "Oh,

yes. We'll think of something. Maybe we can say you've picked up a summer job working at the same restaurant that your uncle is working at. That way it's not even a lie. But Eva and I won't be able to accompany you every time."

I looked at my little sister, conked out in the seat next to me in the back, her head tilted to the side and her mouth drooling.

"It's probably for the best, Mom. I think she can only take so much fabulousness at this point in her life."

In the following weeks, Beaucoup Buko's Karaoke Show turned out to be a big success. Downtown office workers looking for a fun way to kick off the weekend flocked to it. And as word of mouth got around about my unique singing skills, more people started to attend, people who were curious to see me who then became fans, coming back week after week.

At first, I only sang the opening and closing songs. But I watched Beaucoup as she emceed, paying close attention to her every move. She'd do more than just say a few words before each singer and then leave the stage. Each introduction was a chance to make the audience laugh, to connect with them. Even when someone else was performing, Beaucoup was still part of the show. She mingled with the patrons and stood by different tables to join guests as they watched. Her presence was like a battery, placed here and there to energize certain parts of the crowd when she felt they needed a little more to keep them entertained.

Finally, I was ready to do more than just sing, and for the

rest of the summer, Beaucoup split the show hosting duties with me. I still sang a song or two of my choice, but now I was emceeing just as much as she was. I had so much fun hosting that, as soon as a show would finish, I'd ache inside, knowing I'd have to wait seven more days to get to do it again.

I also had something else I looked forward to every Friday evening. Ivan.

"Hey, why do you come here every weekend?" he asked me one time, jerking his head over at Tito Melboy, who was pulling our suitcases out of the trunk of the car. "And what's in those suitcases that you always bring?"

I hadn't told him what we were doing on purpose. Ivan was super-friendly and flirtatious, but I wasn't sure he was gay, and I didn't know if I should let him in on my secret. Looking at his kind eyes and his easygoing smile, I had a hard time imagining him as being judgmental about something as simple as dressing up for karaoke. And besides, Dreamland was only two blocks away and was a famous tourist destination. He had to have known about it.

"The suitcases are for w-work," I stuttered. "At Dreamland. You know that restaurant—"

"Let's go, Rex!" Tito Melboy said, yanking me out of the parking booth by my collar.

Ivan laughed. "See you later, bro."

I waved goodbye, unable to breathe as my uncle choke-pulled me out of the garage.

"You shouldn't have told him where we work," he said when we were out of the garage. "Not a good idea."

"Why?" I pushed my lopsided collar back into place. "I think Ivan likes me. Like, *like* likes me."

My uncle shook his head. "Perhaps as Rex. But not as Regina. If a man is attracted to you as a man, then he will not love you as a woman."

My uncle was overreacting. I didn't know if Ivan would be interested in drag, but I was almost positive he was interested in me. It would be fine. He could come see me perform one night. He'd be so impressed with my talent that any unfamiliarity he had with drag would be instantly obliterated. I had the best drag mother there was. Beaucoup Buko had helped me become a sensation, a star.

I had learned so much from her all those years ago. And now, I have my own chance to pay it forward and teach someone else to be good at drag. Paolo.

Well, sort of. I have no expectations of Paolo becoming America's next drag superstar. I'm not sure I'd ever be a good enough drag mother. And more importantly, drag is a personal art form. A way to express oneself. And what I'm doing is asking Paolo to express who *I* am—not himself.

But still. It would be so much fun to drag up his life.

If I can figure out how to convince him to let me.

CHAPTER 13

"WHAT DO YOU THINK?" I ASK.

Eva steps back to examine my face. She makes a circle with her finger, and I twirl. My pink wrap dress flows outward around me like flowers floating in the breeze.

"Much better," she says. "I'll chalk up last Saturday's makeup disaster to you being a little rusty."

Eva's at my condo to take pictures and videos for us to use for an official social media campaign on both the Pink Unicorn's sites and Regina Moon Dee's.

"Sit for a sec," she says. "I want your eyes to really pop in the pics."

I sit down at my desk. Eva sorts through my makeup, finds a light primer, and starts applying it on the inner corner of my eyes.

"Have you asked Paolo to help you with your crazy doppelgänger plan yet?" she asks.

"Not yet."

Eva switches to my white inner corner highlighter. "He seemed very into you as Regina last weekend. Like, he couldn't take his eyes off you."

"What?" I say. "That can't be true."

"Trust me. He almost missed a few karaoke cues last Saturday because he was so busy watching everything you were doing."

"That doesn't necessarily mean he likes me or anything."

"I didn't say he likes you. I'm saying he was fascinated by your drag. It might not actually be that hard to convince him to try it."

"Oh." It wasn't actually Rex who Paolo was interested in. Why would he be? "Right. That makes sense."

"Why don't you invite him over here before the show on Saturday so he can see you get prepared. You'd have to explain it all to him anyway if he says yes, right? Might as well give him a sneak peek. Get him excited about the world of drag. And then slip in your request."

A sneak peek. Into my process. My world.

"Great idea. You always were the smart one."

"Yeah, yeah, and you're the pretty one," Eva says. "Now pucker your lips. I want to make them pinker."

Eva adjusts a few more things, making sure my wig and dress are on straight, and then takes a series of pictures and video clips. It's a lot like when I used to make my homemade music videos, but also not. Eva uses different filters, effects, and captions—all things I never did with my YouTube videos. She works on writing the copy, doing the tagging, and optimizing everything for maximum exposure, choosing several hashtags for the posts: #guesswhosback, #dragislife, #ReginaMoonDee, #queerkaraoke, and of course, #KaraokeQueen. I'm in really good hands with Eva. Just like I was with Mom, and later with Tito Melboy. Just like Paolo will be in mine.

If he says yes to me, that is.

I TEXT PAOLO AFTER EVA LEAVES, asking him if he'd come over to my place a little earlier on Saturday for extra karaoke night "training." I leave it at that.

Within seconds, he responds, Yes. What time on Sat?

I'm relieved. He always seems to have Saturday nights free from AquaMarine in order to KJ at the Pink Unicorn, but last weekend he was late coming from the restaurant. I wasn't sure if he'd be available to come earlier. Getting an affirmative answer from him so quickly makes me excited. But then I remember that the hard part is still to come. Convincing him to be Regina.

Is 6:00 okay? I ask.

Totally. I'll be there, he responds.

Thank you, I text, adding a few smiley faces and hearts and then erasing them all before just sending my address instead.

For the next few days, meeting up with Paolo is all I can think about. Even that Friday night—as I spend time at the bar with Aaron during his shift, reminiscing about our nights at Kilpatrick's and trying to get him to remember how great we were together—I still think of Paolo and how fabulous he would look in my drag.

Saturday evening rolls around. I hear a knock on the door. True to his word, Paolo arrives on time.

"Come iiiinn," I sing.

"Hi," Paolo says, opening my unlocked door. "So what are we—whoa!"

I'm a little bit of a mess, I admit. I'm still in a bathrobe and wig cap, and my face, streaked with foundation and concealer, hasn't been finished yet. I wanted to give Paolo the chance to see the final steps of my process so that he sees what he'll be getting into. And I hope it's more inspiring than horrifying.

Paolo, at least, looks much more fetching. He's got on a chino blazer over a V-neck T-shirt, his hair is slicked back, and his tortoiseshell glasses bring out his dark brown eyes.

"Thank you so much for coming over so early," I say, motioning to my couch. "Please. Sit."

My condo is technically only a studio, but at least it's completely new. The building is an old cannery that was refurbished into two hundred or so modern residences. I'm the first person to own my unit, with high-end appliances and tall ceilings that make it seem more spacious.

I turn in my desk chair in the living room to face him.

Paolo's eyes roam around my face. Something about the way he does this makes me feel devoid of makeup. Like he can see my naked skin underneath. The tips of my ears start to get warm.

"You know, not many people get to see what's behind my drag queen curtain," I say, fanning myself.

"I appreciate the chance to have a peek," Paolo says with a smirk. "So, you said we're training?"

"Yes."

"I was assuming it was on the karaoke program, but..." he says, swiveling his head around, "I don't see the KJ laptop anywhere."

"Right. We'll have to go over that some other time." I make a mental note to myself about this. He really does have to start figuring out that program soon. "It's a different kind of training. How much do you know about drag?"

"Drag?" Paolo's eyes widen. "I mean, it definitely fascinates me."

"Yes, I sort of got that sense."

"Oh, yeah?"

"Eva said you seemed very interested in me last Saturday. Uh—interested in my drag, that is."

"Your sister's very observant." Paolo's eyes twinkle. "I was *very* interested."

I feel my cheeks heat up. So much so that I check myself in the mirror to make sure my foundation is concealing any embarrassing redness.

Satisfied that Paolo can't tell how hot under the makeup

he's gotten me, I lean in close, as if I'm about to let him in on a secret. "So...have you ever thought about what it would be like to do drag yourself?" I ask.

"Me? Not really. I don't think I *could* do it myself."

"You could!" I say. "Drag is for everybody. Anyone can do it, with the right teacher. I'd certainly love to show you." I watch him, cautiously gauging his reaction. "But only if you're up for it, of course."

Paulo looks at me curiously, as if waiting for some sort of punchline. I just sit there, silent.

"I don't get it," he says, shaking his head when I don't say anything else. "Is this some sort of accreditation? Do you get points for teaching, or something?"

"Actually, it *is* kind of a rite of passage for drag queens to mentor—to become a mother to someone else. But in this particular case, it's really more of a favor," I say, smiling shyly. "For me."

Paolo squints.

"A big favor," I add.

"Okay," he says. "I'm listening."

"I would like to train you because..." I peer at him from the corner of my eye. "I want you to be me. I need you to be Regina Moon Dee."

Paolo's face goes blank. He blinks once. Twice. Then he bursts out with laughter. "You want me to be you? To take over hosting karaoke night?"

"Not to host karaoke night."

"Then what?"

"This is going to sound weird, but I need you to be my double. Rex needs to be seen with Regina, in the same place, at the same time. So someone won't suspect that she and I are the same person."

"Oh," Paolo says, his smile vanishing. "You mean Aaron."

His obvious disapproval hits me harder than I expect. I stand up and start to pace around my little living room. "Aaron can't find out I'm a drag queen, Paolo. Or at least not right now. He wouldn't understand. And all the work I've been doing for the Pink Unicorn—"

"Is for him. All for him," Paolo says. "And here I was thinking maybe if I..."

"What?"

"It doesn't matter." He hangs his head.

Without thinking, I sit back down, reach out, and take his hand. It's nice and warm.

I begin to pull away because, yet again, I've intruded on his personal space. And I know how freezing my hands get when I'm nervous.

But when I try to let go, Paolo holds on. "You're serious about this?"

"I know I'm asking a lot," I say. "But Regina is pulling in so much business for the Pink Unicorn. She's good for the bar."

"She's just not good for your potential relationship with Aaron," Paolo says. But despite the sadness in his eyes, he doesn't let go of me. "Don't you want to be with someone who accepts you for who you are? All of you?"

I stand up, breaking our connection. "He will. One day. It just takes Aaron a while to get used to ... gay things."

He mutters something to himself that sounds like, *That might take longer than you think.*

"What did you say?" I ask.

I look at Paolo, expecting to see those same sad eyes. But instead, they're filled with determination now.

"You'll really show me how to be Regina?" he says.

"Yes."

"In order for this to work," he says, "I'll have to be your twin. You'll have to show me how to walk like you, talk like you, be you. That's going to take a lot of work. And time."

"Yes," I reply. "We'll have to spend a lot of time together."

He grins. "Then let's do it."

Relief rushes through me, along with something else.

"Wonderful," I say, looking through my makeup. "For now, you can get a sense of what some of the steps are while I finish my final touch-ups. And then we'll figure out another time to work together through the entire process."

"How about tomorrow?" he offers.

I hadn't intended for us to do it so soon. But no time like the present. "What time?"

"Nine o'clock in the morning?" Paolo says. "I know it's early, but I'll bring breakfast."

"How can I say no to that?" I say. "Nine o'clock it is. Now where the heck is my lipstick ... ?"

I sort through everything on my desk and in my kit. Still

not able to locate it, I get down on the floor, crawling all around my desk and failing to find it anywhere.

"Found it," Paolo says.

He's standing above me, holding the opened lipstick. He smiles, and a swath of crimson lies streaked across his lips.

I stare at his mouth for much longer than I should. "Hey, stop fooling around."

He smiles a glossy red smile. "I thought I'd get a head start," he says.

I take the lipstick from him.

"Aren't you going to clean it off me again?" he asks.

Something stirs in me, deep and low. I grab a moist towelette and toss it at him. "Quit distracting me! I need to finish getting ready." At this point, it's going to be a struggle to fully focus on my final touches.

By some miracle, though, I manage to finish with enough time to spare. Paolo's presence over the next hour somehow switches over from being disturbing to grounding, even calming. He stays quiet by my side, asking questions here and there, but mostly watching intently as I work, almost as if he's taking notes in his mind. Not even Eva as a kid ever paid such close attention to my makeup process. He even makes me more confident in my makeup choices. I don't doubt for a second that I look beautiful after I'm done. One look at Paolo's face tells me that I am.

When it's time to get tucked and dressed, I excuse myself to go to my bathroom. I don't want to shock him with the whole tucking process, but also the thought of being nearly naked in front of him makes my heart race so fast I can barely breathe.

I'd decided earlier in the day to wear one of my big gowns and a short pixie-cut wig, but after Paolo arrived, I changed my mind. I felt the inexplicable urge to show off my legs. And arms. And chest. And to have longer hair. So I've thrown modesty to the wind and have switched to a one-piece bikini-style bodysuit, bejeweled with silver rhinestones and trimmed with white ostrich feathers, topped with a long, pink, wavy wig.

I emerge from the bathroom and do a seductive spin for Paolo. "How do I look?"

"Wow," he says, his eyes getting very big very fast. "Just...wow."

It's the effect I expected from him but it still thrills me to see it. "Thank you, darling. Shall we get going?"

"I'm ready," Paolo says, his eyes glued to me. "And I'll be watching you all night. To prepare for when I have to pretend to be you, of course."

"Of course." I head for the door, quietly fighting against the irrepressible smile growing on my face.

CHAPTER 14

I WORRIED THAT MY FIRST NIGHT HOSTING KARAOKE at the Pink Unicorn was just a fluke. Old fans rushing out to see what happened to me and then, having satisfied their curiosity, moving on and deciding they had better ways to spend their Saturday night.

But I was wrong. If anything, my second night hosting karaoke is bigger and better than my first.

Eva's social media campaign has brought in even more people, resulting in a line down the block and around the corner. And Paolo's skills with the SYNGX program have somehow improved. He's now figured out how to project a QR code onto the video screens for the SYNGX app, which allows patrons to request songs electronically and even allows them to interact with the show by sending chat messages that pop up on the video displays.

I'm more comfortable and having even more fun than last weekend. And perhaps the main reason for that is because Aaron isn't here.

Not because I don't miss him. It's just easier to be myself without him around.

In fact, there's really only one thing that makes me uneasy. At one point during the night, I catch Loretta filling up a glass of ice with soda and handing it to someone in a dark hoodie. Something about him seems familiar, but his hood is pulled way over his head and the lighting at that end of the bar is too dim, so I can't get a proper look at him. It seems sad to me, that someone in such a fun, welcoming environment would want to keep themselves hidden. And it reminds me of the fact that I've been hiding who I am to people. To the public. To my dad. And to Aaron.

But everyone has their own journey. It takes time for people to be comfortable with things they're not used to. I tried to rush things the last time I was with Aaron, and it didn't work out. I need to be patient and, when the time is right, tell him why I've been hiding my drag identity.

At the end of the night, after leading a final group sing-along of "Don't Stop Believing," I check my phone to see if Aaron has texted me. I'm hoping he's invited me over since he's no doubt already done spending time with Joey.

Not a peep.

Which is okay. Really. It's been a fabulous night, but my feet are swelling past the straps of my slingbacks. I'd love to just soak them in my bathtub while I unwind with a glass of wine, which I just might do. Because tomorrow will be another long day of drag.

Although this time, it won't just be me putting it on.

PAOLO SHOWS UP AT MY CONDO in Emeryville at nine a.m. on the dot, standing there in his motorcycle jacket and jeans, bright and chipper.

"Breakfast," he says, holding up a paper bag.

"Thank you," I say, stifling a yawn. "Come in."

As he passes by me, a blend of leather jacket and woody cologne wafts by, making my insides perk up and finally begin to wake.

He follows me into the small kitchen area, where I've managed to brew a pot of coffee. I get two mugs and plates and bring them to the tiny table. Paolo opens the bag and takes out two humongous bagel sandwiches.

"Wow," I say. "Where did you get these giant bagels?"

"Nowhere. I made them."

"You made the sandwiches?"

"And the bagels."

"Really?" I grab one and take a bite. It's incredible. A firm, snappy crust on the outside, chewy on the inside, with a hint of roasted garlic. A fried egg oozes over thinly sliced cucumbers, tomatoes, and beef tapa. "It's like a bagel sandwich version of tapsilog."

Paolo lights up. "Exactly! Do you like it?"

"Ohmigod, yes," I say, trying not to let my eyes roll up into my head. "You're very talented."

Paolo grins and digs into his own sandwich. "You're one to talk," he mumbles with his mouth full. "You were amazing last night. Again."

"Thank you," I say. It should be getting easier to receive Paolo's compliments, but for some reason, I feel even more self-conscious hearing them now. "You didn't do so badly yourself. You really upped your game on the SYNGX program."

"Yeah. I watched a couple of YouTube videos on it this past week. Learned a few new things."

"Then why did you agree to come over to my place yesterday?"

"Because you asked me to."

"For training. Which you said you assumed was for the KJ program. If you already trained yourself on it, why'd you come?"

He smiles. "Because I was interested in whatever it was you were going to teach me."

Lacking the words to respond to that, I take another bite of my sandwich—a big one—and chew in silence, nodding dumbly.

"Soooooo," Paolo says, "what exactly do we have planned for today? You going to show me how the whole makeup thing works now?"

I pour us both some coffee. "Not yet. You have to learn how to walk before you can run."

"Walk before I..." Paolo says, trailing off. "Oh. I have to learn how to walk in heels."

Ask any queen what the hardest aspect of drag is, and she's likely to say any one of a variety of things. Padding. Corseting. Tucking. But the thing most men have difficulty with first is the shoes. The center of gravity is so different, and muscles that have never been paid attention to before start working overtime. Most of all, walking in high-heeled shoes hurts. Especially when big feet are squished into small shoes.

I sip my coffee, enjoying the way it pairs with Paolo's tapsilog bagel sandwich. "It's not easy. But I'll guide you through it."

"Who taught you how to walk in heels?" Paolo asked.

"My mom did, actually."

"Seriously? Your mom taught you how to do drag?"

"Well, my uncle Melboy taught me the actual art of drag. He's a queen, too. Beaucoup Buko is his drag name. But my mom taught me the basics of makeup and women's wear before I even met him."

"You're lucky to have a mother that open-minded," Paolo says. "There's no way my mom would ever do anything like that. She told us that what we wore reflected on our family, so she basically picked out our clothes until we were teenagers. And since I was a bigger kid, there weren't that many choices. Everything I wore was from the husky section."

"You were a big kid?" Underneath his motorcycle jacket, a T-shirt stretches tight across his chest and lean abdomen. "I wouldn't have guessed that."

"I grew out of it. Besides, you can't tell everything just by looking at someone, right?" he says with a wink, which jolts me into being aware that I've been staring at his chest.

"Right," I say, and focus on my bagel sandwich.

After we're done eating, Paolo makes us more coffee while I head over to my drag trunk and rummage through my collection of shoes.

"Here's my starter pair." I hold up a pair of character shoes with a sensible heel of two and half inches.

Paolo wrinkles his nose. "Those? They're so unsexy."

"Sorry if they don't go with your hot leather jacket," I say.

He tugs on his jacket. "You think this is sexy?"

"What? No, I didn't say that. It's just heavy and thick, so it's hot. You must be hot. You're hot, right?" I say, groaning internally.

Paolo chuckles. "My dad gave it to me for my sixteenth birthday. His way of saying I was a grown man, I guess. It was back when we were still on good terms. I wear it to remind myself that I love him. It's easy to forget sometimes."

I sit down on the floor next to my trunk, tucking my legs under me. "I didn't always get along with my dad, either. I know he supports me. But he hasn't always."

"Dads just want the best for their kids," Paolo says, sitting on the edge of my bed. "But I think too much of their pride and identity is tied up in their children. Their sons, especially. Mine keeps reminding me about my responsibilities to the family business. He wants me to take over for him when he's too old to do stuff. I don't know if I want to do that."

183

"What's your family business?"

Paolo shakes his head. "It's not important."

He looks so sad. A lot like he did back at the restaurant, when he said he was jealous of me. For having a passion for something that I'm good at doing.

I put the character shoes back in the trunk and trade them for a more fun pair of pink platforms with four-inch heels. "Okay, you want sexy, I'll give you sexy. Try these."

Paolo's eyes bulge. "Whoa. Those heels are really high."

"You know what *Kinky Boots* says about heels."

"The higher the heel, the closer to God?"

I hand him the shoes. "Close enough."

"You're not going to put them on me?"

I can't tell if he's kidding. His face isn't giving anything away.

I motion for him to take his shoes and socks off. He complies without a word, though I finally detect a faint smile.

When he's done, I take one of his feet in my hand. The skin is surprisingly supple on top, with a smattering of hairs on the toes. The bottom of his heel is rougher but not calloused. Just thick. Heavy. His foot smells earthy and unusually sweet. He tenses a bit.

"Ticklish?" I ask, looking up.

He shrugs and smiles.

I slip the shoe on. It glides onto him with no more effort than a simple swoop. I pull the strap around his ankle, slipping it just underneath the hard knob of bone that juts out on the side.

"How's that feel?" I ask.

He closes his eyes and, in a low voice, says, "Great."

It's not until I see the curling of his lips that I realize I've been stroking the knobby bone on his ankle with my thumb.

I pull my hand back. "Oh, uh, looks like it fits. Let's get that other one on."

We repeat with the other shoe, but this time I make sure to be as clinical as possible. No more accidental touching of his skin or lingering on the feel of his foot. I just put it on him and strap him in. Tight.

"Good," I say. "Now let's try walking—"

"Okay." Paolo stands straight up from the bed and takes a step.

I reach out. "Wait!"

His right ankle buckles. And as if in slow motion, all parts of him crumple, and down he goes, landing face-first in a pile of clothes on my floor.

"Ohmigod! Are you okay?" I ask.

"Please tell me this is clean laundry," he mumbles into the pile.

"It's clean laundry."

Paolo's head pops up from the pile, a purple thong hanging from his ear. "Somehow, I don't believe you."

I yank the underwear and toss it back on the pile. "Here." I reach underneath his arms to help him stand back up. "Let's try it again. More slowly this time."

His ankles wobble again, but this time I'm prepared and grab his hand, propping him up until he can find his balance.

He looks at the ground as if it will disintegrate beneath him. His legs tremble. I keep holding on to him.

"Take a deep breath," I say. "That's it. Stand up straight. Look ahead, not at the ground. It's okay, I've got you."

I try to convey strength through my hold on Paolo's hand. His grip slowly begins to ease until he's no longer holding on to me for dear life. We're just holding hands.

"You good?" I ask.

"Yes. Very."

"Good. You passed the first test. Now I'll demonstrate."

I put on a pair of stiletto heels about two inches higher than the ones he has on and walk around the room in demonstration.

"Jeez. How do you not howl in agony in those?"

"Trust me, I want to. But beauty is pain. Now try to copy what you see."

He's gotten his balance enough to stand with confidence, but once he starts trying to follow me, it's a disaster. His gait is too choppy. He can't seem to keep his stride flowing or to get enough sway in his hips.

"Ugh, Paolo. It looks like you're stomping on bugs."

"I'm trying!"

"You're thinking too much. Or maybe you're thinking about the wrong things. Let go of everything you've ever learned about walking."

I come up from behind him. "Picture every supermodel you've ever seen on the catwalk. How fierce they are. And channel all that into here." I place my hands on his hips gently, coaxing them from side to side.

The movements of his hips smooth out, becoming more seductive, feeling liquid-like and luxurious in my hands.

"Work! Now try moving forward again."

Paolo takes a small step with more swish in the hips. And then another. The more steps he takes, the more confident they get. And sexy. I feel a rush of something. Pride, perhaps. But something more than that, too.

"Holy crap," he says, stomping around my room. "I think I'm actually getting it. Am I getting it?"

"Oh, yes. You're definitely getting it."

Paolo laughs. "I feel freaking hot."

He is. Extremely.

Stop fixating on Paolo's hips, Rex. Focus. You've got a job to do.

"All right," I say. "You can take off the shoes. We'll do this in different stages. Phase two. Time to try serving some looks."

Paolo nods vigorously. "What do I get to try on first?" He sits at my desk to undo the straps of my high heels.

"First things first. The tuck."

"The what?"

I point toward my groin. "Have you never noticed that this area down here is smooth as a baby's butt when I'm in drag?"

"I just assumed you had a fun-size penis."

"Hey! I have a very not fun-size penis. I mean, it's plenty

of fun. I mean, it's an above-average-size penis." I groan. "Why? How big is yours?" Warmth floods to my cheeks. "Nope, forget I asked you that. Tucking is where you pull your flaccid dick and scrotum back in between your legs and tape it in place behind you."

"Don't your balls get smashed?"

"No, because you put them up inside you."

"You what now?" Paolo asks.

"You'll put your balls up inside your body."

"No. I won't be doing that. They can't do that."

"It's actually pretty natural. You know when it's really cold outside and your ballsack kind of shrivels up? It's because your testicles are traveling up closer to your body to stay warm. And when it gets really cold, they go all the way up inside your pelvic area. To keep all those floaties nice and toasty and ready to make babies. Although, ew."

"*That's* the part you're *ew*ing about? The fact that sperm helps create life? Not that your balls actually move of their own volition up into your stomach?"

"They don't travel that far. But let's get back to you."

"I don't know if I want to do this anymore."

"All right. We'll skip the tuck." I knew it would be a tough sell. "I just thought, if you were man enough to walk in heels, you'd have enough balls to tuck. Although it's a bit better if you don't have big balls so your tuck isn't as meaty, but—"

"Okay, I can't believe I'm saying this," Paolo says, "especially since whatever a meaty tuck is sounds hideous. But I'll try it. Only if you demonstrate for me, though. To help me make up my mind?"

Again, I can't tell whether Paolo's playing with me, flirting with me, or neither. Whatever he's doing, I'm not about to drop my pants and yank my penis back with him watching.

"We'll just find you some sort of big skirt to wear instead."

I start sorting through the possible outfit options in my trunk. "Ooh, this one!" I pull out the dress I wore for my first time hosting Friday karaoke at Dreamland—a blue sequined bodysuit top that flares out into a poofy, pink tutu. It's long so it'll cover up Paolo's privates and still look wonderfully girly. Another great thing about the dress is that it matches perfectly with my pair of platforms. High and dramatic, but much easier to walk in than regular stiletto heels. And there's no need for a breastplate. The ensemble works better with a flat chest.

"Let's have you try it on so you know what to expect."

I avert my eyes out of respect as he undresses. And maybe because I'm also afraid of the reaction I'll have if I see him without clothes on.

I instruct him to lay the dress on the ground and then step into it, pulling it up and around himself. After he's done that, I step in to assist. There's no real need to pad the hips with the tutu, but the top is essentially a corset. It's important that Paolo get a sense of how that feels.

"Putangina!" Paolo yelps as I cinch him in. "That hurts! Does drag always feel like this?"

"If it feels like your organs are trying to escape upward and out of your mouth, then yes. Now shut up and be a man about it."

"Can we reassess the tucking thing? Maybe I'll do that instead if I don't have to wear a corset."

"No matter what we choose, there's going to be discomfort involved. We drag queens are warriors. We get used to the pain. We have to."

This seems to quiet Paolo. He grins and bears it as I finish getting him into the outfit and shoes.

Afterward, he even manages to walk around with a bit of sass.

I snap my fingers. "Werk it, henny."

"I'm getting used to it," Paolo says.

"Very good. Now that you know how it feels, you can take it off. This next step—the makeup—is more for my sake. I want to make sure I'm able to replicate Regina Moon Dee's face on you perfectly so that no one can clock you."

"About time," he says.

I help him out of his dress, shimmying it down off his body until it lays like a poofy flower on the floor. There's no avoiding his undressed body now. I can't help but take in all of his physique. He's lean, not thick and brawny like Aaron. His muscles are long and sinewy. The tutu tulle on the ground surrounds Paolo in a pink corona, making him look like a male version of Venus, the goddess of love and beauty.

It's only after he clears his throat that I realize that I've been staring at his nearly naked body for who knows how long.

"Well, don't just stand there," I say, standing up abruptly. "Put your clothes back on."

Paolo takes just a few seconds too many before finally putting his pants and shirt back on.

I mindlessly rearrange the makeup and other materials on my desk while Paolo dresses, glad to be moving on to something that doesn't involve him taking his clothes or shoes off or me putting them on him.

But doing his makeup doesn't distract me from my thoughts about him. If anything, it just makes it worse.

As soon as he sits down in front of me and takes his glasses off, my heart swells. At first, I think it's only the thrill of doing someone else's makeup. I've never had a drag daughter of my own, so I've been looking forward to this act of sharing my art with someone else. But I haven't been this close to Paolo's face since last weekend, when I smothered his face with a surprise kiss. Knowing I'll be sitting this close to him, our faces only inches from each other for the next hour or so, fills me with something that's hard to ignore.

"Are you going to be okay without your glasses?" I ask.

"I should be fine. Things only get slightly fuzzy without them. When things are up close, they're okay. Like, I'm able to see you just fine," he says, in a way that makes it seem as if he likes what he sees. Something deep inside me stirs.

I put a wig cap on him and then move on to start blocking his brows. I notice that my hands are shaking.

"Something wrong?" Paolo asks.

"Don't move your face like that," I say. "You'll mess up the glue."

"Sorry. You just seem to be a little nervous."

I sort through my makeup kit, stalling to try to think of some way to respond. "I'm fine. I'm just..." And then I notice that I'm missing one of my favorite eyeliners, which is a bummer. They don't make that exact kind anymore. "I can't seem to find my liquid eyeliner."

"Oh," Paolo says, sounding disappointed.

"It's okay. I'll use another one." I push forward and start applying foundation to his face, hoping to get lost in the work.

Only now I'm acutely aware of my hands brushing against his skin. How nice it feels. How familiar. In some ways, it's a lot like touching my own face. We have comparable complexions and hair. Our noses are somewhat alike. Our eyes are both shaped similarly. We're not exactly the same, of course; anyone with decent eyesight can tell us apart. But it still feels as if I'm working on an extension of myself. It's exhilarating.

"You really like this," Paolo says.

"I do," I say, thankful I can answer him honestly. "I love makeup. I'm not always the best with matching colors, but it always feels so satisfying putting it on. I've never done someone else's face before, so I thought it might be different. But it's sort of the same."

"Or maybe *we're* sort of the same," Paolo says. "We have

a lot of things in common, you know. We're both Filipino. We're around the same age. We love karaoke. And..."

"And...what?"

He keeps his face still, like I asked him to. But I can sense something underneath, wanting to show itself. "And," he says, "we'll both do whatever it takes to please the people we love."

I force my gaze to shift, to focus on his cheeks, his nose, his brow. Anything other than his eyes on mine.

"Well, it's a good thing we're so alike," I say, "because when I'm done with you, no one will be able to tell the difference between you and me."

He makes this funny little snort. I can't tell if it's annoyance or amusement. In any case, I keep forging ahead, knowing that, if I put anything less than one hundred percent attention into the makeup, I'll lose my focus completely.

There's a benefit to being a bundle of nerves, at least—the makeup goes on quickly. I go at a faster tempo than usual, though still managing to get all the Regina details right. The thicker lining, the dramatic contouring, the signature eyebrows drawn with upward strokes that reach almost to the hairline, and the lips that are slightly overdrawn. I'm able to paint Paolo's face in a little under an hour, a record for me. It helps that he's stayed mostly quiet for the whole thing, only speaking to ask a few questions about what I'm doing. There's a part of him that probably understands that I need silence in order to work. He's being respectful of the process. Or maybe he senses that I'm too preoccupied to talk.

Whatever it is, every trace of the agitation I've been feeling over the past hour evaporates when I'm finally done and step back to fully examine my work.

"Take a look." I turn his chair around to see himself in the mirror.

His face freezes. "No fucking way."

"Do you hate it?"

He swivels his head from side to side, examining every angle.

"I love it. I'm so beautiful," he finally says.

I lock eyes with him in the mirror and am momentarily stunned. Paolo's right. He is absolutely gorgeous. And not only that, he's beaming. Brimming with so much pride over his own feminine beauty that it spills out and floods over me.

I can't deny it any longer. I'm really, really into Paolo.

I need to get him out of here. I'm trying to be with Aaron now. And everything I'm doing, the improvements to the Pink Unicorn, this whole doppelgänger plan, is for Aaron. I can't let any confusing feelings about Paolo mess that up.

"Well, I think we're done for now," I say. "I, uh, have other plans for today. I'll help you get out of makeup so you can be on your way."

"Wait," Paolo says, his eyes pleading. "Let me keep it on. I'll take it off when I get home."

"Seriously? Why?"

"I'm not ready to let go of Regina Moon Dee yet."

He puts his motorcycle jacket back on and places his glasses on his face. The effect of those things with my makeup still on him is like seeing the two of us mixed up together. And I love how it makes me feel.

I walk him to my front door, trying not to stare at him.

"When can we do this again?" he asks.

"Soon," I say. "We need to, I mean, we *should* do it again soon. And maybe a couple more practices after that. We'll take our time. To make sure we get everything right."

"Good," Paolo says to me before turning to leave. "Because I really want to take our time and get this right."

CHAPTER 15

"I HAVE TO DO IT NOW?" Paolo says loudly into the phone, making me pull it away from my ear. It's Monday morning, and I'm taking a quick coffee break in one of the empty conference rooms. "You said it was going to take a couple of training sessions before I was ready. I can't do it today," he says.

"Tomorrow night, not today. That gives us more than twenty-four hours," I say. "I'm sorry. It's just, I messed up and Aaron's getting more suspicious now."

Late Sunday night, after still floating on a high from a wonderful day of drag with Paolo, I received a text from Aaron. And not the kind I'd been hoping for. It was a picture.

Of my liquid eyeliner.

Is this yours? he texted. I found it at my place.

I stared at my phone for an eternity before figuring out how I could respond.

Nope. Regina might have stuck it in my jacket and it fell out at your place? She's always leaving me little gifts everywhere, that silly prankster. But it's for sure not mine. I def do not put on makeup.

After shooting off my response, the three horrible, haunting text dots hovered, blinking on and off for an eternity until, finally, they were replaced by OK.

I sat there, a hundred follow-up excuses flooding my brain when Aaron then texted, You free for dinner tomorrow night? My running friends got us a 6:30 pm reservation at Comal in Berkeley. I'm getting off work early. They want to meet you. It'll be a double-date kind of deal.

Yes! I texted back immediately. But that was all. I didn't know what else to say.

All I knew was it was time to implement the Regina doppelgänger plan. Right now.

"I'm having dinner with Aaron and his friends tomorrow night, Paolo. And if we don't get rid of his suspicions before then, it's going to be the worst dinner of my life."

"I can't pull it off yet, Rex," Paolo says.

"You can. I promise. I'll get you prepared, and I'll coach you, and—aieee!!" I see Kat's face pressed against the window of the conference room door and stretched out to comical proportions.

Paolo laughs on the other end. "What the heck was that?"

Kat slips into the conference room. I set my phone on the table and put Paolo on speaker. "Kat scared the crap out of me."

"You have the most adorable shriek, Rex," she says as she sits down next to me. "Who're you talking to?"

"It's Paolo," he says from the phone. "Rex says I have to be Regina Moon Dee tomorrow."

"Already?" Kat asks.

"He's ready," I say. "Paolo, you've got the walk down. And I'll get you into the clothes and makeup. You're going to look exactly like me. All you have to do is sell it."

"I'm not sure," he says.

"You can do it," I say. "I know you can fully inhabit me."

Kat gives me a weird look.

What? I mouth.

Fully inhabit you? she mouths back, trying not to laugh.

"Well, if you put it that way, I'm down," Paolo says.

"Perfect," I say, smiling to myself. "What times are you working tonight and tomorrow?"

"I'm working until late tonight, but I don't have to work tomorrow," he responds.

"Oof. Okay. Tomorrow will have to do. The legal team will be out of the office all day for a continuing education seminar, so I can leave work early. Be at my place by two o'clock. That should give us enough time to get you prepped and ready. Aaron will be bartending tomorrow night. I'll arrive around five. You'll come in, say you're on your way to a gig and are just passing by to pick up your eyeliner from me. It'll take five minutes. Sound good?"

"Ooh, ooh," Kat says, bouncing up and down on her seat, "can I come?"

"Sure, why not," I say.

"I'll help you, Rex," Paolo says. "But only if you can answer me this—who are you really doing this for? Rex or Regina?"

"What does that even mean?" I ask.

"I get that Aaron finding out about your true identity jeopardizes things. But what, or who, are you really trying to protect?"

I don't say anything.

"What are you really afraid of?" Paolo asks.

I still don't respond.

Paolo says, "Just think about it. See you tomorrow at two," and hangs up.

Kat sniffs. "I think I know what he means. Do you?"

No, I really don't. Aaron has made it clear to me that, while drag is good for the Pink Unicorn, it's not good for him. Ergo, the need to remain separate. Rex for him, Regina for the bar. That's all there is to it.

That's what I keep telling myself, at least.

BY THE TIME PAOLO arrives at my place the next day at two o'clock, I've already set everything up. The makeup is laid out on my desk, the wig is washed, dried, and styled, the ballerina outfit with its tutu fully fluffed hangs in my closet, and the shoes are unstrapped and ready to be slipped onto Paolo's feet.

He's quiet. I am, too. The silence isn't exactly uncomfortable, though. We're concentrating on the task at hand and know that it's going to require both our full attentions to pull this feat off. This is all still so new for Paolo, and I don't have my mother or drag mother or even Eva, who's at a new internship right now, to help me make sure everything is correct.

We get down to business.

To be honest, I'm thankful for the stress the ticking clock has put on me. Being singularly focused on turning Paolo into Regina Moon Dee means I can concentrate more on her and less on him. Because if I'm allowed even a second to think about Paolo, I'll never get this done. Being this close to him, being so attuned to his face and his body, it's almost too much. It makes me question everything I'm doing.

Why am I doing this?

Who am I doing this for?

I don't want Aaron to know I'm a drag queen. I know that. But is it because I know he'd never date me if he knew? Or is it because I'm afraid of his reaction? Would he be upset that I've fooled him? Furious, even?

A familiar pain rustles in the pit of my stomach. What am I afraid of?

After about two and a half hours of careful preparation, Regina Moon Dee stands before me in fully realized form.

Paolo looks at himself in the mirror. He's serene, poised, as if he's spent all that time in the chair gathering himself, working on transforming the inner parts of himself while I worked on the exterior. He truly does seem like Regina to me.

I have him practice walking around the room in the shoes while I go over the game plan.

"You don't need to say too much," I say as he walks. *"Hello, I'm here to get my makeup back. Goodbye.* Got it?"

"Got it." With every step, he becomes Regina Moon Dee more and more.

"And pitch your voice up a bit when you talk," I remind him. "Channel your inner queen as much as possible." I look at my watch. "We should leave in about twenty minutes. You can relax your feet until then."

Paolo nods, clearly relieved to be able to rest for a while. He attempts to sit down on my bed but is unsure of how to handle the tutu. He pushes it aside, and then he tries to spread it out from his backside, reaching around to pull it forward. Finally, he just pulls the whole thing up and around his body. He smiles triumphantly at me.

I laugh.

"What?" he asks.

"You look like a big, gay daisy."

"I'll take that as a compliment."

"I owe you more than just a compliment for doing this."

"You don't owe me anything, Rex. I'm happy to help. But you do owe yourself something." Paolo leans forward, the tutu fanning around him. "An answer to the question I asked you last night. Do you have one yet?"

My forehead begins to throb. "Actually, let's head out now. There's always a little more traffic around this time of day."

Paolo frowns, and his flower tutu seems to wilt.

I help him off my bed, and we head off to the Pink Unicorn.

We both park our cars around the corner in a more secluded part of the neighborhood where Paolo can sit and wait safely for a while. When I get inside the bar, Kat is already there chatting it up with Aaron while he stocks more liquor on the shelves. Bryan is, as usual, snacking and watching TV. This time, it's pretzels and reruns of *Cheers*, which feels appropriately meta. He acknowledges me with a smile and goes right back to his show.

I lean up against the bar to give Aaron a hug. He smells salty and peaty, like he's been eating Bryan's pretzels while sampling some of the scotch he's been putting away.

"You're just in time," Aaron says. "Kat was just about to pitch me some ideas for more themed nights."

"Oh, yeah?" I ask, sitting on the stool next to Kat. "Like what?"

"You remember my ex, Sal?"

"The poet?"

"Yes, which was literally the only good thing about him. Well, that and his adorable pudgy python."

"Is that a euphemism?" I ask. "Anyway, please continue."

"He's got lots of friends who are always looking for a place to do their poetry slams, and the stage here would be perfect."

Aaron starts mixing up some drinks for us. Something with Aperol and fresh oranges. "Not a bad idea," he says. "But speaking of stages, why not have your band come play?"

"Are you guys actually getting back together again?" I ask.

Kat crinkles her nose. "Kind of? I was just telling Aaron we've been having more jam sessions together. Been coming up with some new material."

"It'd be great for the bar, Kat," Aaron says, carefully cutting an orange peel for her drink. "We haven't had live music here in a long time. What else?"

We discuss other possibilities. Trivia nights, bingo nights, even hosting a speed dating event. After a round of drinks, I start to worry about Paolo's absence. Almost half an hour has gone by since I arrived, and still no sign of Regina Moon Dee. I'm about to send a text when she comes tripping in.

Literally.

Paolo-as-Regina walks into the Pink Unicorn waving and saying, "Hiiiiiiii—" and then his right ankle wobbles, and he falls to the ground. A horrible feeling of déjà vu washes over me.

"Oh, shit!" Kat says.

I run over to the entrance, but Paolo manages to pick himself off the ground without too much effort before I reach him. Luckily, the massive amounts of tulle seem to have absorbed most of his fall.

Bryan hops off his stool. As he helps Paolo up on his feet, Bryan blinks a few times and squints at him. He turns to me and gives me a funny look.

"Are you okay, Regina?" I ask.

"I'm fine!" Paolo says. "I think I just over-sillied that walk."

"*Sissy*," I whisper into Paolo's ear.

"Hey, no need to be rude. I'm trying my best," he mutters.

"No, the phrase is—"

Aaron wipes his hands off with a bar towel. He hesitates for just a second—a moment that seems to stretch out indefinitely as I wonder whether or not he's able to see through the makeup and see Paolo underneath.

He smiles and reaches his hand out to shake Paolo's. "Nice to see you again. And, uh..." He gives me a questioning look. "I don't know. Is this the right way to greet a drag queen?"

"Oh, honey, I'll take hugs, kisses, handshakes, and any other hand gestures," Paolo says playfully. He stretches out an arm, leading with the wrist. "Enchanté. You stay."

Better, I mouth silently to Paolo.

"So, um, why exactly are you here, Regina?" Kat asks, trying to move the charade along.

"Ah, yes. Just here to pick up my eyeliner from Rexie here," Paolo says. "Don't you just love finding my things? It's like leaving behind little kisses."

I smile and nod. So far, so good. I root around in my jacket for the makeup but can't seem to find it.

"You were great your first night here," Aaron says while I continue to search. "But everyone's been telling me what an even bigger party it was last weekend. I'm hoping to be able to switch to Saturdays soon. Wait, you're not working here tonight, are you?" Aaron gives Bryan a look, who shakes his head at him. "Am I missing something? Why are you all dressed up?"

I panic for a few seconds, praying Paolo's gotten his story straight.

"Just on my way to another gig in the city," Paolo replies. "Now that you've gotten me out of retirement, the floodgates are open, and the offers are just pouring in."

"Yes, well, try to keep those floodgates closed a bit," I say. "Or you'll spread yourself too much. I mean, you'll spread yourself too thin."

Paolo's face cracks as he tries not to laugh at me.

"In any case, you look very pretty tonight," Aaron says to Paolo.

"You really are!" Kat says, glancing sideways at me. "I'm so fucking impressed!"

I take another look at Paolo. I can't help it. It's not just that he looks and sounds so much like me as Regina Moon Dee; it's that I'm experiencing what other people feel when they're around me. Paolo-as-Regina is buoyant, effortless. Fun. She's someone I want to be around. It makes me sad that I've kept my other persona hidden for so many years. And it makes me want to spend more time with him.

More time *as her*, I mean.

Paolo brings a hand to his chest. "Why, thank you both."

And then I notice that Paolo has frozen, his smile angled into something like a scowl.

Kat squints at him. "Are you okay, Regina?"

Paolo nods slowly, his strange smile still stuck in place. "Mm-hmm."

"You sure?" Aaron says.

"Mmph," Paolo mumbles. "It's...just..."

"What?" Kat says.

"Mytk," he says quietly through gritted teeth.

"Your what?" I ask.

"My tuck," Paolo whispers.

"Your *what?*?" we all say.

"Excuse us for just one second." I pull Paolo aside. "What's this about your tuck?"

Paolo whispers, "It's coming loose. Like, really loose. I don't think I did it right."

"You're tucked? Why the hell are you tucked? I chose that outfit specifically so you didn't have to!"

"I know, but I just wanted to go all in. So I learned all about it online and tucked before I got to your place."

"Oh. That's why you were so quiet the whole time."

"Yeah. It felt weird, and I was trying not to think about it. And now I'm pretty sure I didn't do it right because—oops. There we go."

"Your penis is fully untucked now, isn't it?" I ask.

"Completely," Paolo says.

"You should probably get going," I say.

"Yes."

I move back toward the bar. "Nice seeing you, Regina," I say with lots of enthusiasm, pushing him toward the front exit. "Have a wonderful gig tonight. Wherever you're going."

Paolo, however, squirms while walking, as if he has a load in his pants. "Actually, I'll just use the bathroom before I go," he says, before rushing off to the back.

"Maybe I should go help her out?" Kat says, looking concerned.

"Wait," I say, but it's too late. She's gone after Paolo and entered the bathroom behind him.

"Sweet sausages, what the hell am I looking at?" we hear Kat yell from behind the door.

FIFTEEN MINUTES LATER, Kat and Paolo re-emerge from the restroom. Paolo looks much more comfortable, his face tranquil and the tulle of his tutu nicely fluffed.

Kat, though, looks as if she's just walked out of a combat zone triage center.

Paolo smiles at us. "Aaron, so nice to see you again. Rex, ta-ta. And, Kat? I owe you." He floats out of the bar, giving Bryan a goodbye air-kiss as he leaves.

"That is *not* what I thought tucking meant," Kat says, still shell-shocked.

Aaron scrunches his face in confusion before shrugging and attending to a bunch of new people who have shown up at the bar.

I sit back down on my stool and feel a lump in my pants pocket. "Dammit," I say, pulling the liquid eyeliner out. "That's where it was."

I hurry out the exit, and then realize there's no need. Paolo can only go so far so fast in my shoes.

"Hey," I say.

Paolo turns around. "How did I do?"

"You were perfect," I say. "I was totally into it."

"Yes, I could tell," Paolo says, lightly tapping me on the chest. "So why did you come running after me so fast? Aren't you heading out to dinner with Aaron and his friends?"

Why *did* I go after him? The makeup is mine, not his. My heart is still racing, even though it wasn't that far for me to chase after him.

"I just..." I say, staring at him.

"What?" Paolo's red lips curl up into a smile.

And then, without even thinking about it, I hug him. "Thank you," I say.

The massive tutu crinkles and gives way between us. The tulle becomes thinner until it's not even there. Paolo holds me, saying nothing. He smells of perfume, and underneath that, his sporty soap and slight perspiration, which makes me—

"Rex, is that you?"

I turn my head around to the voice next to me.

My jaw drops. "Tito Melboy?"

CHAPTER 16

"WHAT ARE YOU DOING HERE?" I ASK.

Even though it's been over ten years since I last saw my uncle, he looks as if he hasn't aged at all. His skin is still smooth and sun-kissed. His hair is longer than ever, draped to one side and cascading down the front of his body. And he's just as pleasantly plump, filling out his large tropical shirt and powder blue shorts.

"Eva said you would be at that Pink Unicorn bar," Tito Melboy says. "I came here because—wait a second." He stares at Paolo. "Who are you, and why are you dressed as my nephew?"

"Hi." Paolo waves. "I'm Paolo."

"Hey, Aaron sent me to check on you," Kat says, walking up to us from the bar. "What's the holdup?"

"Rex." Tito Melboy *tsk*s as he examines Paolo's face. "Why did you choose this color palette with this dress?"

Kat gasps. "Is this who I think it is?"

"Uh, can I get out of these shoes now?" Paolo says, flexing one of his feet and nearly falling over.

"Okay, you guys—Kat, this is my uncle; Tito Melboy, this is my best friend and work-wife, Kat; Paolo, yes, you can take your shoes off." I look back at the Pink Unicorn, checking to make sure Aaron hasn't come outside for any reason. "Sorry to be so abrupt, but Aaron and I need to be at the restaurant soon for our dinner reservation. Can we save in-depth introductions for another time?"

"Fine with me. I'm on my way out," Kat says. "That was one hell of a show, Paolo. Maybe more than I ever needed to see, but still."

"I have a good drag mom," Paolo says, glancing at me.

"What's this now?" Tito Melboy asks. "Have you become a mother now, pamangkin?"

"He has indeed," Paolo says. "And he's already punished me by making me wear these." He slips my high heels off and holds them up by the straps.

"I'll get them back from you some other time, okay?" I say. "Along with my other stuff. And thanks again for what you did for me back there."

"You'll make it up to me," Paolo says before turning around and heading to his car.

"I'm going that way, too. I'll walk you." Kat puts her arm around Paolo's waist. "Have fun on your date!" she says, turning back to me. Paolo keeps looking straight ahead. I watch them leave, getting smaller down the sidewalk to their cars.

Without even turning my head, I know that Tito Melboy is looking at me. I can feel the heat of his stare on my right cheek.

"So you're back doing drag again, ha?" he says.

"It's a long story. I can tell you all about it later tonight. You'll still be around, right?" I ask. "Are you just visiting? Or are you back here for good? I thought you were living in Palm Springs now."

"I'm back at Dreamland. I started doing a few shows at OASIS, too."

"Does my dad know you're back?"

He grunts. "Your mother told him. But he's not talking to me. You know how he feels about my life choices. It still makes him so angry after all these years. That dad of yours is so hardheaded."

He's got that right. I want to tell my uncle how much happier Dad got after I quit drag. And how proud he is of me now that he thinks I'm pursuing a completely different career path. But before I can say anything, my phone buzzes with a text from Aaron.

We're still doing dinner, right?

"I'm sorry, but I have to run. Aaron's getting antsy."

"This Aaron, he's your boyfriend?" Tito Melboy asks.

"Not exactly. Not yet, at least."

"And let me guess—he doesn't know that you are a drag queen."

"Good guess. Don't worry, I learned the lesson you tried to teach me. About keeping myself safe. About not letting men see everything about me."

"I don't—"

My phone buzzes again. Any second now and Aaron will be poking his head out the Pink Unicorn door, wondering where I am.

"Can I call you later?" I ask, edging back toward the Pink Unicorn.

Tito Melboy nods. "Of course, Rex. I'm just glad to see you again. Ask your mom for my new phone number, okay?" He throws his arms around me, and I'm surrounded by a familiar, soothing feeling that I haven't felt in years.

"I will," I say, eventually tearing myself away to head back into the bar.

AARON AND I DRIVE OVER SEPARATELY TO COMAL, about ten minutes from the Pink Unicorn. We get there in what seems like an instant. I'm so preoccupied with the many thoughts running through my head—Paolo's performance as Regina Moon Dee, Tito Melboy's reappearance—that I don't even realize it when I arrive, parking right next to Aaron in the garage.

"Everything okay?" Aaron asks as we walk from the garage to the restaurant. "You're pretty quiet."

He looks at me with genuine concern, that same kind look on his face he has whenever he talks to patrons when he works. So many of them unload their problems on him. It's common enough to do with a bartender, but Aaron actually enjoys listening to people's problems. He's a good guy that way. A great guy, even. I should be open with him, too. I should tell him the truth about me. Why can't I seem to do that?

"I'm okay," I say. "Maybe a little nervous about meeting your running buddies."

He places his arm around my shoulder. "Don't worry, you're going to love them."

Aaron cares about me. I know that. If he wants me to meet his friends, then he's as serious about getting back together again as I am.

Maybe what Tito Melboy said about men liking me only as either Rex or Regina isn't completely true. Maybe I should trust that Aaron will be able to see and accept all of me. Maybe it's time to tell him the truth.

If everything goes well tonight, maybe I will.

We enter into the cacophony of the restaurant. Comal, unlike the subdued, romantic AquaMarine, is bustling. Its modern take on Mexican cuisine is extremely popular, so the sleek wooden banquettes, communal tables, and outdoor patio are always packed. The lobby is a mass of people. Aaron makes a beeline to the side, locating his two friends in an instant.

Aaron bro-hugs them both. "Sorry we're late. Rex, this is Etienne and Miguel."

Etienne's jacked body strains against his button-down

shirt as he shakes my hand. "Really nice to meet you." His voice lilts with the musicality of someplace in the French Caribbean. I have a hard time imagining his football-player physique in a running club.

It's easier to see that Miguel is an avid runner, though. He's got a slim build in his designer jeans and long-sleeve Henley. He smiles kindly at me. "Aaron says you guys met in Bloomington while you were at Indiana University?"

"We did, indeed," I say.

"Bummer," Miguel says.

Aaron laughs at my confused look. "Miguel went to Purdue," he explains.

"Oh, so I probably shouldn't be saying 'Go, Hoosiers' at any point tonight?" I say.

"Grrrr," Miguel growls playfully. We laugh.

"Are we waiting for a table?" I ask.

"We have reservations, but they wouldn't seat us until everyone was here. I'll let them know we're ready," Etienne says, and walks over to the host stand.

"Rex, I understand you're in biotech?" Miguel asks.

"I work in the legal department at a sustainable resources company. You?"

"Mechanical engineer," Miguel responds. "At Tesla. Etienne's there, too."

"Sounds like a tough job," I say. "Is he an engineer, too?"

Aaron smiles at Etienne as he rejoins us. "Oh, no," Aaron says. "Etienne's job is much harder."

"What do you do?" I ask.

"Human resources," Etienne says. "Trust me, I'd rather work on wheels and driveshafts than intervene in employee squabbles."

"Well, who wouldn't want to work on driveshafts all day long?" I say. "Yass, give me all of that torque and screwing."

They stare at me blankly.

"Uh, I mean—"

Miguel laughs. "Nice. You have a cute sense of humor." He rubs my arm lightly, grinning.

"Oh, ah. Thank you." I cough and clear my throat. "So where are we on the table situation?"

"They're a bit behind," Etienne replies. "There are stragglers at all the four-toppers. She suggested we get some drinks while we wait."

Miguel motions to the bar. "Shall we, then?"

"Let's," Aaron says. "I hear this place has some original cocktails. Maybe I can pick up some new ideas."

He heads to the bar with Etienne, leaving Miguel and me to trail behind them. I notice Etienne saying something into Aaron's ear, making him laugh. A small knot twists in my stomach.

A small group at the bar leaves for their table just as we arrive, so we're all able to snag stools. The bartender—a stylish young femme who looks like one of the Queer Eye guys' younger brothers—sashays over to us to ask for our orders.

"What'll it be, sirs? If you need any suggestions, I'm more than happy to assist."

"We might need a sec," Aaron says. "Do you have a drink menu?"

"Absotootley," the bartender says, pulling up some menus from behind the counter and placing them on the counter in front of us. "Just wave when you're ready, sweeties."

After the bartender whisks back over to the other end of the bar, Aaron hands the menus to us. It's surprisingly long, with endless margarita variations. We decide on four different ones.

When our bartender delivers our drinks, we're about to clink our glasses when he asks us, "Is this a special occasion? Do you guys want me to take your picture?"

We look at each other and shrug wordlessly. *Why not?* Aaron gives the bartender his phone, and he snaps a few shots.

We scroll quickly through the pics. The three of them nod and go back to their discussion of the Golden State Warriors' chances for the playoff, while I give the pictures a second look.

As I usually do these days when my picture is taken, I've tried to appear butch, posing with my jaw set, forming a smile that's barely there. It's closer to a sneer than anything else. Miguel and Etienne look similarly imposing, and Aaron by my side is hunky as hell. We look like four masculine men. I should feel happy about what I see. But I'm unsettled. As if what I see is warped somehow. Wrong.

The hostess approaches us at the bar. "Etienne, party of four? Your table's ready."

"Go on ahead," Aaron says to Miguel and Etienne. "We'll close up the tab here." They nod and accompany the hostess while Aaron gestures for the bill.

"You doing okay?" he asks me.

"Yeah, why?"

"I know you're not into basketball. I'm sorry if you feel left out."

"Oh," I say, relieved that that's why he thinks I looked distressed. "It's fine. Really. As long as we don't talk about it all night," I say, trying to smile reassuringly.

The bill arrives. Aaron slides his credit card inside the check holder. "Want to talk about drag queens instead?" he asks.

"What? No. Why? Are you not happy with Regina Moon Dee? I can give her suggestions, if you or Bryan want her to—"

"No, relax. She's the best thing to happen to the Pink Unicorn in years. I just thought it'd be a more interesting topic for you. Though, to be honest, I think Etienne and Miguel are like me. Not as into it as you are."

"I'm not *into* it," I say. "I just happen to know Regina."

"Got it," Aaron says. "Oh, and one more thing before we join the others." He reaches out and holds on to my shoulders. My heart starts beating faster. He's going in for the kiss now. The one I've been waiting for. I close my eyes, waiting.

"Miguel's really into Filipino food," he says.

My eyes pop back open. "What?"

"I told you his stepmom is Filipino, right? He grew up eating a lot of it."

"Okay."

"I just wanted to make sure you had something to talk about."

"What," I say, laughing, "are you and Etienne planning on leaving us alone?"

I look at him, waiting for him to laugh with me. He doesn't. In his eyes, that look of concern resurfaces. "Are you not into him?" he asks me.

"Am I not into who? Miguel? What do you mean? Are you..." Oh no. I take a step back, searching his face, as if I'll find some alternate explanation for what he's talking about. My shirt suddenly feels too tight. I undo the top two buttons, but it doesn't help.

"Are you and Etienne here together?" I ask. "The double-date thing—it's you and him...and me and Miguel?"

The bill comes back. Aaron signs the bar tab and takes back his credit card. "I thought you knew," he says. "I told you I thought you'd like one of my friends in particular. Just talk to him. I'm sure you'll like him once you get to know him."

The knot in my stomach has now bloomed in size and tightened so hard that I almost keel over.

"Actually, you know what?" My face twists. "That mango margarita hit me kind of weird. Maybe the fruit was bad or something."

"Oh, no," Aaron says, "I'll go ask and see if the restaurant has some antacids."

"I don't think those will help." I grab my stomach with both arms crossed over, hugging myself. "Look, I don't want to make a bad impression on Miguel. After all the trouble you went through to set us up. Could you just tell them something came up? I need to go be near my bathroom."

"Yow. Okay." He goes to give me a hug, but I dodge it, pointing to my tummy, and I exit quickly out the restaurant, hoping at first that Miguel and Etienne don't see me leaving, and then realizing that I really don't give a damn if they do.

"I CAN'T BELIEVE I thought I ever had another chance with Aaron," I say, lying down on my side on Tito Melboy's futon couch and staring at the wall, where an old stained-glass lamp casts its pretty, mosaic-like light. His studio apartment in the Castro is tiny but cozy. A Japanese folding screen separates his bed from the living space, cluttered with vibrant fabrics all in various states of being transformed into drag garments. "I was so stupid."

"Don't say that, Rex," Tito Melboy says from his makeup area in the living room, an old sewing station with a large vintage mirror. "You're being too hard on yourself. Here," he says, putting down his lip liner and retrieving a hot herbal tea from the nearby microwave. "This will calm you."

"Thanks, Tito." I breathe in the minty lemon steam rising from the mug. "And thanks for letting me come over. I couldn't reach Kat or Eva. And Mom wanted to go to bed early tonight."

"I'm glad to be your fourth choice."

"You know what I mean," I say.

"I know," he says, sitting next to me on the couch. "So what happened? Did he get upset that you do drag?"

"No. It wasn't that."

"He was okay with it?"

"It wasn't that because I didn't tell him."

"Ah. So it's not that he didn't like Rex because of Regina. He just doesn't like Rex."

"Okay, I'm going home now."

"Joke *lang*!" he says, tickling me and making me spill some of the tea on the floor.

"Hey, you're making me make a mess."

Tito Melboy waves at the floor. "It's already dirty anyway. Who cares."

I set the tea down on the coffee table and hunch over, resting my elbows on my knees. "I tried to follow your advice, you know."

"Which one?"

"What you said about not confusing a guy you like. How if a man is attracted to you as a man, he won't love you as a woman. And vice versa."

He shakes his head. "That might not have been my

best bit of advice. I think people are more sophisticated nowadays."

"I was going to tell him eventually, after he got used to the idea. Doesn't matter now, anyway. I guess there was just something about me he didn't like. That he didn't fit with."

Tito Melboy rubs my knee and then goes back to his makeup station, outlining his mouth with lip liner. "Or maybe it was the other way around, Rex," he says, smacking his lips.

From the first moment I laid eyes on Aaron, all I ever saw was someone unattainable. And when we finally got together, I thought I'd become someone better, worthy enough to be with someone who was my idea of the perfect guy.

But was Aaron really so perfect? Did it really matter how big a stud he was when there was always something there that I was afraid of? Something that made me not want to reveal myself?

Because there's someone else who's seen that part of me and supports it. Adores it, even. Paolo loves the fabulosity that is Regina Moon Dee. I know that.

What I don't know is how he feels about plain, old Rex.

"Rex," Tito Melboy says as he puts his wig on, "do you want to accompany me to OASIS? We can chat some more on my break."

"Thanks, Uncle. But it's getting kind of late for me. I have to work tomorrow. Thank you for letting me come over, though."

"Any time."

"I'm so glad you came to find me," I say. "Really. I missed you."

"I missed you, too, pamangkin. So very much."

I slide off the couch and give Tito Melboy a kiss on the cheek. "You've given me a lot to think about."

"Call me tomorrow if you want to talk. Or for anything else, okay? I'm here for you. I'm not going anywhere. I promise this time."

"Good," I say. "I'll hold you to that."

CHAPTER 17

THE PHONE FEELS HEAVY IN MY HAND, plastered against the side of my face as I try to take in what Aaron's just said to me. How in the world am I supposed to respond to that?

TWELVE HOURS EARLIER

I'm so lost in my thoughts about Aaron and Paolo at work the next morning that I don't even notice that Kat's come up to me until she sits on my desk.

"What's going on with you?" she says, swinging her legs. "You have a weird sad-but-not-sad look on your face."

"My dinner with Aaron and his friends last night was not what I thought it was going to be. He was trying to set me up with one of his friends."

"He was trying to... Oh, shit. I guess Aaron Part Two is a no-go, then," Kat says. "Aw, babe, are you okay? You must be okay because you're here instead of on your couch eating Cheetos and watching *The Real Housewives of Atlanta*."

"I'm fine," I say. "I know I should be devastated, since I've been dreaming about a chance like this for years, but I don't know. Something's changed. I talked to my uncle about it last night, and he made me feel better about the situation."

"Ohmigod, your uncle. I know I only met him for, like, two seconds, but he's my new favorite person. I'm so glad you guys reconnected." Kat scratches her chin. "Actually, do you think we can hang out with him together or something? I think it would be so much fun. He's exactly like you except there's more of him to love. Ooh!" she says.

"What?"

"Do you think he'd adopt me? I could be one of his drag daughters."

"Possibly," I say. "I'll put in a good word for you."

"Thank you! And in return," she says with a huge grin, "I'm giving you a present."

"If it's another subscription from your cheese-of-the-month club, I'm not interested. There's a gorgonzola smell in my fridge that I still can't get rid of. At least, I think it's gorgonzola."

"Gross. No, it's not that. I snagged you an invite to Susan's party tonight. She's hosting a fancy dinner for the execs and the board of directors at her place. I'll be there, and I'll have a surprise for you. Two, in fact. You'll adore the theme. Glitter and Be Gay. My idea! Inspired by you, of course. Though Susan nixed the rainbow-colored caviar because she has

HORRIBLE TASTE," Kat says, yelling that last bit so Susan can hear.

"Sure. I'll come," I say.

"Yay! It'll be the perfect way to forget about Middle-American Meathead." Kat slides off my desk. "Dress to impress. Although not an actual dress. It's not that kind of a party."

"You said the theme was Glitter and Be Gay."

"True," Kat says, strolling back to her desk. "Wear what you like."

AFTER WORK, I dust off my suit and drive over to Orinda for a night of canapes and corporate conversation, thankful for the distraction from my tumultuous love life.

As I park along the side of the long gravel driveway, I hear the squeal of electronic equipment being plugged in, followed by the snap of a stick against a snare and several thumps of a bass drum.

I walk in through the open oak doors and am floored by what I see. Susan's place is incredible. It's a ranch-style home, furnished with Nordic-style furniture, with an expansive view of the redwoods. Through the floor-to-ceiling windows in the back I see a lit-up terraced patio and garden area. A few caterers are there, just starting to set up.

Along with Kat and her band.

"Rex!" Kat yells when I make it out to the back. She's in a gold sequin crop top, leather skirt, and black stilettos. The

Nine Tails girls are also dressed to kill and setting up their instruments and audio equipment in a corner of the enormous patio.

"Okay, this is definitely a nice surprise," I say. "I was going to ask you when your first gig would be."

"This is it! When I told Susan that I got back together with the girls, she said she'd hire us for something."

I look inside and see Susan milling about with a few early guests, having casual conversations and making a backless black halter jumpsuit look like a million dollars.

"She's so calm right now. I've never seen her like that," I say.

"Her job is so stressful. So she ends up screaming a lot."

"Yeah, at you."

"Eh. I don't mind. Actually, she kind of reminds me of my mom. We yell at each other all the time, too. But that's just how it is in our family. We're just as loud when we laugh about how dumb our fights are after. And I'd rather Susan lose her cool with me than with the other execs. Those wussies couldn't take it like I can."

Susan sees us watching her through the window and waves. Kat waves back.

"You're something else, Kat Sniegowski," I say.

"Hells yeah I am!" she says, pushing me inside. "Now go get something to drink in the kitchen. We're about to start our first set. You'll find your second surprise there."

I wander back in, admiring the dark hardwood floors and modern light fixtures. They don't look as great with the iridescent streamers, brightly colored flowers, and rainbow decorations that have been placed throughout, though. Rainbows aren't always the way to go.

I'm trying to make sense of a sparkly dining table centerpiece that looks like it's been glitterbombed by children when I stop right in my tracks. "Paolo?"

At first glance, someone else might have mistaken him for another one of the caterer's waiters. He has on the same black slacks, white dress shirt, and black bow tie as everyone else, but to me, he stands apart, exuding an air of authority that's a bit surprising and extremely sexy. He's also frozen in place, staring at me as if he's just seen a leprechaun among all the rainbows.

"Rex? What are you doing here?"

"Kat invited me. We both work for all those people out there. She's the one that hired you guys, I'm assuming?"

"Kat's here, too? I had no idea. I haven't been out back yet. AquaMarine doesn't usually do catering jobs, but the CEO of your company insisted. Something about wanting to please her favorite employee. You look nice, by the way."

I flip my wrist casually over my ensemble. "Oh, this old thing?"

Paolo lights up at the gesture and looks as if he's about to say something but doesn't.

"What?" I ask.

He smiles and shakes it off. "Nothing. It's just nice to see you. How did things go with your...uh, dinner date?"

"Not great," I say.

He smiles, lighting up the room. "Oh, yeah?"

A glass crashes in the kitchen, followed by an expletive from one of the waitstaff. We both turn. The floor is now bright red with a huge splotch of gazpacho.

"I should go help them," Paolo says, touching my arm.

"Yes. Please," I reply. "Go do your thing." I grin as he hurries off.

After snagging a glass of wine from the kitchen, I head back outside to listen to Kat and Nine Tails play one of their original songs and try not to spy inside, watching Paolo as he helps clean. It's hard not to admire him, kneeling down on the ground, mopping up the mess with the other cater waiters in his fancy starched white shirt, tailored to flatter his torso, and his pants, so beguilingly tight at the—

"Impressive, no?"

I spit out the sip of wine I've just taken.

"Sorry for startling you," Susan says, placing a hand on my back as I gently cough.

"No, I'm sorry. I was just lost in thought. What did you say?"

"I said—impressive, right? Kat and her band?"

"Yes! Right. Impressive. So impressive," I say, still watching Paolo out of the side of my eye, despite myself. I try to focus on Kat and Nine Tails. Though there are only a few guests so far, and Kat and her band are really here for background music only, they look as happy as if they were performing in front of a sold-out auditorium.

"You did a nice thing, hiring them to play," I say to Susan.

"It's the least I could do." She sips her champagne. "Kat takes very good care of me at work."

"Funny. She said sort of the reverse. That you reminded her of her mom," I say. Susan crinkles her brow, and I immediately regret telling her that. "No, I mean—"

"Yes, that is funny," Susan says. "I've never had a daughter. I've always wondered what it would be like. A lot like what we have, I suppose? Complicated. A little messy at times. But it's something I don't think I could live without."

Kat turns with her microphone, singing directly to us.

"Mother-daughter relationships can be that way. Things get rocky," I say, thinking initially about Eva and my mom. And then I think of Tito Melboy and me. "We just have to work through it."

"I'll drink to that," Susan says, holding her glass up to mine. "Cheers."

"Cheers," I say, looking back inside again to see Paolo done with cleaning and now serving a tray of mini-empanadas to some newly arrived guests.

"Do you know him?" Susan asks, following my gaze back inside the house. "You can't seem to take your eyes off him."

"Him who? The waiter?"

"He's not a waiter. Those are his people."

"His people? What do you mean?"

"AquaMarine is his restaurant," she says. "Sorry, would you excuse me?" Susan gently squeezes my elbow and saunters over to one of the directors.

My brain jolts with awareness. I try to think back to the

times I've seen him at the restaurant. He served food. He also seemed to cook the food sometimes? He worked when he wanted, where he wanted. I could never figure out what it was that he actually did.

And now, as I look back inside, I realize that he's managing the others. Telling them what to do and where to go. Showing them how to operate the equipment and assemble the serving plates and make the cocktails. Paolo's not just one of the workers. He's their boss.

I make a beeline for Paolo, who has gone back into the kitchen.

"Back so soon?" he asks.

"Are you the manager?"

He chuckles. "Why? Do you have a complaint?" He adjusts his shirt, re-tucking it into his pants. I notice that it might be one size too small for him. It strains at the buttons, bulging out and showing a little bit of skin underneath.

I make myself look up at his face. "I'm serious, Paolo. Do you own AquaMarine?"

"No, but my family does," he replies. "And six other restaurants like it. Only two here in the States, though. AquaMarine in SF and Bamboo Fork in Los Angeles. The rest are in the Philippines."

Even I've heard of Bamboo Fork. It made this year's *New York Times* list of the top one hundred restaurants in America. "How did I not know this?" I say.

"I told you we were in the business, didn't I?"

He did. But stupid me, I assumed he was talking about one tiny little restaurant in the Philippines.

"My dad hosts this TV show," Paolo adds. "Where he goes around the world to try different dishes and then goes back home to try to replicate what he's eaten. It's called *Eats Meets West*. I don't know if you've heard of it."

My mind reels. Mom and Eva watch *Eats Meets West* on TFC every Saturday to vacation vicariously and get good cooking tips. It's been on the air for years. "Your dad is Sonny Sazon?"

"Yes," Paolo says.

Sonny Sazon's mother, Ligaya Sazon, is one of the most influential Filipino cooks of all time. Her cookbook, *Cooking with Ligaya*, is in every Filipino household. My mother used to refer to hers all the time when I was growing up. I can still see it, sitting on top of the microwave, its yellowed pages folded over and worn down from constant use.

Paolo is Filipino food royalty.

"My mom and Eva are big fans of your family," is all I can manage to say.

"I can come over and cook for them sometime."

"You'd really like to, wouldn't you?" I ask.

"Uh, yes? That's why I just offered."

"No, I mean..." My face gets warm. "You really seem like you're in your element right now. Making all the food. Like how you were at my place when I told you how much I loved your bagel sandwiches. You look happy. Really happy."

231

Paolo stares at me. Through me. As if the words I've just uttered are a jumble on the wall behind me, and he's attempting to put them into the right order.

"You're right," he finally says. "I am happy. This makes me happy."

"Good," I say. "And—"

"And you make me happy, too," he says quickly, as if making sure he doesn't lose the nerve to say what's on his mind before stopping himself.

"Me?" My breathing stops. No air seems to be reaching my lungs. I force myself to inhale. "I...I..."

A cater waiter yells, "Hey, Paolo, can you help us? The fires under the chafing dishes are kinda out of control."

Paolo doesn't respond to the call. He just looks at me, his face full of anticipation.

"Paolo!"

He shakes his head. "Sorry, I don't want the place to burn down," he says, looking slightly upset. He heads back to the servers.

My mind struggles to process what he's just said. Not because I don't believe him. But because he's just confirmed that he feels exactly like I do.

Paolo makes me happy, too. More happy than I've ever been. Because not only does he know and like me, he knows and likes all of me. Regina *and* Rex. Every part I've been scared to show the world. And to my dad. And to Aaron. I've never felt afraid to be myself around Paolo. With him, I've never felt like being Regina Moon Dee was something to be ashamed of. I realize that, from the minute he first laid eyes on me, he's always made me feel beautiful. Not just when I was in drag. Even that first night, when he looked up at me through those Clark Kent glasses of his, smiling at my dumb outfit and excited that I might sing something for him.

I like Paolo. A lot.

Aaron and I were never meant to be; that much is clear now. It should be easy to just tell Paolo how I feel. But I'm having trouble coming up with the words. And this isn't exactly the best place to have a heart-to-heart. Not when we're both on the job. Also, will it be an issue working together at the Pink Unicorn? Will that make things weird?

My first instinct is to ask Kat for advice, but I see that the band is on a break and she's talking to Susan. They're drinking together, having a good time. I don't want to disturb them.

I text my uncle. Hi Tito. Can I talk to you about something if you have a minute? Call me when you get the chance.

Three dots pop up in response, and I watch them, waiting for the full reply to appear.

My phone rings. I click immediately to accept it. "Hello?"

"Rex?" says a voice that is not Tito Melboy's.

I double-check the caller ID. It's Aaron. "Hey," I say, exhaling a stress breath. "Listen, I'm really sorry about bailing on dinner last night."

"That's fine," he croaks. "It's not that."

"Wait, is everything okay?"

"No, everything's not okay." His voice is wobbly, raw. He sounds in bad shape.

"What's going on?"

"My mom..." he says, then stops.

"Is she all right?"

"She's fine. She did have a health scare. An ulcer. But for some reason, she thought she was dying so she had this come-to-Jesus moment and called me. Said she wanted to tell me something before it was too late. Something she kept from me about her. And Bryan."

I already knew Aaron's mother had known Bryan. His mom was the one who had told Aaron to get in touch with Bryan when he moved to the Bay Area. "What is it?" I ask.

"They've been lying to me. This whole time. My mom said my dad was just some jerk who left her and never came back. I guess that's the truth, come to think of it. Because that jerk is him."

"What?"

"Bryan," Aaron says. "Bryan is my dad."

CHAPTER 18

"OH. WOW."

Bryan had always seemed invested in Aaron's happiness. I chalked that up to Aaron being a great bartender and the Pink Unicorn's manager—not because Bryan was secretly Aaron's father.

"How could he not have told me?" Aaron asks, his voice catching.

"Maybe he felt it was better to keep it from you?"

"Why?"

"I don't know. He was afraid of how you'd react?"

"I'm more mad at him now for not telling me the truth all this time."

The truth. A voice whispers in my ear, *I've been lying to him, too.*

I look around at the people in Susan's home. Everyone

has finally arrived at the party. The executives, the board of directors, and their plus-ones. Kat and Nine Tails. The Aqua-Marine caterers. And Paolo. All of whom are completely oblivious to the revelation that Aaron's just shared with me.

"Rex, I'm taking a few days off, flying back to Indiana tonight on the red-eye. I need to see my mom. Make sure she's okay."

"I thought you said it was just an ulcer?"

"She still felt bad enough that she thought she was dying. And I don't think I can face Bryan right now. Could you just tell him I'll be gone for a while?"

"Why don't you two just talk. Ask him why—"

"I can't. But thanks for listening. You've been amazing these past few weeks, Rex. All the stuff you've been doing for the bar. And for me. I'm glad we ran into each other again."

"Of course," I say. "I'm here for you."

"I know you are," he says. "Talk later, okay?" He hangs up before I can respond.

Kat and Paolo are outside on the patio. Kat is, unsurprisingly, stuffing her face with lumpia while Paolo is trying to wrest the plate of food away from her to give to the other guests.

She stops mid-chomp when she sees me coming. "You look paler than me at the Brazilian bikini waxer. What happened?"

"Aaron's flying back to Indiana."

"Why?" Kat asks.

"He needs to talk to his mom. She told him that Bryan is his dad."

"What?" they both say in unison, almost dropping the plate of hors d'oeuvres.

"Apparently, that's how Bryan knew Aaron's mom back in the day."

"Does Bryan know that Aaron knows?" Kat asks.

"No clue," I say. "But I do know that Aaron doesn't want to talk to Bryan. Or even see him. I don't even actually know when he's coming back," I add.

My phone rings. It's Bryan.

"Rex? Do you have any idea where Aaron is? I've been trying to reach him. He was supposed to work tonight."

"He's not coming to work, Bryan," I say, pausing. "And I don't know how to tell you this, but he's really upset with you. He's flying back to Indiana tonight, in fact. His mom told him you're his dad?"

"Ah, hell," Bryan says. "I was afraid that's what happened. I got this weird voicemail from Tonya saying she was sick and was going to call Aaron and—" He starts choking up. "I tried to call him and...damn."

"Just give him a day or two to calm down. He'll come around," I say.

"No. He's never gonna forgive me for what I did. Leaving him. Lying to him." His voice sounds even worse than Aaron's did. "Forget it, I'm sorry I bothered you. I'll just sit here and try to forget about it somehow."

"Let me see if I can talk to him," I say.

No response.

"Bryan? Hello?"

He hasn't hung up yet, but I don't hear anything on the other end of the line. He must not be in the bar. Maybe he's home. Alone. I start to worry.

"Bryan? Are you there? Where are you right now?"

I hear a ragged inhalation of breath before he says, "I'm at the Pink Unicorn. In the office."

"Stay put, I'll be right there. Fifteen minutes or so. Okay?"

Silence.

Finally, he says, "Okay," before hanging up.

"Well?" Kat says. She and Paolo are staring at me.

"I need to go," I say.

"Right now?" they both say.

"I'm worried about Bryan. He sounds pretty bad. I should go check in on him. Father-son stuff, it's never easy to begin with, let alone in this case."

"But you just got here," Kat says.

"And we were going to talk," Paolo says.

Kat perks up. "Talk? About what?"

Paolo and I glance at each other.

"Ha! I knew it," Kat says. "I one hundred percent freaking knew something was going on between you two."

"Nothing's going on!" I say.

"Please. I've felt major vibes between you guys since that first karaoke night. I told you," she says, pointing at me, "I saw a spark."

Paolo grins, which makes me grin, too.

"Raincheck?" I ask him.

He nods. "I kind of have to work right now, anyway."

We stand there smiling at each other for a brief moment before Kat squeals, "Eeeee! I love what's happening here right now!"

"Okay, I'm leaving," I say. Every bit of my being wants to reach out to Paolo—to touch him, hold him—but I know if I do, I'll never leave. So before he or Kat can respond, I wave at them both quickly before rushing out of the kitchen, through Susan's giant oak doors to my car, suppressing the urge the entire time to run back into the house.

WHEN I GET TO THE PINK UNICORN, Loretta's busy making drinks for a decent-size Wednesday night crowd. At least half of the tables are filled, and there's even a short line at the bar. Meanwhile, Bryan has emerged from the office and is sitting on his usual barstool at the end. At first glance, he seems fine. But when I get closer, I notice the tracks of tears on his face.

"Hey, Bryan," I say.

He nods quietly and wipes his eyes with a cocktail napkin. "You didn't have to come all the way here, Rex. I'm fine."

"You don't look fine," I say. "But I'm here, if you want to talk."

Bryan shakes his head wearily. "Nothing to talk about.

Aaron ditched, and I don't blame him. It's exactly what I did to him."

I sit down on the barstool next to him. "Can I ask why you left him in the first place? I don't mean to pry. But I want to help somehow. Maybe if I know more, I can get him to talk to you."

"I didn't do it on purpose," Bryan says, blowing his nose on the napkin. "Aaron's mother, Tonya—we grew up together in Indiana. She had decent folks, while my dad was a nasty sonofabitch. So I spent most of my time at her house. We were so close, I think everyone expected us to end up married. Even though I didn't really know I was gay at the time, I knew we would never do that. I think she did, too."

Bryan plunges his hand into his snack bowl, grabs a fistful, and tosses it in his mouth. He chews slowly, his eyes glassy. "One night my dad got drunk," he continues. "Spent the whole time yelling at me. So I went over to Tonya's and spent the night there and, I don't know. One thing led to another. She was trying to comfort me physically, and I really needed it. We didn't talk about it after that. Then an old high school buddy of ours called me. Said he'd moved to San Francisco and wanted me to visit. So I drove out there. I needed to get away from my dad for a while. I asked Tonya if she wanted to come, but she said no. Said she had other things to attend to. Little did I know that that thing was Aaron."

"She never told you about him?" I asked.

"Not at first. Maybe she thought she'd just tell me when I got back from my trip."

"But you never went back home," I say.

Bryan looks around at the people in the bar, buzzing with conversations. "I stepped one foot in here, and I knew I'd found the home I'd been looking for. Everything hiding inside me came rushing right out. I finally understood what it was my dad hated so much about me. And why I could never go back home again."

"Tonya told you about Aaron eventually, though, right?" I ask.

"Yes. But not until Aaron was in grade school. We'd fallen out of touch by then. Her parents helped her raise him. They didn't need me. I was too involved in myself, anyway, exploring, experimenting. This was at the height of the AIDS epidemic, mind you. Tonya and I both agreed I should just stay out here and live my life. Let her and Aaron live theirs."

"Later on, didn't you want to see him?"

Bryan's eyes well up. "I did. But by then, Tonya had told him that his father was just a stranger who breezed through town and never thought twice about knocking her up. I know she didn't mean it that way, but I became the dead-beat dad. Years later, when she called saying that Aaron was coming out here with his boyfriend? By god, I just about fell off this damn barstool. My son was gay. My son! So I told her to send him my way. I'd help them get set up, give him a job, whatever he needed. But when he was here, I couldn't bring myself to tell him the truth. I tried. But the first time I brought up the subject of his dad, his eyes went cold. 'Whoever that bastard is, he can stay the hell out of my life,' he said. So I kept my mouth shut. What else could I do? I'd just found him. I didn't want to lose him again. But it didn't matter. I ended up losing him anyway."

"You had him here next to you, all this time. Even though you could never find a way to tell him you were his family," I say. "You know, he told me working here felt like home to him for some reason. Now I know why."

"This place is home. For both of us." Bryan suddenly looks up. "I think I have an idea. Will you excuse me?" he says, slipping off the barstool to head back to the office.

I watch him go, hopeful that he's come up with something that might help him salvage his relationship with Aaron. "Hey, Loretta, could I have a cosmo?" I ask.

She nods and prepares my drink. "Bryan's like a father to us all," she says. "But especially Aaron. I'm not really surprised he's Bryan's son."

"But Aaron is," I say. "And he never had a clue."

Loretta slides the cosmo over to me, the cold sides of the glass beaded with condensation. "I really like Aaron. He's a nice guy. Great manager. But not the most aware person. Notice how he always calls everyone *buddy*? It's because he can't remember names or recognize faces to save his life. He doesn't always see what's right in front of him."

That certainly explains a lot.

Bryan shuffles back from the office. "Aaron said he'll

come back," he says to me and Loretta, not looking as happy as I expect him to be.

"You're not telling us something," I say.

"I wanted to apologize," Bryan says. "I was going to make an offer to him. He wouldn't let me talk. Said he'd be ready to listen once he gets back." Bryan smiles weakly. "But he wouldn't tell me when. Could be tomorrow. Could be next month. Who knows?"

Loretta places a can of soda and a glass of ice in front of Bryan. Without even looking, he opens the tab with a snap and pours the soda into his glass, the bubbling liquid hissing as it slides over the ice.

"But thank you for trying to help." Bryan swirls his soda mindlessly. "At least we've got Regina Moon Dee. Without her, this bar would be two nights away from shutting down. Another thing I have to thank you for. I tell you, I'm really looking forward to Saturday now. Your friend's gonna save me from my sorrows."

We both drink in silence. I'm glad that I'll be cheering Bryan up this weekend, but that seems so far away. There must be something I can do now. I mull over various things I could say to Aaron to try to get him to hear Bryan out and cut him slack for lying all this time.

But the fact that I've never been fully honest with Aaron pricks at me, making me uneasy about attempting to be some voice of reason.

My phone vibrates in my pocket. It's Eva.

"Don't kill me, big bro," she says.

"What happened?"

"I made a mistake."

"You're supposed to be the smart one," I say. "What, did you mess up a recipe?"

"Way worse than that. I kinda told Dad where Mom and I have been going every Saturday. To see you."

"What?" I slip off my stool and exit the Pink Unicorn so that I can hear Eva better. "Say that again. I must've heard you wrong. You would never make a mistake like that."

"Don't worry, I didn't say anything about you being back in drag. Just that you've been working there on Saturdays. We were singing karaoke at home, and I said the Pink Unicorn had this fancy new request system now and that you kind of figured out how to use it better and now a lot of people go there on Saturdays. Including me and Mom."

"Eva!"

"Sorry! It just slipped out! I mean, you already told him you were helping Aaron with some ideas for improving the place, right?"

I stare out into the night. Long, gray clouds crawl across a tiny sliver of a moon.

"Yeah, I did," I say. "I guess it's not so bad."

"Except..."

"Except what?" I ask.

"Except now he wants to come to karaoke night at the Pink Unicorn to spend time with all of us. This Saturday. When you're hosting as Regina Moon Dee," Eva says. "And he won't take no for an answer."

CHAPTER 19

"THIS IS BAD," I WHISPER TO EVA. We're at my parents' house, in the kitchen while she's preparing dinner. Even though Mom and Dad are in the living room watching TFC with the volume turned up, I want to be completely sure that they can't hear our conversation.

"Gee. Thanks, Rex," she says.

"I meant the Dad-coming-to-karaoke thing," I say. "Not the food. What you made is actually really good." Eva's stepped up her game and tried to put her own twist on a Filipino classic, making something she calls a *deconstructed arroz caldo*. Instead of the usual one-pot meal of chicken and rice, she's separated things out. The chicken was simmered to make a homemade stock, which she used to cook the rice. She then shredded the chicken, crisped up the skin, fried some shallots and garlic, and put those things—plus chopped scallions, soft-boiled eggs, and calamansi slices—in separate bowls for people to add as much or as little of each to their rice as they wanted. My own serving has extra dark meat and lots of fried garlic with a big squeeze of calamansi. "It's a home run, sis."

"Thank you," she says, tossing more raw garlic slices into the frying oil. "And again, I'm sorry I told Dad about the Pink Unicorn."

"Are you sure he really wants to go?"

"He's been talking about it all week," Eva replies. "Maybe Regina Moon Dee can call in sick this weekend?"

"And disappoint all my fans? Plus Bryan said he's specifically looking forward to seeing me on Saturday. It's the only thing that's going to cheer him up."

"Then you're screwed."

I put the bowl of arroz caldo down on the counter. "I think I just lost my appetite."

"I'm kidding. Come on! You have the solution staring you in the face. Just get Paolo to be Regina again."

"Being Regina for five minutes to fool one person who doesn't really know her is one thing. Doing an entire show to a packed house full of fans? There is no way on earth Paolo would be able to do that."

"Not for the whole show, then. Just a part of it. What if you have someone else co-host? Like Kat?"

"She's got a gig on Saturday. She can't come until later."

"Tito Melboy?"

"He can't come at all. He's working at Dreamland.

Besides—he and Dad aren't really talking. I don't think an appearance from Beaucoup Buko is what we need on the night we're trying to keep Dad happy."

"Could Uncle ask around? He's got to know someone that could help."

"Maybe." I grab back the bowl of arroz caldo and start eating again. "But even if we could find a co-host, Paolo would have to do more than just show up looking like me; he'd need to perform at some point. And Paolo can't sing to save his life."

"You're forgetting something, big bro," Eva says. "What's most drag queens' number one talent?"

A light bulb goes off. "Lip-synching."

"All you have to do is pre-record you singing a song or two, and Paolo can lip-synch to them."

I finish my last spoonful of Eva's arroz caldo and attempt to get more, but Eva slaps my hand away. "Ow!"

"Now you just have to convince him to do it," she says. "Think you'll be able to do that?"

When I asked Paolo to impersonate me the first time, he asked: what was I doing it for? I know the answer to that now. I was afraid of revealing myself to Aaron because I was afraid of his reaction. I didn't want him to reject Rex—but I was even more afraid of him turning on Regina. Now I'm asking Paolo to protect me again, but this time from my father's inevitable anger and dismay. Given Paolo's complicated relationship with his own father, he should be able to sympathize with that.

"I'll be able to convince him," I say.

"And don't forget that you have less than two days to get him lip-synch-ready."

"Don't worry. It's totally doable," I say. "But not all by myself. It'll have to be all hands on deck."

Eva claps her hands gleefully. "Are you going to ask me and Mom to help? And Tito Melboy? We'll definitely be able to get him into shape. Once we're done with him, he'll be able to lip-synch for his mother-tucking life!"

"What is this about mother tucking?" Mom says as she comes into the kitchen. "Are you making fun of the clothes I wore to church last Sunday? I knew I shouldn't have listened to Marybel. She's the one who told me to tuck in my blouse. My breasts are too voluptuous. I don't look good like that!"

"What's this about voluptuous breasts?" my dad says as he enters the kitchen.

"Bastos!" Mom says, hitting Dad on the shoulder. "Take your mind out of the gutter."

Dad laughs as he tries to avoid more of Mom's playful slaps. "Hoy! Tigilan mo nga yan!"

"You guys! Get out of here," Eva yells. "I'm not done cooking yet."

"Okay, okay," Mom says. "After dinner, Rex, will you practice my audition for the church solo with me?"

"What are you singing?"

"A good Christian song! 'Like a Prayer' by Madonna."

"Uh, I'm not sure that's such a great—"

"Thank you, anak," Mom says, heading back to the living room.

"Rex," my dad says, his face suddenly solemn.

Eva and I give each other a nervous look. Has he been able to hear what we've been talking about?

"I heard you are working regularly at that bar now," he says.

"Oh," I say, trying to look as nonchalant as possible. "It's not a big deal. Just helping my friend, Aaron."

"And you're sure it's not affecting your day job? And your plans to go to law school?"

It's definitely not affecting my plans to go to law school, since I don't have any. "I'm sure."

He stares at me unblinkingly for a few seconds. "Good. You are going in the right direction. Keep going, okay? I'm proud of you, Rex." He grips my shoulder strongly, like a vise.

"Thanks, Dad," I say, so quietly that I barely hear myself.

"You're welcome, anak," he says, releasing me to rejoin Mom in the living room. "And hurry up with the food, Eva," Dad says over his shoulder. "We're getting hungry."

DRIVING BACK TO MY PLACE AFTER DINNER, I patch my phone through my car's Bluetooth and call Paolo, intending to leave a message since he's probably still at the restaurant.

He picks up immediately. "Hey!"

"Is this a bad time?" I ask. "I can call back."

"Nah, I'm just in AquaMarine's office, going over some things."

It's still not clear to me what his official position at the restaurant is, beyond being the son of the owner. "So, what exactly is it that you do for your family's business, can I ask?"

"A little bit of everything. I don't have an official title. It was my dad's idea for me to familiarize myself with every job here, from dishwasher all the way up. That way I can learn every part of what goes into running it. Right now, I'm shadowing Melissa, the manager."

"And how's that going?"

"Just a second, let me step out of the office." I hear Paolo mumble something to another person. A few seconds later, the sounds of the kitchen come crashing through. "Ugh! It's so boring. I don't want to be a manager. It's the most unexciting part of the business."

"It's also one of the most important, unfortunately. I'm assuming that's why your dad wants you to do it?"

"Yeah. He wants me to learn from Melissa and then move down to SoCal. The manager at Bamboo Fork is going to retire soon, and he wants me to take over when she's gone."

"Oh. And you...don't want to go?" I ask. "Right?"

"I thought maybe I did," Paolo says. "Until I met this very interesting guy and his drag alter ego at a dive bar. Makes me really appreciate how good my KJ gig is."

I smile to myself. "I'm sure your dad will think that's a much more viable career option."

"And what do you think?" Paolo asks.

On a whim, I reply, "I think that I'd like to continue our conversation in person. When do you get off?"

"Whenever I want."

"Can I come over to your place?"

"Yes!" he says, his voice suddenly charged. "That would be great." An address pings through via text.

"Okay, see you soon." I hang up, and instead of taking my usual exit to go home, I zip past it and head toward San Francisco, trying not to break too many speed limits as I go.

When I arrive, I double-check the address Paolo sent me to make sure I'm in the right place. It's one of those fancy new remodels—boxy, slate gray, and sleek in comparison to the old Victorians around it. I search around for multiple doorbells assigned to different floors and residents, assuming he only lives in a portion of the building. But there are none. Just one doorbell below a sophisticated security camera and intercom system. I ring it.

No answer. I ring the doorbell again. Nothing.

I'm about to resort to knocking on the door when it opens. Paolo is standing in the doorway in just gym shorts and a loose T-shirt. Both his glasses and his hair are a little askew, like I've just interrupted him in the middle of doing something physical. I swallow hard.

Paolo's smile makes my heart skip. "Don't just stand there," he says. "Come in."

The interior of his house is just as impressive as the exterior. But where everything is slightly cold on the outside, inside it's warm and inviting. Parquet floors of honey-hued oak. Cream-colored couches with fluffy pillows and macramé throw blankets. And above the fireplace, a massive landscape painting of a winding blue river crisscrossing green rice paddies.

"It's beautiful in here," I say. "Did you do the interior design?"

"A little. Mostly it was just me looking through a lot of magazines and watching a lot of HGTV."

"That's kind of how I learned to do makeup," I say.

"Wow, I must've been watching the wrong HGTV shows," Paolo says.

I follow him into the living room. He waits for me to sit down on the couch and then hovers nearby, as if trying to decide how close to me he should sit. And though I want to pat the spot next to me on the couch, I can't be that close to him yet. Not until we've talked. And not until I've asked what I've come here to ask.

Probably sensing my hesitance, he sits on the leather lounge chair across from me.

We stare at each other across his coffee table with its perfectly curated assortment of books and flowers, a vast landscape that separates him from me.

"Thanks for letting me come over," I say. "You must be tired after working at the restaurant."

"Not tired. Just frustrated. Melissa was going over all the bookkeeping stuff. Ordering, scheduling, payroll. But I just wanted to be in the kitchen helping the cooks."

"Can't you just tell your dad you'd rather cook than manage?"

"Maybe," he says, falling back against the back of his lounge chair. "But even then, I don't know if what I want to make is the stuff we have at AquaMarine or Bamboo Fork. Not everyone can afford to eat at our restaurants. I'm more into casual food. Making Filipino food more accessible."

"You don't have to be at your family's restaurant to be in the restaurant business."

Paolo raises an eyebrow. "You mean start my own place?"

"Why not?"

"I don't know. Do I even have what it takes to do that?" he says, more to himself than to me.

"Yes," I say immediately, thinking of how in-charge Paolo was at Susan's party. "Absolutely no doubt about it."

He smiles. "Of course you'd have no reservations. You're Regina freaking Moon Dee. Even for the few hours I was just pretending to be you, I felt like a superhero. Like I could do anything I wanted. Do you feel that way, too?"

"Actually, yeah," I say. "As far back as I can remember, there's always been this feeling inside, wanting to come out. When I discovered drag, that part of me was so happy to be free. When I can really express myself, I'm filled with so much possibility. And positivity. And yeah, strength. I think it's because I'm able to channel all the energy it takes to keep things hidden into being the fullest, fiercest version of myself."

Paolo sighs wistfully. "God, I could use some of that. I

need Regina-level courage to tell my dad that I don't want to work for him anymore. Which I know will probably never happen." He gets up suddenly. "I could use a drink. Want something?"

"Sure," I say. Speaking of courage, I could use some of the liquid form to talk to Paolo about what I really came to talk about. "What do you have?"

"A little bit of everything."

I'm flabbergasted by what I see when I follow him into the kitchen. There's a massive stainless-steel refrigerator, a six-burner gas stove with an industrial range hood, and a quartz kitchen island the size of a real island. To the left is a closet with a see-through door, which I realize is not a closet at all but an aboveground wine cellar. Next to that is a small counter with barstools and a fully stocked alcohol cabinet behind it.

"You weren't kidding about having everything," I say.

"Wine? Beer?"

"How about a scotch?" I ask. "And don't make me choose between all your different expensive ones I've probably never even heard of. Whatever you've got open is fine."

He takes down a half-empty bottle of Highland Park 19, pours a generous amount into two highball glasses, and hands me one.

We clink glasses and drink. I don't have the most sophisticated palate, but I can tell when something is top shelf, and this definitely is, tasting like smoky molasses.

"Good?" Paolo says.

"So good," I say, smacking my lips.

We drink in silence for a bit. The awareness of us being alone at his house together late at night creeps into my consciousness. The warmth of the scotch magnifies, blooming in the back of my throat.

"So," Paolo says, breaking our silence, "you never finished telling me about your date with Aaron. You said it didn't go well?"

"It's kind of inaccurate to say my date with Aaron didn't go well. Because it ended up not being a date at all. At least, not with Aaron."

"What?"

"It was a blind double-date. Aaron and his guy, and someone else he was trying to set me up with."

"Oh, damn. That's messed up."

"Looking back on it now, I think I just misread Aaron's feelings toward me. I know he cares about me. Just not in that way. Not anymore. Maybe not ever, actually," I say, sighing. "I don't know."

"And...how do you feel about that?"

"I'm okay with it," I reply.

"Really?"

"Yeah." A smile starts to grow on my face.

"What?" Paolo asks.

"You know what you said last night at the party, about me making you happy?"

"Yes?" Paolo says, not quite looking at me, as if afraid to meet my eyes.

"Did you really mean that?"

"Yes. One hundred percent."

"Well I...feel..." The same. Happy. More than just happy. Giddy. When I'm with Paolo I feel supported. Accepted. Appreciated. I want to tell him that and so much more, but the words don't seem to come. It's strange. With Aaron I was willing to just throw myself at him, do or say whatever I needed to be wanted by him. And now that there's someone I truly care about in my life, who sees all of me and likes it, I don't know what to say. I don't know how to say yes to the possibility of being loved for who I really am.

Paolo's face falls. "It's okay if you don't feel the same."

He doesn't move or say anything more. The house has gone incredibly quiet. I hear the rush of a car down the street. The rustle of a bird, roosting on a tree branch outside the kitchen window. And the sound of my own heartbeat, beating so wildly in my ears now that it takes over everything.

And then I reach out, pull Paolo's face toward mine, and kiss him.

God. I always thought all kisses were alike. A kiss is just a kiss.

But this. This.

It's like nothing I've ever experienced before. It's more than just his lips on my lips. It's more than the taste of caramel and vanilla and a wisp of smoke finding its way across my mouth, dancing across my tongue, and going down, deep, into the very center of me, lodging itself in my core and making me shudder.

It's a gift I'd never known I'd needed. A connection to someone I'd never known I was looking for and didn't know would make me feel so complete until now.

With one single kiss.

I pull back suddenly. "I'm sorry. Why do I keep doing that to you?"

"It's okay," he says, breathing heavily. He grasps the sides of my face and caresses me, his fingertips hot against my skin. "I've been wanting that, too. A proper follow-up to the first time," he says.

I stand there, wishing I could feel his hands on my cheeks and the warmth of him lingering on my lips forever. But I remember then that I need to ask him a big favor. Again.

"Uh-oh," Paolo says, letting his hands drop. "Was I that bad?"

I shake my head. "Nothing could be farther from the truth."

"But...?"

"But I need to ask you to do something for me," I say. "Good news is, you've already done it before. The bad news is, you'll have to pump it up a notch. Or ten."

Paolo's eyebrows crease. He picks up his glass from the counter and takes a long sip of the whiskey. "Go on."

"My dad's coming to karaoke night this Saturday. And I don't want him to know I'm doing drag again. But I don't want to let down the fans. And I definitely don't want to disappoint Bryan, especially now. Regina Moon Dee has to be there."

Paolo closes his eyes and sighs. "I can see where this is heading."

"Would you be me again? Just one more time? Pretty please?" I ask, making each word sweeter and higher than the one before it.

Paolo laughs out loud, though not at my ridiculous baby voice. "You want me to host an entire karaoke show as Regina Moon Dee?"

"No. We're figuring out a plan for that. You'd just have to do one itsy-bitsy little lip-synch. Maybe two."

He raises an eyebrow. "A lip-synch, huh?" he says, downing his whiskey with a big gulp. "I've actually always wanted to do one of those."

"And I'll teach you how," I say, finishing off my own drink.

"Could be fun," Paolo says. He reaches for the bottle and pours us some more. "Okay. Let's hear the plan."

We keep drinking as I go over all the details for the upcoming karaoke night.

Close to midnight, I look at my watch and realize I should probably get going. Only I've had a little too much to drink.

"You can crash here," Paolo says, seemingly reading my mind.

As much as I want a repeat of that kiss, I know I'd feel better if we were sober when we did. I'm not sure I'll be able to resist Paolo if he wanted to go further, and I definitely wouldn't want to be drunk for that. "Mmmm, I don't know."

"I promise, no funny business. Not tonight at least," he says with a smirk, intuiting my thoughts again. "You can stay in my guest room."

My head begins to throb from a little too much scotch. "Okay."

We go upstairs. He leads me to the guest bedroom. A California king with towering mahogany posts takes up half the room.

Paolo inches toward me. It feels as if he's about to embrace me or even push me onto the bed. Both scenarios play out in my head tantalizingly as I try to give no indication of wanting anything more than just a—

"Good night," Paolo says, touching his fingertip lightly on my nose.

"Good night," I reply, half relieved and half disappointed he's kept his promise about being a gentleman.

He walks backward slowly, watching me with every step before finally turning around and heading into his bedroom down the hall and shutting the door softly behind him.

I sigh and fall onto the enormous bed. The comforter poofs up around me, surrounding me in a soft cloud smelling of orange blossoms. I want to burrow under the covers and wrap myself in the memory of our kiss.

Instead, I make sure to text everyone with the plans for tomorrow.

It's not until I've sent out those messages that I notice I have an unread one from Aaron.

Hey Rex. I've decided to stay here for the week. Can you let

Bryan know? He wants to talk, but I'm not ready yet. I'm still mad at him for lying to me. You think you know someone, right?

That last part stings a bit.

Oh, and Miguel sent me this pic. Forgot to show you. Maybe you guys can give it another go sometime?

A shot of me, Miguel, Aaron, and Etienne at Comal, raising our glasses at the bar. To any casual observer it might seem like a perfectly normal picture. Four men having a nice time out on the town. No one would know that there's something not quite right about it, that the look of contentment on one of those men's faces is only a half-truth, a fantasy. Because what he's presenting to the world in that picture is just an illusion.

Fantasy and illusion. There's nothing wrong with that, right?

After all, isn't that what drag queens do best?

CHAPTER 20

PAOLO SHAMBLES INTO THE KITCHEN with his eyes half closed and his glasses not yet on.

"Thanks for making coffee," he says, yawning. He walks up to the person at the coffee maker. "Can I have some?"

"Sure. Do you like it black? Or creamy and sweet, like me?" Tito Melboy says, turning around with a mug full of piping hot coffee.

Paolo blinks and puts his glasses on his face. "Tito Melboy?"

"The one and only," Tito Melboy replies, jiggling his hips.

"When did you get here?" Paolo asks.

Tito Melboy hops up onto one of the stools at the massive kitchen island. "About an hour ago."

"Hey." I come up from behind Paolo and nestle a cup of

coffee into his hands. "Looks like you might need this. You were so sound asleep you didn't even hear the doorbell ring."

"Not that I mind, but why are you here, Tito?" Paolo turns to me. "Rex, I thought we'd be heading over to your place to practice, since that's where all your stuff is."

The doorbell rings. Paolo gives me a *what now?* look before heading to the front door.

I trail behind. "Um, about that—"

Paolo opens the door to see Kat.

"I invited Kat, too," I say.

"Good morning!" Kat says, posing briefly in the doorway.

"Hey," I say, "was Susan okay with you taking today off?"

"Oh, totally. She's super happy about how her dinner party turned out. The execs and board raved about me and Nine Tails. We were a hit! Well, us and Paolo's food." Kat flashes Paolo an appreciative smile.

"Oh," Paolo says, looking pleasantly surprised. "That's awesome."

Kat takes in her surroundings. "Nice place you got here! Give me a tour."

"Okay," Paolo says. "This is the main sitting room—"

The doorbell rings again.

Paolo's eyes bulge at me. "More, Rex?" He opens the door, and Eva and my mom are there, holding on to two suitcases.

"I needed them to bring all my stuff," I say. "Hey, Eva. Hi, Mom." I drag their suitcases inside and hug them both.

Mom stares wide-eyed at everything. "Wow, Paolo! Ang

ganda ng bahay mo! I didn't realize being a karaoke assistant paid so well."

"Oh. That's just a hobby. I don't really get much money from it."

"He also works at AquaMarine," Kat says, already making herself at home on one of Paolo's plush couches.

"And he also kind of owns AquaMarine," I add.

"What?" Kat and Eva say at the same time.

"You own a restaurant?" my mother asks.

"Not exactly." Paolo's face reddens slightly. "It's my dad's."

"He's Sonny Sazon's son," I say.

Eva and my mom shriek.

"Ohmigod!" Eva screams. "Are you that little chubby kid who used to help Sonny make food on *Eats Meets West*?"

Paolo covers his face with one of his hands. "Yeah, that would be me."

My mom clasps her hands together. "That's my favorite show!"

"What's all the commotion?" Tito Melboy says, standing at the entrance to the kitchen with his coffee.

"Melboy!" my mom calls out. "Did you know Paolo is one of the Sazon kids?"

"Talaga ba?" Tito Melboy says.

Paolo nods.

Tito Melboy, Eva, and my mom all look at one another and scream.

"This is all way too much for a Friday morning," Paolo says.

"Would you be willing to teach me a thing or two?" Eva asks.

"Please do," my mom says with a pleading smile. "She needs as much help as she can get."

Eva swipes at her shoulder "Mom!"

"Actually, I'd be happy to," Paolo says. "I love to cook."

"He's good at it," I say, grinning. "Really good."

Paolo smiles back. "Thank you."

We stare at each other for a few moments before I realize everyone else is watching us.

"It's hot in here already, and you haven't even turned the stove on yet!" Kat says.

Paolo blushes but probably not as much as me. Fittingly, it feels as if I'm staring into an oven door that someone's just opened.

"How about this," Paolo says. "Everyone who wants to help make some breakfast, come with me."

Eva, Mom, and Tito Melboy follow him into the kitchen. Kat and I trail behind and pour ourselves some coffee before sitting at the kitchen island to watch. Kat's just like me: a big lover of food but more than happy to leave the actual preparation of it to others.

Paolo starts pulling out ingredients from his humongous refrigerator—a plastic tub of leftover white rice, a carton of eggs, and some vegetables. From the freezer, he pulls out packages of meats and then gathers a few vegetables and a long, green papaya from the kitchen counter.

"Are we making silog?" Eva asks.

"Yep," Paolo says. "But I like to freshen up the meal by adding a salad—what I like to call a quick atchara. Tito Melboy, would you mind making the fried rice? Tita Sharon, I'll defrost the longganisa and tocino so you can cook it up with the eggs. And I'll show Eva here how to make the salad."

As my mom passes by Kat and me to get to the refrigerator, she gets close and whispers, "Rex, I like Paolo for you. He's very nice. And talented. And rich and haaandsoooome," she singsongs.

"Mom, shhh!" I whisper back, though I'm pretty sure everyone's heard us.

"It's okay now if you don't learn how to cook. He will do it instead!" Mom adds.

I shake my head. I see Paolo, who is setting up his mandoline slicer, attempting to suppress a smile.

"So what's the plan for tomorrow night? Walk me through it," he says. "Eva, can you slice the veggies?" He sets the mandoline, a few carrots, an onion, and two red bell peppers next to her.

"The plan for karaoke night is straightforward, really," I say. "It's really all about the lip-synchs."

"The good thing is, that's pretty much all you'll have to do," Eva says to Paolo as she juliennes the carrots. "We've planned it all out so you'll only have to appear for two songs. One at the beginning and one at the end."

Paolo preps the green papaya for her by peeling it and then halving it to take out the seeds. "What will I be doing between the two songs?" he asks.

265

"After you kick off the night, you'll pretend to get a migraine and excuse yourself to the office for a while," I reply.

Tito Melboy dumps the container of rice into a pan of hot oil. The air fills with the crispy sound of the rice kernels flash frying. "And I have exactly the right person to help step in to host karaoke for the bulk of the show. They're in town visiting from Los Angeles and are very happy to help us. You just need to focus on your two lip-synchs, Paolo."

"Which songs?" Paolo asks. "Hopefully not something with a lot of choreography?"

"No, we're keeping it simple. They'll be standard park-and-barks," I say.

"What?" Paolo asks.

"Oh! I know that one," Kat says, stirring scary amounts of sugar into her coffee. "Those are songs where you just stay in one place and sing,"

"Standing still sounds easy enough," Paolo says.

"It might seem simple," Tito Melboy says, spooning garlic slices that my mom has prepped for him into the frying rice. "But lip-synching is a real art form. Many a queen have based their entire careers off this. And separately, impersonation is also an important and difficult skill. You're going to have to be perfect at two things at once."

"Luckily, we have a true master in the house," I say to my uncle. He winks back at me.

"Okay. I know why Tito Melboy is here," Paolo says. "How about the rest of you?"

"Mom and I are Regina Moon Dee's biggest fans," Eva says.

"If you can fool us, you'll be okay," my mother says, frying up the longganisa links and tocino. The sweet smell of pork, paprika, and pineapple drifts over to Kat and me, making my stomach gurgle.

"I can give you some stage presence tips," Kat says. "But mostly, I just didn't want to miss out on this learning-to-lip-synch montage moment."

"I guess it takes a village to make a drag queen," Paolo says.

"It takes more than a village," I say. "It takes a family." I look at everyone around in the kitchen, taking in the beautiful picture that I see. One that feels more authentic to me than the one Aaron sent last night.

But we are missing one important piece.

Paolo shows Mom a foolproof way to finish off the eggs she's frying next to her sausages by placing a sheet pan on top of the skillet, allowing the steam to gently cook the tops of the eggs without having to flip them over. The eggs slide out onto the serving platters perfectly set with deep orange yolks just on the verge of firming up.

Everyone takes seats at the large, reclaimed-wood table and promptly digs in to the food my family and Paolo have prepared for us. Tito Melboy's fried rice is steamy hot and redolent of garlic, Mom's longganisa are so juicy their casings burst, and the tocino is thick and meaty. Paolo and Eva's quick atchara is the perfect complement to everything, with vibrant papaya and fresh veggies, a tang from rice wine vinegar, and a rich sweetness from muscovado sugar.

"This food is freaking amazing," Kat says. "Especially this ah-cha-cha salad stuff."

I'd say something to concur, but I'm too busy inhaling my food, like everyone else at the table.

But I do manage to catch Paolo's eye when Kat gives her compliment and see the unmistakable sense of pride there, bright as day. I smile and keep eating.

AFTER BREAKFAST IS DONE, Kat helps Eva and Mom clean up so that Paolo can begin "Lip-Synch Camp."

First, Tito Melboy shows us videos of his favorite non-dancing lip-synchs. Latrice Royale performing "(You Make Me Feel Like) A Natural Woman." Jujubee doing "Black Velvet." And Jujubee and Raven lip-synching for their lives to "Dancing on My Own." No props or cartwheels or shablams. Just communicating the lyrics to the audience.

"You see, Paolo?" Tito Melboy says. "How they make you forget that they're not the ones actually singing? Their lips, their mouths, even the way they breathe is in sync."

Paolo watches each video intently. Kat, however, floats in and out of the room, watching sometimes but mostly checking out everything in the house, flipping through Paolo's books and sitting on every piece of furniture she sees (even the ones not meant for sitting).

"Now we watch Regina Moon Dee do the songs you'll be

lip-synching," Tito Melboy says, navigating to a video of me doing Sara Bareilles's "Gravity" at Dreamland.

"Ooh, I love this one!" Kat says, wandering in from who knows where. Eva and Mom join us from the kitchen later and sit next to me on the couch to watch.

We all observe me sing it once. Twice. Both times, Paolo scrutinizes my performance, sitting perfectly still to take it all in. By the third time, he's able to mouth some of the words and move his body a little bit like mine.

"You sound so beautiful, anak," my mom says, rubbing my knee. "And your dress is so pretty."

"Thanks, Mom. I found it at a consignment store, but Tito Melboy altered it for me."

"Was this the last performance you did there at Dreamland?" Mom asks.

"No. This was the week before Baby Buko's farewell," I say. "Before I stopped going."

"Before I asked Rex to stop," Tito Melboy says.

"You asked Rex to stop?" Eva says. "Is that why you quit drag?" she asks me. "You never told me why. Or why you and Tito stopped talking to each other."

Tito Melboy turns the TV volume down, and we're suddenly surrounded in silence.

"He was just trying to protect me," I say.

"From what?" my mom asks.

"He didn't want me to get hurt again. For..."

"For what, anak?"

"For being a drag queen," I say quietly.

"Why would anyone do that? No one would do that," my mom says. "Drag queens don't hurt anybody. They only bring happiness."

Tito Melboy looks at me sadly.

"I think it's time they heard the full story, Uncle," I say.

"Okay then, Rex," he says. "Tell them. Let's get it out in the open."

CHAPTER 21

THE SUNDAY BEFORE LABOR DAY was Baby Buko's final performance before heading to New York. Beaucoup Buko had planned a big going-away celebration for her at Drag Brunch, going all out with food and drink specials, plus American flag cake for the kids. Mom and Eva wouldn't be able to join because they'd be with my dad at a church barbeque. But Beaucoup and I would be there to see Baby off.

Tito Melboy created a special outfit for me, a modernized version of the Filipiniana dress with humongous butterfly shoulders. Underneath the diaphanous piña fabric, I'd wear a red, white, and blue body suit. The layering of the traditional Filipino on top of the modern American was a statement of what it meant to me to be a drag queen. I was two things at the same time, one just under the other.

I had suggested doing a duet with Beaucoup as a joint

parting gift to Baby. She loved this idea and scheduled us to perform last.

What I didn't tell my uncle was that I was also planning on finally asking Ivan to come see me perform that day.

As we drove into the parking garage, my heart sank. An older man sat in the parking attendant booth instead of Ivan.

"I see your friend's not here," Tito Melboy said as we parked, not even attempting to suppress the sound of relief in his voice.

"Maybe he's on a break?" I said, hoping.

Through the large office windows, I watched as Ivan appeared from the bathroom at the back, dressed in regular street clothes.

I rushed over to him from the car. "Hey! Are you not working today?"

"I'm off this weekend. Just came by to get my paycheck."

"Do you want to come see a show?" I asked him quickly, while Tito Melboy was still wrestling with our suitcases.

"What kind of show?"

I had underestimated my uncle—he could move that hefty body of his quickly when he needed to. Before I knew it, he was at my side, tugging at my sleeve. "Rex, don't," he said.

I ignored him. "It's at Dreamland," I told Ivan. "Just two blocks down from here on Folsom."

"You mean the one with the red door?"

"That's the one."

"I thought that was just a Chinese restaurant or something."

"It's more than that. They have performances there."

My uncle pulled at me again, harder, forcing me so off-balance that I nearly fell. "Huwag na, Rex," he hissed. "Tara na. We're going to be late."

Before I could argue with him, a group of rough-looking guys around Ivan's age came in from the street.

Ivan straightened up. "These are my homies," he said to me.

His friends stared at us, sneering. Their eyes filled with something thick and venomous.

Thankfully, Ivan seemed to sense the hostility building up in his buddies. "Don't want to keep you, man. You should probably get going."

"See you," I said, grabbing both rolling suitcases and nudging Tito Melboy ahead of me out of the garage.

The dressing room at Dreamland bubbled with excited chatter, but Tito and I got ready in silence. I was forcing myself to forget what had just happened and focus on getting prepared for the brunch. I assumed my uncle was, too.

The restaurant was crowded, full of people who had come out to send Baby Buko off. As a result, the brunch was even more festive than usual with all the girls lip-synching their favorite performances for Baby. Ever the professional, Beaucoup Buko showed no signs of unease as she co-emceed Drag Brunch with her drag daughter. Baby and Beaucoup's improvised dialogue between the acts seemed easy and relaxed, as if they'd rehearsed for weeks.

As the show came to an end, Baby Buko got up a final time to announce our closing number. Beaucoup and I waited by the side of the stage for our cue to go on.

"For our last song, we're going to hear our two emcees from Friday's Karaoke Happy Hour. Regina Moon Dee and Beaucoup Buko, her drag mother. Who is also my drag mother! Family is important to us here at Dreamland." Baby Buko waved at some of the children at a nearby table, who giggled in response, covering their mouths with their hands.

Baby's face beamed at the children and then went slack. Her gaze was drawn toward the sound of some raised voices on the side. There was a disturbance at the hostess stand. A group of young men was arguing with Benta Box.

Ivan and his friends.

They looked as if they were trying to get a table, but Benta seemed to be refusing to let them in for some reason. They seemed inebriated, and Ivan looked dazed, as if he couldn't figure out where he was. He kept looking at different spots in the restaurant. First at the hostess, at the girls waiting tables, and at Baby onstage.

And then at Beaucoup and me.

All the blood in my body went straight to my head. I held on to the handrail on the steps, feeling perilously close to passing out.

Baby Buko excused herself from the stage and rushed to

the hostess stand. Beaucoup showed her experience as a live host and quickly went up to continue the show.

"Regina Moon Dee, why don't you come up here and join me?" she said, seemingly unperturbed. As I stood close to her, though, I could see that her hands were shaking.

Baby managed to quiet Ivan and his friends down and moved them toward seats at the bar. They grabbed their stools and turned them around, where they sat and watched us, simmering. Ivan must have told them about my invitation to the show, which I completely regretted now.

I mustered as much positive energy as I could, plastered a huge grin on my face, and said, "Bon voyage, Baby Buko!"

The karaoke music for the Mariah Carey and Whitney Houston duet "When You Believe" started playing. And although Beaucoup was clearly a baritone, she sang with a clear, dulcet tone that matched my high alto voice nicely.

As the song went on, I was able to lose myself in the hopefulness of the lyrics, letting the happy faces of the diners make me forget about Ivan and his friends at the bar. Everything was going great.

Until one of Ivan's friends yelled something out loud.

"Hey!" he said. "I see kids here! At some of the tables. What are you all doing letting kids in here? At this freak show?"

Even over the music, I knew everyone had heard him. Beaucoup and I stopped singing.

Within seconds, Baby and some of the girls gathered to

try to boot them out. They refused to move, laughing in their faces. Ivan did nothing. It looked like he still wasn't even sure where he was.

I was about to go back to help get them when three of the cooks emerged from the kitchen—tall, built, and more than capable of kicking the guys' asses.

Ivan's friends threw up their hands and exited the restaurant at last.

The patrons clapped and whistled their appreciation. Beaucoup and I smiled with relief and started our song over again from the top, managing to end the show on a positive note.

As the patrons started paying their checks, Baby Buko took Beaucoup and me aside. "Who were those people?" she asked both of us, but I could tell she was addressing me primarily.

My heart was still racing—not in the usual intoxicating way it did after a performance, but in a way that made me feel terrified, as if it might not ever come back down again. "One of them is a friend. Sort of."

Baby clucked her tongue at me. "Regina, none of those men are your friends."

"That's what I was trying to tell her," Beaucoup said. "You're courting danger when you befriend rough trade like that. But if you do, and they know you as a boy, then you stay that way with them. Don't confuse them. Otherwise they can turn on you and get violent. Trust me. I know from personal experience."

Beaucoup and Baby looked at each other, something dark passing between them.

Baby took my hands. "You must be careful in this business. You need to know where it's safe to be who you are. And with whom. Not everyone will understand or accept you."

I couldn't look at either of them and just nodded at the floor.

"Good." Baby patted my head. "Now, go help your sisters bus the tables."

I helped close out brunch. My uncle and I changed, cleaned up, and packed our things. Feeling remorseful, I offered to take care of both our stuffed suitcases while Tito Melboy held a plate of American flag cake. He happily scooped spoonfuls of it into his mouth as we walked back to the parking garage.

But we didn't make it all the way there.

As we neared the entrance of the garage, we were blocked. By Ivan's friends. Ivan, though, was nowhere in sight.

They pushed us sideways into a nearby alley. My uncle dropped his plate of cake. The porcelain plate shattered onto the sidewalk with a clatter that no one paid any attention to. We were alone on the street.

We tripped through the alley as they shoved us, splashing through puddles slick with gasoline. It was dimly lit, secluded. Everything smelled like urine and trash.

"What the hell?" I said. I looked over at my uncle to make sure he was okay but also for guidance.

Unfortunately, Tito Melboy had curled into himself with his head bowed. I wouldn't be getting any help from him.

I looked around for a way to escape, but the guys blocked our exit from the alley. One took a suitcase and was rifling through its contents.

"Hey!" I yelled. "Leave that alone!"

A red shock of pain burst across my face. Tito Melboy screamed into his hands, making a muffled, high-pitched strangle of a sound. One of the guys had slapped me hard with the back of his hand. I grabbed my cheek. Heat and wetness. My fingers were colored with a small, bright splotch of blood.

I stared at the man who had slapped me. He wasn't a man at all. Just a boy. Not more than a year or two older than me. None of them were.

"What the hell do you want with us?" I said.

"That was some show you did back there," one of the other boys said.

"That wasn't us. Please," Melboy said, begging. His voice was wobbly.

"Bullshit," another boy said. "We watched you. We followed you. We wanted to make sure Ivan wasn't getting himself into some faggot shit."

"Don't call us faggots," I said.

The guy who had been sorting through my suitcase lifted up my wig. It looked ghastly in the air, like a wraith loosed from a grave.

"We can call you anything we want," he said, throwing it at me. The loose hairs whipped across my face.

"Fuck you," I said.

Another burst of pain, this time in the stomach. A punch to the gut. I bent over and gasped for air, retching and coughing. It felt, for an endless time, as if I were drowning. The boys' laughter made it harder for me to catch my breath somehow, as if they were sucking the oxygen right out of me. I fell to my knees beside my uncle, who looked like he couldn't bear to watch what was happening. He'd shrunk in on himself even further.

My scalp exploded. One of the boys gripped my hair and yanked my head upright. "Listen," he spat at me. "Don't ever talk to Ivan again. Don't park in his garage. Don't go inviting him to your ladyboy club. We see you anywhere near him again, you'll end up looking worse than all your shit over there." He nodded over to the boy with both our now-open suitcases, who was pouring some sort of liquid onto their contents. I blinked, trying to see through the pain searing through me.

A spark of light. A blaze of fire. The smell of smoke.

The boy threw my face toward the ground. My forehead hit the cement with a wet thump. As my eyes closed, I watched four sets of feet walk away from us, out of the alley and into the light of the street, while two suitcases of clothes burned, and my uncle kneeled and bent over, separate and away from me, crying and crying and crying.

CHAPTER 22

TITO MELBOY CRIES INTO THE PALMS OF HIS HANDS. "I'm sorry, Rex," he says. "I'm so sorry."

"Don't be sorry," I say. "It wasn't your fault. You didn't do anything wrong."

"Diyos ko." My mother brings her hand to her mouth, curling it into a fist. "How could anyone do that to you? To my beautiful boy?"

"Rex," Eva says, "why didn't you tell us?"

"Tito Melboy said to forget it. And you were too young anyway. I wanted to protect you, I guess."

After Ivan's thug buddies left, we went back to Dreamland for help. Baby was still closing up. She gave me some first aid and, shaking with rage, encouraged us to file a police report. But Tito Melboy refused. When we got back home, he told everyone we'd been mugged and instructed me to take a break from Dreamland and, most importantly, from drag. A week later, he found another place to stay in San Francisco and moved out of our house for good. It was the last time I saw him until this week.

"I should have done something to protect you, Rex, instead of just crouching there like a coward," he says.

"What could you have done, Uncle? I tried to stand up to them, and they beat me up. They would have done the same to you."

"I was paralyzed."

"It's okay."

"No," Tito Melboy says. "Let me explain. Do you remember how I warned you not to tell Ivan that you were Regina? That's because I had an experience before, in the Philippines."

He takes a few slower breaths, his head still bowed. "There was this young man whom I met at one of the bars where I worked. He used to give me big tips when I would perform. Eventually we became close, and we began to see each other. But only there at the bar. And only when I was in drag. Then one day, I ran into him at the market. I took him aside to say hello but he pushed me away, as if I were a stranger. At first, I thought he didn't recognize me out of women's clothes. And then I realized, it's because he was there with his wife. If I had been dressed as Beaucoup Buko, it might have been better. He would have just laughed and boasted to his wife about being irresistible to women. Instead, he cursed and spat on me. I'm lucky he didn't do more. I could see it in his eyes.

The fear of being found out. If it weren't for his wife pulling him away, I know his reaction would have been worse.

"I was just trying to warn you, Rex. My experience with men at that time told me they would all be the same, that they don't want to be confused by how we present ourselves to them. But I'm sorry I couldn't do more to protect you in the alley. I don't blame you for not talking to me again after that."

I kneel down in front of Tito Melboy and take his hands in mine. "Uncle, the reason I stopped talking to you isn't because you didn't stand up for me in that alley. It's because you told me to pretend like it never happened, instead of working through it. Processing it. That's what I needed to do. And I wanted you to help me do that. But you didn't. And then you just left me," I say.

Tito Melboy shakes his head, leaning over and still unable to look at me. "That was such a mistake, pamangkin. I thought if you could just let everything go, even me, you would eventually forget the pain." His tears fall, splashing onto our hands.

"But pain is part of drag," I say. "Not just in the uncomfortable clothes and shoes. It's in the ache that comes out of us when we perform. The hurt that we transform into art. It's in the way we pay tribute to queens who've inspired us, who've suffered just for existing. Like you. Without people like you and everything you've gone through, there would be no Regina Moon Dee."

"I never realized how much suffering you went through,

anak," my mom says, wiping tears from her eyes. "I see now why you thought you had to stop doing your drag. I never understood it before."

"I know I disappointed you, Mom. That you always liked having a famous kid."

"No, Rex." She pulls me up on the couch to sit between her and Tito Melboy. She puts her arm around me. "Listen to me. My happiness for you never had anything to do with that. Yes, it's true, when I was a girl, I wanted to be an actress. And I always resented that your lola and lolo did not support me. So I encouraged your creativity. I saw how much happiness was in your heart when you wore your favorite colors or clothes. Or when you sang and danced to your favorite songs. That's all I ever wanted for you. That's all any parent ever wants for their child—to be happy! But more important than that, to be safe. And it breaks my heart to know that there are people out there who don't want you to be who you are meant to be. How can I protect you from that?" She looks at my uncle. "How can any of us?"

"We can be there for them, Sharon," he says. "And most of all, not tell them to hide themselves away. That is not the way. I know that now. Rex taught me."

"My whole life I've known I'm different," I say. "And yeah, sometimes it's been hard. Especially these last few years. But I never would have had the strength and courage to find myself as a kid—to discover drag, to become Regina Moon Dee—if it hadn't been for you, Mom. For as long as I can remember, you've always been my biggest fan. Not just

Regina's. *Mine.* How many kids out there have someone who made them feel beautiful, and accepted, and loved every single day? The world's full of people who hate people like me. Just because of who I love or how I express myself. But you loved me so much it all got drowned out. I never had to listen to them because I had you. You are the best mom any kid could ever have. You both are."

I put my arms around Mom and Tito Melboy and pull them into me. My shoulders get wet as they cry into my shoulders.

Kat hands a box of tissues to Eva. They both wipe tears from their faces.

And Paolo stands in front of us, his eyes full of so much care and concern that it feels as if he's embracing me, holding on to me as much as I'm holding on to my mother and uncle.

I look around at them, my face slick with tears. How lucky I am to have these people in my life.

"Okay, enough crying," I say, shaking my uncle and my mom lightly. "We've got work to do."

AFTER A QUICK BATHROOM BREAK, we put my music video back on. This time, Paolo and I lip-synch to it together. The rest of the group observe, helping Paolo to capture every tilt of my head, every flick of my finger, and every inflection of the words in my expressions. Tito Melboy stands beside us, making suggestions and adjusting Paolo's body as he goes.

We move on to the second song—karaoke night's finale— and repeat the process. This one involves a surprise bit of choreography in the beginning, which we make sure to go over carefully with Paolo.

By the time he's gotten the basic moves down, the cloud cover in San Francisco has mostly evaporated, revealing a swath of sun over the neighborhood. Everyone wanders into the kitchen to get some food for lunch. I grab Paolo's hand and pull him aside.

"Can I have a look at your back deck? I haven't seen it yet," I ask, enjoying the heat his hand brings mine.

Paolo laughs. "Is that code for something?"

"Trust me," I say, squeezing, "when I want to do more than talk, you'll know."

We head out through the sliding glass doors beyond his dining room onto the deck. While not large, it's smartly designed, utilizing every bit of space for relaxing in privacy. Thick arborvitae trees line the sides, and stalks of bamboo border the back.

We sit down on the outdoor love seat overlooking the deck. Above, a single, silken cloud edges its way across the sky.

"Your family is so amazing," Paolo says. "I wasn't so sure we needed that many people here, but I'm glad that they are."

"I am, too. And I feel so much better now that my mom and Eva finally know the truth about what happened outside of Dreamland," I say. "You, too."

"What happened to you and your uncle was so horrible."

"It was. But what was worse was not telling my family about it. I don't know why we thought it was better to keep everything buried. It wasn't."

Paolo leans his head against mine. The feel of it is substantial and feather-light at the same time. "I can see how it would be easy to associate being in drag with hiding," he says, his words vibrating against me. "It's all an illusion, right?"

"I used to think that," I say softly. "But it isn't. Not to me, at least. For me, drag is heightened reality. It's not about lying, it's about revealing the truth in a different way. My truth. I see that now."

I feel Paolo smile. "I like that."

"And on the subject of truth..."

"Uh-oh. I don't know if I can handle another bombshell revelation."

"Just hear me out." I look out onto the bamboo in the back, swaying in the slightly chilly wind sweeping through. A tiny shiver runs up my body, and I move even closer to Paolo. "I need to tell my dad the truth about my drag. Not tomorrow, obviously. But one day. And I really think you should tell your dad that you don't want to manage one of his restaurants. That there's something else you want to do with your life, something that you're damn good at. So let's make a pact with each other to come out to them soon. And to be there for each other when we do it."

"Yeah. I'm in."

"Good."

"So," he says, "how am I doing so far, being you?"

"Mmm, so far, so good," I reply. "Now you need to practice in the outfit and wig. So you'll get a better idea of how everything will look and feel."

Paolo strokes my hand with his thumb. "I can't wait to see and feel it. All of it," he says with so much loaded intention that my insides tingle.

"Maybe we should go inside now," I say quietly.

He nods but doesn't move, still stroking my hand. I know that I should just get up and bring him inside with me. But I stay there, letting him hold on to me. We watch as the edge of the cloud above briefly covers the sun before revealing it again.

I chuckle. "Hey, do you remember the first night I hosted karaoke?"

"Of course I do. Every minute of it."

"There was this moment when I started seeing you differently. Do you know when?"

He shakes his head.

"It's when you sang. With your lovely voice."

"My lovely...hey!" he says, pulling back with an indignant smile.

"No, but seriously, you left everything out on the floor. I really respected that."

"That's why I love karaoke," Paolo says. "It's a chance to be free. To not have to care about what my dad thinks or worry about running a fancy restaurant. It's just me and the music. And the people willing to put up with me."

He smiles at me. I smile back.

And then he gives me a brief, light kiss on the lips.

I want to stay there. Return the kiss. Make it a longer, deeper one.

But one of my family members could come outside and interrupt us at any moment. And we still have to finish working on the final song.

"Okay," I say. "Before you get me into any trouble, we should get back to practicing. We need to make sure your lip-synchs are perfect."

CHAPTER 23

PAOLO'S LIP-SYNCH is an utter disaster.

THREE HOURS EARLIER

In other circumstances, applying my makeup to Paolo's face could be an intimate act. Something we'd share. Something private. Sexy.

But there's nothing sexy about having your mother and drag mom looking over your shoulder and critiquing you while your sister runs around the room trying to prep your clothes.

"More contouring on the nose, Rex," Tito Melboy says, pointing. Paolo stares at the tip of Tito Melboy's finger hovering right between his eyes.

"And more red on the lips, anak," Mom says.

"Dude, this dress is so wrinkled!" Eva shouts. "Why did you store it like this? I'm never going to get this ironed right."

"Hay naku!" my mother says. "That's so easy. Let me show you."

I sigh. Yes, it takes a family to prep a novice drag queen. And this particular family is driving me nuts.

To save my sanity, I try to ignore them all and just focus on the face in front of me. Luckily, it's a face I can easily get lost in.

"You all set with the plan?" I ask Paolo.

"Mm-hmm," he hums. "A cold open lip-synch. No intro. Afterward, I pretend to get a headache, and you ask Tito Melboy's friend to host."

"Ujima Jones!" Tito Melboy adds. "They're a star. Everyone's going to love them. No one will even miss Regina Moon Dee."

"Thanks, Uncle," I say.

Tito Melboy pinches my cheek. "You're welcome."

"I'll hide in the office," Paolo continues. "And then you'll come get me when it's time to do the second song. I leave right after, letting Ujima explain that I'm going home to get some rest. Then they'll close out the show."

I brush excess powder from Paolo's nose contour. "Good. Bryan and everyone else will get their Regina Moon Dee fix, and Dad won't know that I'm back in drag."

Our plan is to get to the Pink Unicorn an hour early so Paolo can hide in the office before most of the audience gets there. Mom will plan to arrive with Dad right when the show starts. He, and most everyone else, will only really get to see Regina while she's performing her two songs onstage.

Tito Melboy bows out early to get ready for his own show at Dreamland. "Break both of those beautiful legs of yours," he says to Paolo before leaving.

Later, at seven o'clock, when we arrive at the bar, things are still fairly quiet. The few people already there stare at us as we escort Paolo in. Not a surprise because he looks absolutely stunning. His face is properly beat, his long, wavy hair cascades over his back, and his dress, a custom-made Beaucoup Buko special of draped piña fabric studded with lapiz shells, sparkles in the light. He makes Eva and me—in jeans and T-shirts—look like slobs.

Bryan sees us when we enter and heads over from his seat at the bar. "You're here so early," he says. "Can I get you all anything?"

"Just a club soda for Regina," Eva says. "She feels a headache coming on."

"Actually," I say, "can she just rest in the back office until it's time to go on, Bryan?"

"Sure. I'll bring your drink there."

"Thank you, Bryan," I say. "Oh, and just FYI, Paolo can't make it tonight, so Eva will be filling in on tech."

Bryan briefly gives Paolo-as-Regina an odd look but shrugs and says, "Fine with me."

Eva and I accompany Paolo to the back office and breathe a little sigh of relief once we close the door behind us.

"Okay. We can relax a bit now," I say.

A knock at the door makes us all jump.

A bald, brown head pushes its way through the door opening. "Am I interrupting?" it asks.

"Manny!" Eva says. She runs to the door and pulls someone in. I recognize him as a friend of hers from grad school. Someone she met in a Philippine folk dance class. "I asked Bryan if he needed help with crowd control, and he said yes. So I asked Manny to come. I figure he could help *manny* the door. Haha! Get it?"

"Don't quit your day job, sis," I say.

Eva's made a good call, though. The Pink Unicorn risked getting cited by the fire department last week for having too many people inside the bar at one time. We don't want to chance it again. At six foot two, Manny towers over all of us. That, plus his shaved head, the indigenous tattoos that cover his arms, and his bulky frame make him the perfect doorman, which—if I recall correctly—he's done before for some high-end lounge in SoMa.

"Dang, who's the sexy lady?" Manny asks.

"Regina Moon Dee," Paolo says, holding out his hand. "The pleasure is all yours."

Manny kisses the top of Paolo's hand, and a little surge of jealousy runs through me.

"Okay, we're all going to give Regina her space now," I say, opening the door and waving Eva and Manny out ahead of me.

Paolo frowns as they exit. "You're not going to stay here with me?"

"I can't. I need to get Eva set up and keep an eye out for my dad, in case he arrives early." Which is true. But mostly, it would be a bad idea for me to be all alone with Paolo in the room. I don't know if I'd be able to control myself, even when he's dressed as Regina Moon Dee. Actually, the fact that he looks so stunning in drag makes him even sexier. Best to not think about it at all and hang out in the bar. "I'll be back to escort you to the stage when it's time to go on."

"Wait!" Paolo reaches for my face. He touches my cheek with his press-on nails and pulls them back. In between his fingers is a single, long lash. He puts it in the palm of his hand. "Make a wish and blow."

I puff the lash out of his hand. "There you go. A drag queen just earned her first pair of Spanx."

"What did you wish for?" Paolo asks.

"I can't tell you. That would ruin it," I say, giving Paolo a quick peck on the cheek before leaving him alone in the office.

On the stage, I go over the SYNGX system with Eva. We check the audio, video, and request system. It takes us at least half an hour, but between the two of us, we're able to figure out most of the controls.

"This SYNGX program is not the most user-friendly," Eva says. "No wonder Paolo took so long to figure it out. Like, why are these light and sound buttons so close together? You would think this is the volume, but..." She presses it, and the disco ball turns on.

"You don't have to get fancy, Eva. Just keep us on track.

Literally. Remember that the most crucial thing is to make sure my vocal tracks for both of Paolo's songs are uploaded and synced up to the karaoke tracks."

After she seems comfortable with that key detail, I leave her to it. She pumps EDM music through the speakers as I slowly make my way back to the bar. I scan the entire place to see if my parents have arrived early and spot someone familiar sitting alone at a table in the corner of the main room. The mysterious person from last week. His hood is pulled tight over his head again, and his face shrouded in shadows because of how he's positioned himself under the lights. Something about him makes my pulse race.

But I don't dwell on it long because I'm distracted by Manny at the front entrance. He's almost tripping over himself to usher someone inside—a statuesque Black woman in a sleeveless bodycon dress and a Kente African print head wrap, radiating so much regalness that I half wonder if she is actually royalty of some kind.

Manny offers his arm to the woman and escorts her over to me. "Rex, I think this is the guest you've been waiting for?"

"The one and only Ujima Decadence Fabricant Jones. She/they," the woman says, smiling affably.

I try not to stare, but it's hard not to gawk. "So happy you could be here. I'm Rex, Beaucoup Buko's nephew."

I lean in for a polite air-kiss, but Ujima says, "Girl, come here," and wraps their long arms around me. They smell so sweet and their skin is so soft that it feels as if I've been wrapped in rose petals.

"BB's told me so much about you. I feel like I already know your sensational sissy-singing, style-challenged self!"

Strangely, even though I've just met Ujima, it feels like I already know them, too. "Did you two meet at Dreamland?"

"No." Ujima snags an empty barstool and sits. She's so tall that she doesn't even have to hoist herself up on it, merely needing to rest gracefully on its upholstered surface. "I was in LA on the last leg of my *Strange Loop* bus and truck. Beaucoup was doing a show at Hamburger Mary's, and one of the girls got sick at the last minute, so I got pulled in to sub. She didn't know me from Eve, but she still offered me a bag of her homemade lumpia," she says, tilting her head at Beaucoup. "You've tasted her cooking, right? I was hooked, baby. Shablam! Instant sis! And we've been good friends ever since. In fact, your mama reminds me a lot of my bestie— another fabulous Filipino. Who isn't quite as round as Beaucoup, but still."

"Well, thank you so much for coming," I say.

"Of course," Ujima says, leaning in close to speak more softly. "You're BB's daughter, so you're basically my niece. And I'll always help family."

"So you know what you need to do tonight?"

Ujima nods. "I've got you, girl."

We continue to chat and gossip. The bar fills up steadily as Manny slowly lets in more and more people, many of whom I recognize as returning customers and loyal Regina Moon Dee fans.

And then, finally, my parents arrive.

I motion for them to come join Ujima and me at the bar. They take their sweet time getting to us. Mom keeps greeting the new karaoke friends she's already made while my dad cautiously takes in his surroundings.

"Mom, Dad, this is Ujima. They're a friend of Tito Melboy."

Both my parents' eyes widen—my mom's from obvious delight and my dad's from apparent shock.

"So nice to meet you both," Ujima says.

"Wow, I've never seen anyone so impressive in my life!" my mom says. "Don't you agree, honey?"

My dad continues to stare. "Uh, sure."

Ujima leans over and whispers in my ear, "I can see why you decided to keep your identity a secret from this one. He looks easily disturbed."

I wish Ujima wasn't right. But even as my father eases out of his initial apprehension and shakes Ujima's hand, I know that he's only okay with Ujima because they're a stranger to him, free to do whatever they want with their life. That same open-mindedness doesn't extend to Uncle Melboy or me.

Now that my parents are here, though, we're ready to proceed with the plan. I lead all three of them to a table Bryan's reserved for them at the front, where my dad can have an unobstructed view of Paolo as Regina Moon Dee.

It's eight p.m. Time for the true test: Paolo's opening performance.

I head to the office to retrieve him.

"Are you ready?" I ask, poking my head in.

He's seated at the desk with his hands on his lap and his eyes closed. "Mm-hmm." He nods, smiles subtly, and opens his eyes to look at me. There's an unease there that I empathize with. We've prepared as best we can, but things could still go wrong. Seeing him vulnerable and feeling exactly the same makes me want to shut the office door behind me, pull him in close, and hold him until we both feel better. But there's no time for that.

"Come," I say, holding out my hand to him.

Once we get to the back of the stage, Eva fades the background music and turns the house lights down. Paolo emerges from the darkness at the back of the stage and steps into a semi-hazy spotlight (Tito Melboy's idea, for more drama and to keep him partly shadowed). So far, so good.

After the karaoke track for "Gravity" begins and my vocal track successfully kicks in, I begin to breathe easier. Paolo nails the accompanying lip-synch. He blends his body movements with my vocals so seamlessly that he almost makes me believe he's actually singing. I check the audience. Their pleased expressions tell me he's fooled everyone else, too. Including my dad, who looks rapt, as if discovering for the first time what a drag queen can do.

I keep watching my father, checking for any glimmers of

recognition on his face, to see if he's able to identify my voice on the track. Thankfully, he doesn't. It's been years since I've sung in my upper range in front of him, so he's hopefully forgotten the sound of my natural singing voice. Mostly, though, it's due to Paolo's perfect execution of the lip-synch.

After Paolo's song is over, instead of making any introductory remarks into the mic, he brings a hand to his temple and walks off the stage as planned. I rush up to him to see if he's okay and then make a big show about talking to Ujima, ensuring that everyone can see me asking them to take over.

Shortly after, I escort a clearly declining Regina Moon Dee back to the office.

Paolo flumps onto the sofa, slips his shoes off, and nudges them aside. "How did I do?"

"You were incredible," I say, sitting beside him and soaking in the post-performance heat coming off him. "I don't think anyone had a clue that you were lip-synching."

"Good! Now can I take off this dress for a while? I am melting in these outfit layers."

"Yeah, you can relax for a while. Kat will help you put it back on before you need to perform again."

Paolo pulls his long hair over the front of his shoulder and turns his back toward me. "Can you help me with this?"

I unzip the dress, but the zipper gets stuck close to the bottom. "Hold on a sec."

"That should be enough for me to take it off," Paolo says.

"I know, but we won't be able to zip it back up if it's jammed like this." I scoot in closer to him, trying to move the slider in either direction. "It won't budge. Can you stand? I think it snagged on some of the bunched-up fabric."

We get up off the couch and I try again, grunting as I pull. After a couple more attempts, I'm finally successful.

"Got it," I say. "Except..."

"What?"

"I think I just made it worse."

The zipper slider has moved, but I've jammed it up with so much force that it's gotten caught on the fly of my pants.

My crotch is now attached to Paolo's rear end.

He tries to turn around and look. "What did you—"

"No, don't move." I hold his hips and bring his backside even closer to me. "You'll ruin the dress."

"Well, this is an interesting position to be in," Paolo says.

A knock on the door. "Hello?"

It's my dad.

"Crap!" I whisper.

"Rex? Are you in there?"

"Um, yes?" I call out.

"Ujima said Regina wasn't feeling well," Dad says. "Does she need any help? Do you want me to get some medicine for her?"

The door handle jiggles. I realize I didn't lock it or put the dead bolt in. It starts to open.

Paolo and I throw our bodies against the door, slamming it shut. "Don't come in!" I shout through the door. "I mean, Regina's resting and needs some quiet time alone."

"You sure she's okay?" Dad asks.

"Yes!" we both yell.

And then we hear someone say, "Stop worrying, honey."

Thank god. Mom to the rescue.

"Rex has it handled," she says. "Just come back to the table."

Paolo and I stand there, his body pressed to mine. I feel the rapid pace of his breathing as his back expands into my chest. In any other situation, the area down below where he's pushing up against me would become a bit more... crowded as a result. But right now, being stimulated is the furthest thing from my mind.

Finally, we hear my dad say to my mom, "Okey dokey."

A few seconds pass. A minute.

I crack the door open and take a look. They're gone.

I close the door again.

Another knock.

"Shit!" Paolo and I whisper.

"Guys? It's me, Kat. Can I come in?"

Paolo and I let out a sigh of relief. I open the door to let her in. "I'm so glad you're here. We could use your help."

She stares at us for a few moments. Her eyes travel downward slowly, eventually landing on Paolo's butt. "I don't think adding another person to whatever's happening here is going to help. But I'm open to trying new things."

"Kat, please," I say, exasperated.

"Yeah, yeah," she says. "Let me take a closer look. Paolo, could you lean over so I can have a better view of what's going on?"

Paolo bends over at the waist.

Kat bursts out laughing. "Ohmigod, I didn't think you'd fall for that. Hold on, I need to take a picture of this."

"Kat!" Paolo and I shout.

"Okay! Okay," she says, giggling.

After about five minutes of tugging, Kat finally manages to coerce the dress's zipper all the way open, freeing us from our compromising position. "Et voilà," she says.

"Thank you," I say, finally able to step away from Paolo. "Let's not do that again."

"At least not in public," Paolo says, grinning at me.

I smile and shake my head. "Okay, you guys hang out here while I head back out to be with my parents. I'll come get you both when it's time for the second song. And, Kat, don't forget to lock the door behind me."

"Will do," Kat says.

Despite that little hiccup, everything else continues to go according to plan. Ujima is a natural host, telling stories and jokes in between songs and singing one of their own, too. I'm stunned by their voice—hot, sweet, and golden, like melting honey.

And my parents seem to be enjoying themselves. My mother gets her chance on the mic with "Say a Little Prayer"—I wonder if it's another one of her potential church solos—and my dad even sings along with her from his seat.

An hour later, it's time for Paolo to do his second and final lip-synch. At the bar, Bryan stays busy fulfilling drink orders next to Loretta, and the crowd adores Ujima. I guess my uncle was right after all. They don't even miss Regina Moon Dee. Do we even need Paolo to do the second lip-synch at this point?

We rehearsed the second song so much, though. It would be a shame for Paolo not to show his stuff. Plus, he and Kat must be so bored being stuck together in the room. I should go rescue them.

But there was no reason to be worried.

Kat holds up her phone when she lets me back into the office. "I've been showing him old Kat and Nine Tails performances!"

"And I've shown her a few clips from *Eats Meets West*," Paolo says.

"You were an adorable kid," Kat says.

"Aw, thanks!"

"And your dad is smoking hot," she adds.

"Uh, thanks?"

"It's showtime," I say. "Paolo, you set?"

"Yes," he says. "Good to go."

We wait for the current karaoke singer to end her number, and then Kat and I take Paolo back to the stage. Eva sets up the cues for Paolo's last song.

Ujima outros the last singer and intros Regina Moon Dee. "Look who seems to be feeling a bit better!" they say. "Our fierce Filipina phenom is back for a very special song."

Paolo gets into place by the KJ console. I see Eva say something to him. He bends down and looks at the laptop screen, squinting—apparently unable to see well enough without his glasses—and points at something. Eva checks the screen. Her face crumples. She's about to say something back to him, but Ujima has left the stage and Paolo has already moved into place.

Eva shrugs and hits the cues.

The lights onstage dim except for one odd one in the back that doesn't want to come down. I see Eva pout, shake her head, and press a few buttons, though the light still doesn't change.

It doesn't matter, though. All eyes are focused on Paolo, still looking gorgeous in my lapiz-shell-studded dress.

The music track starts. A familiar flute and plucked instrument intro begins.

And then, right before the vocal starts, Paolo tears away the lapiz shell dress, revealing a familiar pink and purple hanfu underneath. People in the crowd gasp. He begins his lip-synch to my rendition of "Reflection" from *Mulan*.

And it's even better than his first performance.

His lips move in perfect sync with my voice. The inhalation and exhalations, the ever-so-slight signs of more exertion on higher notes. His throat even slightly vibrates to mimic my vibrato. It's as if I can feel my own voice being taken out of me and being put into him.

Everything is going to be okay.

Eva starts pressing at a few more buttons on her KJ control screen, probably still trying to turn off that one last light. Instead, a second spotlight gets turned on and starts wandering around the room. At one point it shines on the hooded figure in the back corner, who reels back as if being singed by it. The light crawls on, making people shield their eyes from the sudden glare. I give Eva a *WTF?* look. She shakes her head and pokes at more controls.

The spotlight doesn't turn off, but it at least finally stops moving. It ends up focused at the front of the bar, where it lights up a very annoyed-looking person standing next to Manny at the door.

Aaron.

He's back in town already. Sooner than I expected. Sooner than Bryan expected, too, from the look on his face. He almost drops the drink he's holding when the spotlight lands on Aaron.

And at that moment, just as Paolo-as-Regina gets to the beginning of the first refrain of "Reflection"—where she asks the mirror to tell her who the girl is that she sees there—my vocal track shuts off completely. Eva must have turned it off by mistake while trying to turn the roaming spotlight off.

And Paolo, unaware that he's been left alone with just the instrumental track, keeps on going.

Mouthing absolute nothingness into the air.

CHAPTER 24

EVERYONE IN THE PINK UNICORN STARES in silence at the train wreck happening right in front of them.

For what seems like forever, the instrumental track for "Reflection" continues on with no singing. Though at least Paolo's stopped lip-synching.

Eva flails her hands around the KJ console, pressing every button she can, turning lights on and off and eventually stopping the instrumental track.

Ujima scurries back onstage. "Just a bit of technical difficulty, everyone. I think we accidentally turned off Regina's mic. Why don't we just start over?"

Eva stops cold, her eyes as wide as saucers. She looks at Paolo, who is even paler than the Ben Nye Super White makeup we put on his face. Eva ever so subtly shakes her head *no* at Ujima.

Ujima smiles and nods back *yes*.

Eva shakes her head again, bigger.

They keep doing that to each other until Eva shouts out, "Fine!" and presses a series of buttons. The light cues go back to the beginning, and the karaoke track starts again. And from our table in the front row, I can clearly see that Paolo is trembling, surely hoping that Eva's managed to find my vocal track this time. My own nerves aren't doing much better, sensing the increasing bewilderment in my dad next to me.

The instrumental introduction plays. Time for the vocal line to start. Paolo takes a breath, preparing the phrase.

But my vocal track is still missing.

So Paolo begins to sing. With his own voice.

And it's absolutely the most wretched thing I've ever heard in my life.

Paolo can't find the key. It's too high for him to sing so he ends up only halfway there. Worse, he keeps trying, so he glides from note to note, trying to readjust things. He's also nervous, which makes it all sound even worse. It honestly feels like something inside of me is dying.

Everyone has gone from confused to horrified. They look to Ujima, who doesn't seem to know what to do anymore. Eva has stopped trying to figure things out and is just staring blankly at Paolo.

And then something strange happens.

Before I'm even aware of it, I'm onstage.

I don't know how I've gotten up here. I don't know if

it's because some part of me feels so terrible for Paolo that I just blacked out and jumped up onstage to help him or if it's because the pain in my ears is enough to give me temporary amnesia. Whatever the reason, I find myself taking the spare mic and standing next to him.

And I sing.

Who is this person I see in my reflection, looking back at me?

But I'm not singing to the audience. I'm singing to Paolo.

Even stranger than me suddenly finding myself onstage? Paolo starts to mimic me. He's no longer trying to sing (thank god), but he is moving in time with me. He's not just lip-synching. He's hands-synching, arms-synching, eyes-synching, matching every one of my movements. Almost as if he can read my mind.

He's become my reflection.

I keep singing. About how I've had to hide my heart. That I no longer want to conceal what I think and feel. I sing all this to the entire bar, and to Paolo. But mostly to myself.

It makes so much sense now, why these feelings I've been having for Paolo are so strong. He's helped me to see myself. Literally. To see the things inside I've been too scared to pub-licly reveal to the world. And to Dad and Aaron.

He's been telling me that I'm beautiful. Every swish of my hips and flip of my wrist. Every lisped consonant and high-pitched shriek. I'm extra. I'm feminine. I'm a drag queen.

And I don't have to apologize for any of it.

The song approaches its end. The music fades to nothing. Paolo and I stand there, staring at each other in silence.

My mom gets up and starts clapping. Then Kat and Ujima. Followed by the rest of the bar. Nearly everyone—including my father.

I'm stunned. Dad must know now, like everyone else, that I'm the true Regina Moon Dee, not Paolo beside me. But my dad not only knows it, he's applauding it. Everyone is. Except for one person.

Aaron.

I see him at the front door, closing his eyes hard. Like he's straining to keep out everything he's seeing.

He turns around and leaves.

Bryan hurries to get out from behind the bar and follows him. I thrust my mic back into its stand and hurry off the stage, gently pushing my way through the people, trailing after both of them.

Aaron hasn't gone far. He's just right outside, leaning against the door of the shuttered cafe next to the Pink Unicorn, staring up at the night sky while Bryan approaches slowly.

"Aaron?" Bryan says.

Aaron closes his eyes and sighs. "That's not really Regina Moon Dee in there, is it?"

"No," I say. "It's not."

"I kept thinking something was off about her lately," Bryan says. "But I couldn't put my finger on exactly what."

"So you lied to me?" Aaron asks.

"Yeah," I say.

"Just like you did," Aaron says, opening his eyes to look at Bryan. "Why didn't you just tell me, Rex?" He sinks, slumping down on the concrete sidewalk.

I sit down beside him and lean against the wall. The rough stucco digs into my back. "I was scared."

"Of me?"

"Of a lot of things. But yeah. Of you. Of you rejecting me. I went through this bad thing with this other guy once. It's a long story. But the lesson I learned was that I had to be careful who I revealed my drag identity to. If I wanted to be safe, I had to stay hidden."

"I was afraid of losing you, too, Aaron," Bryan says, sitting down on the other side of him. "You hated your deadbeat dad. I didn't want you to know that that asshole was me."

Aaron doesn't say anything at first. I can tell that he's trying to take it all in.

"Well, I guess I'm not the best person to tell people that they shouldn't hide who they are, since I spent most of my life doing that, too," he finally says.

"You know, Rex, I was pretty excited to see you that first night here. We had a nice thing going on in Bloomington, and I thought maybe we could even try to give it another go. But when we got to talking at my place, I remembered what it was about you that never clicked with me."

"I was never good enough for you," I say.

"No," Aaron says. "That's not true at all. We broke up that first time because I wasn't ready to be with you. I wasn't out of the closet like you were. And to be perfectly honest, I'm

DOMINIC LIM

not completely out yet. Sure, I can work at a gay bar, have a boyfriend. But when it comes to doing things in public— holding hands? Kissing? I can't do it. I'm still too scared. I'm too afraid of what people will say, what they'll think. That's the real reason why Russell left me. He said if I couldn't be completely comfortable with who I was here, then I wouldn't be okay with it anywhere. When you came over to my place that night, you reminded me of how open you are about your identity. And I realized, I wasn't as strong as you. I'm not the person you need to be with. That's why I tried to set you up with Miguel. He's a lot more out than I am. I thought you'd be happier with him."

I let out a long, slow breath as I try to wrap my head around everything he's just said. "The ironic thing is that I *wasn't* brave enough to be entirely open about my identity. Not all of it, at least."

"Looks like the three of us are more alike than we thought," Bryan says.

Aaron chuckles. "Looks like it."

"Coming out can be a long process," I say. "It doesn't happen overnight."

Bryan laughs. "It happened overnight to me. All because of this beautiful bar right next to us," he says, patting the wall behind him. "Which brings me to what I was going to tell you on the phone, Aaron. The thing you weren't ready to hear until you came back."

"What is it this time?" Aaron says. "I'm not ready for another huge secret."

"It's no secret. I want you to be owner of the Pink Unicorn," Bryan says.

"Oh." Aaron knocks his head back against the door softly a few times. "Okay."

"What I did to you and your mom, abandoning you both, it was wrong. Family doesn't do that to each other. So I want to make it up to you by giving you what I—and I think you—see as part of our chosen family. The bar."

Aaron fidgets next to me. "I know how much this place means to you. It means a lot to me, too. And I'm grateful. But I've been managing the expenses for a year now, and I know we're not in good shape. Even with the added business from karaoke night, we're on the verge of shuttering. I get why you want to give it to me. But it almost feels like you're dodging your responsibilities again."

"Dammit," Bryan mutters to himself. "You know that's not my intention, Aaron."

"I know," Aaron says, shaking his head. "I know. But still. It's a lot."

The Pink Unicorn's door cracks open, and music, laughter, and loud conversation spill out. I see Manny's, Kat's, and Paolo's heads swiveling around to find us.

They spot us sitting together against the wall. I give them a tiny *we're okay* wave and they slip their heads back inside. I wonder if Ujima or Eva has given the audience a reason for the Regina Moon Dee double situation, and if my mom has explained it all to my dad. Yet more things my friends and family have been doing to help me. I think about us all at

Paolo's house yesterday, everyone taking time out of their busy day to teach him how to be me. To carry out this kooky plan that's totally fallen apart.

But at least we were together, enjoying a day of drag in Paolo's gorgeous, multimillion-dollar home.

Wait a second.

"How much money do you think the Pink Unicorn would need to get back on its feet?" I ask.

Aaron whistles low. "I'd say at least a hundred and fifty thousand dollars?"

That's a lot. But... "I might have a potential benefactor for you."

"Really?" Bryan says.

"No promises. I'll ask," I say. "I know it's only been a month, but I've come to love this old bar, too. It's helped me to face my fears and get out there again. And it's even helped to reunite with a long-lost family member."

"It has that effect on people," Bryan says. He punches Aaron playfully on the shoulder.

Aaron shakes his head and makes a *pfft* sound. But when I look over at him, he cracks a smile.

I stand up and brush the back of my pants off. "I should let you two have time to talk. Then we can figure out what we can do to save this place. But first, I have a father-son confrontation of my own to deal with."

CHAPTER 25

BACK INSIDE THE PINK UNICORN, Eva has turned on quiet lounge music, and the house lights are up to mid-level again. Karaoke night is over, but the bar is still abuzz.

"Hey," someone says to me as I enter. It's Jenny—Ms. Anaconda-fanny-smacker. She puckers her lips, as if tasting something sour. "Never seen anyone do 'Reflection' like that before. With a surprise real-life reflection. Props," she says, tapping her chest with two fingers and saluting me before exiting.

Paolo, Kat, and Ujima make their way over to me near the entrance. Paolo's wig looks like it's melting, and from the way he's standing, I know his feet are swollen and tired.

"What happened with the rest of the show?" I ask them.

"I told the audience that it was a new gimmick you were

trying out to drum up publicity for the bar," Ujima says. "If it helps, #dragqueendouble is already trending."

"I should just tell everybody the truth," I say.

"The only person you really need to talk to is sitting up front," Kat says.

At the table near the stage, my mother holds one of my father's hands in hers. He nods along as she talks. I wish I could hear what she was saying, but I'm too far away, and my legs don't seem to want to take me any closer to them.

"I know," I say.

"Do you want me to come with you?" Paolo says.

"As sweet as that is, I don't think seeing the physical manifestation of my drag sitting next to me will make things any easier for my dad. But thank you." I reach out and caress Paolo's cheek.

"Rex," my father calls out, waving at me and pointing his lips at an empty chair at their table. His stoic face reveals nothing, and I'm not eager to find out what's really on his mind after my big reveal.

"I guess I should get this over with," I say.

Kat gives me a quick hug before I go. "Whatever happens, we'll be here, waiting."

I wade through the crowd and sit down next to my mom, using her as a buffer between me and my dad. I try to face them, but my eyes twitch and twist away, unable to look at either of them. My gaze shifts to the empty stage instead, focusing on the hazy, soft spotlight still illuminating the lone microphone like a ghost.

"Anak," my mom says, "your father and I have been talking."

I nod, frowning. "About how I've been lying to him." My body tenses, ready to receive a blow.

"About what a hardheaded fool he's been," my mom says.

My ears perk up. "What?"

My dad sighs. "Rex, let me ask you a question. Why do you think I always go out into the garage?"

"I always thought it was because you wanted to be alone."

"That's part of it, yes. But why? Come on, I want you to be honest with me," he says.

"Because...sometimes you feel like you don't fit in with Eva, Mom, and me?"

"I can see how you would think that. But no." He reaches for the nearly empty glass in front of him, ice cubes melting into the dregs of his drink, and knocks back what little is left. "I have a lot of things inside me that I don't always show. Lots of thoughts that I don't know how to say. Except through what I make in that room. I feel more comfortable with my tools and projects. I'm not so good with my words, anak. Not like you or Eva. Do you remember that chest I made for you?"

"Of course," I say. "It's one of my most prized possessions. Maybe the most."

My dad's eyes brighten. "I made you that chest because it was the only way I knew how to tell you how I felt. I also know what it's like to have to express myself through other, let's say, more unique ways."

315

All this time I'd thought my father was the odd one out. That he didn't understand my mom's affinity for performing or my connection to drag. But he was more like us than I knew. He understood that these things aren't just mere hobbies. They're passions. They're what make us feel whole.

"So you made my trunk for other reasons besides my graduation."

I watch as he gathers the bamboo cocktail picks from the empty glasses on the table and begins to untie the knotted head of one of them. "Yes, Rex," he says.

"Because you felt bad about what happened to me and Tito Melboy. The...mugging."

He grunts, nods, and takes the picks in his hand, wrapping one around the others and tying them together.

"Dad, I have to tell you something. We weren't mugged. We were attacked. For dressing up in drag."

In my father's hand is what looks like a small flower made of bamboo.

He places it on the table and pulls a faded handkerchief from his pocket. I assume it's to wipe the sweat that always seems to accumulate at the back of his neck when he gets worked up. But instead, he raises it to his eyes. Something is happening that I've never seen before.

My father is crying.

"Dad?"

"I know what happened, Rex. Your uncle told me everything a long time ago. About your drag. About what really happened to you both."

"He did?"

My mother rubs my dad's arm.

He wipes his eyes. "Why do you think he left the house? Because I told him to leave! I was so angry with him for leading you down that path. Look at where he took you! Straight into that alley, where you were hurt. Where you could have been...Susmaryosep, I don't even want to think about what could have happened."

"Tito Melboy never told me," I say. "You never told me."

"I was going to, Rex. But you never went back to dressing that way. You changed yourself, and I was content, knowing it wouldn't happen again. That box I made? At the time, it was my way of encouraging you, to tell you I thought you did the right thing. To thank you for not putting yourself in danger anymore."

"And I put that part of myself inside it."

"Yes, Rex. Your mom told me. You put yourself inside. But I understand now the toll it took on you."

He leans back in his plastic chair, crosses his arms, and looks up at the ceiling, blinking rapidly, trying to keep the tears at bay.

"You know, anak, when your uncle Melboy left us in the Philippines, I was just a child. I couldn't comprehend why our kuya abandoned us. Why would he choose a life of drag over a life with us? It wasn't until your mom told me something just now that made me understand."

"What?" I ask.

"That your uncle Melboy has been sending money

back to the Philippines for years," my mom says. "To your grandpa, to your uncle Reg, to Uncle Reg's entire family. All this time. More than half of what he makes performing, no matter how little, he sends back to them. He's never stopped taking care of your family, even when your lolo was the one who told him to stop being himself. I've been telling your dad that's exactly what he did to you."

"Your mom is right," my dad says.

"As always!" my mom says.

He smiles, his eyes wrinkling out a few tears that he quickly brushes away with his hand. "When I first saw you in that dress in your bedroom, you were so happy. But I took that away from you. I never again saw that kind of happiness in you, anak. For so many years. Not until just now. Right there on that stage. Where you were brave enough to be yourself again in front of me. In front of everyone."

He blows his nose with his handkerchief. I just stare at him.

"What is it?" he asks. "Do I have a booger on my nose?"

I get out of my seat, walk over to my dad, lean down, and embrace him. I don't think I've hugged him that tightly since I was a boy. The same little happy, singing, dancing, overacting boy that my father said he hadn't seen in years.

"Thank you, Dad," I mumble into his shoulder. "I love you."

"I love you, too, anak," he says, his voice ragged. "I want the best for you. I want you to be yourself. Here. At home. Everywhere. Do whatever makes you happy."

"Which means you don't really want to go to law school. Diba, anak?" my mom adds, lifting one of her eyebrows at my dad.

"Well, if I'm being perfectly honest about everything—"

"Hoy," my dad says, laughing. "One thing at a time. You don't need to rush any other decisions right now."

I'd thought the turning point in my relationship with my dad was the day I decided to put my drag away. I know now that it's exactly the opposite. It's here, years later, at the Pink Unicorn, when we both agree that my drag should never be hidden away again.

Manny holds open the Pink Unicorn's door to let Bryan and Aaron come back inside. From the relaxed looks on their faces, their father-son discussion must have gone as well as ours.

"That guy," Dad says, pointing at Aaron with his lips. "Is that the guy you told us about a while back? The one you're helping here?"

"He must be very happy with the success of karaoke night," my mom says.

"He is," I say. "But it's not enough, unfortunately. Would you guys come with me? I want to discuss this with everyone."

We gather at the bar. My mom and dad, Bryan and Aaron, Ujima, Eva, Kat, and Paolo. Manny even joins, standing next to Ujima with a bashful look on his face. Loretta kindly serves us all a round of drinks.

"Aaron," I say, "could you share what you told me outside

with everyone else? About how the Pink Unicorn still needs more help? We've got a lot of really creative people here. I'm sure we can come up with a solution."

I sit on the barstool next to Paolo and assist with taking off his shoes, listening while Aaron explains the Pink Unicorn's financial difficulties to everyone.

"I was never going to just leave you with all that debt," Bryan says after Aaron has finished. "I wasn't going to just cut and run. Again."

"I know," Aaron says. "But still. Karaoke night may have bought us a few weeks, but not much more than that."

I clear my throat nervously. "Paolo?" I'm embarrassed about what I'm about to ask him, but I know that he loves the bar. "Do you think you might be able to help financially?"

He rubs his foot and groans. I'm hoping it's from the soreness he feels and not from my question. "How much are we talking about?"

"Around a hundred fifty thousand," Aaron says.

"I don't have that much," Paolo says. "Not even close. My house, most of my stuff—it's really all my dad's. I could ask him for a loan, but then I'd have to tell him it's for a gay bar that I KJ for, and I don't think he'd be very happy about it. I can still try, though."

"All right," I say. "Let's consider it a possibility. Any other ideas?"

Eva, the good student that she is, raises her hand like she's in class. "Could we do a GiveFunds campaign? Didn't that help the Alley Bar in Oakland?"

"That's a great idea, anak." My mom puts her arm around Eva.

"Would we make enough money that way?" Bryan asks.

My dad snaps his fingers. "Do you remember the telethons on TV with Jerry Lewis? They used to do fundraising, but they weren't just asking for money. They combined it with performances to motivate people to give. What about something like that?"

"A live fundraiser," Ujima says. "I've done a few drag versions of that before. They even have event platforms we could use, where people could watch the show virtually and donate online."

"Rex," my mom says to me, "why don't you program an evening of karaoke performances? You, and Melboy, and Kat, and everyone else. You can charge admission that night. And whenever someone sings a song, we ask people to donate. We can even ask them to pay for special requests, for themselves or for anyone else. Of course, I'd be very happy to sing whatever songs people would be clamoring for."

"Of course you would, Mom," I say, smiling.

"That's a great idea," Bryan says.

"We can do it in parallel with the GiveFunds campaign," Eva says, "which I could start right away, and then close out at the end of the live event."

"I'm in," Kat says. "And I know the Nine Tails gals would be willing to donate a performance, too. When do we do it?"

"Soon, if we can. But with enough time to get the word out. How about the end of the month, on the last Friday?"

Aaron says. "Actually, wait. Let's do it on the Saturday. I forgot I'm changing my special day with Joey to Fridays. I don't want to miss that."

Bryan gives Aaron an approving look, and I smile. I can tell Bryan's proud of his son's commitment to Joey.

"Good," Eva says. "That gives us about three weeks to get the GiveFunds campaign going, line up the music acts, and get the word out for the live event."

"Sounds like a plan," I say.

"Thank you," Aaron says, looking around at all of us.

"Yes, thank you all for doing this," Bryan says. "For me, and my son."

"Nothing's more important than family," Ujima says, holding up their glass. "Can I get an *amen* in here?"

"Amen!" everyone says.

Paolo and I clink our glasses, making sure to maintain eye contact. For tradition's sake, of course. We sip, smiling at each other. And then his eyelid flutters as he utters a tiny groan.

Your tuck? I mouth silently to him.

Yes, he mouths back, wincing.

"It's time for us to get going," I say to everyone. "Paolo is turning into a pumpkin. I need to take him back to de-drag and untuck."

I get a bunch of knowing looks from almost everyone, except my dad, who looks like he definitely does not know what *untuck* means.

Paolo and I say our good-nights to everyone, and I help him gather his things and hobble to the car.

On the drive home, Paolo leans the car seat back and plucks his wig off. "Ahh, much better. So, how'd it go with your dad? Everything looked like it went okay, from what we could see from the bar."

"Were you guys spying on us?" I ask.

"Possibly."

"It went well. Really well."

Paolo reaches for my hand and squeezes. "Good."

"And now that I've done my part of our little dad agreement..."

Paolo groans. "Okay. Yes. I'll talk to him." He looks at his watch. "It's the afternoon in Manila. I can call him now."

"You don't have to do it now."

"I need to ask him about the money for the bar so I might as well get everything out now. It actually helps that you're here with me."

He rings his dad, who answers right away. And though I can only hear Paolo's part of their discussion, I can pretty much tell what his father says on the other end of the line. Their discussion lasts the entirety of our trip back to my place, and they're still talking when we arrive. Paolo puts his dad on speaker and continues the call in my bathroom so that he can start taking everything off. I can now hear both sides of their heated conversation, so I flip on the TV to give them a little privacy.

When Paolo finally re-emerges, he's taken off all my drag, but still has most of his makeup on. He flings himself onto the couch and lies down, staring at the ceiling.

"Not as good as my conversation with my dad?" I ask, perching on one of the couch's arms.

"Pretty much. He was sort of okay with me not wanting to manage Bamboo Fork, but he couldn't understand why I wouldn't just stay with the family business and cook. He said he'd even let me be one of the cooks there, or even at Aqua-Marine. Work my way up to executive chef eventually. But I told him I wanted to do my own thing."

"And the loan?"

"No go. Especially not for a bar that our family doesn't own. I'm sorry, Rex."

"At least you tried. We'll just have to depend on the Give-Funds campaign and our fundraising karaoke event."

Paolo sits up abruptly. "Hold on. I might have one last trick up my sleeve."

"Really?" I say, batting my eyes. "Spill the tea, please."

"Not yet. Let me finish getting this stuff off, and then I'll tell you. Or not. We'll see," Paolo says, a mischievous grin growing on his face.

"Oh, okay, we're gonna be like that?" I say, sliding off the arm of the couch and onto his lap.

His eyes temporarily widen. I bring my face closer to his. So close I can see the various little color smudges and cracking of foundation around the wrinkles of his eyes. All the tiny imperfections. Which are all so perfectly beautiful to me.

I kiss him. The fruity taste of my own gloss flavors my lips.

"Mmm," he says, smiling with his eyes closed. "You know, if you help me finish taking all this off, I might just tell you my plan."

I grin and hop off his lap, pulling him off the couch and into the shower. Time to finish taking the last traces of makeup off Paolo's face. He looked beautiful as me, but he looks even better as himself. And I finally get to see every last bit of him.

CHAPTER 26

DRAG AND KARAOKE.

Most people see drag as playing dress-up. Being something that you're not. Similarly, people think that karaoke is just singing someone else's song. A sad attempt at re-creating the original.

But they're wrong.

Karaoke is taking something familiar and making it your own. You don't have to sound like anyone else. You can sing to the music however you want. It doesn't matter how you sound, or even how good you sound. All that matters is how good you feel when you do it.

And drag is more than just wigs and makeup. It's an escape from the restrictions that other people put on you. It's a way of telling the world what you feel inside, of sharing your truth.

I've loved both these things for as long as I can remember. But they'd been out of my life for years.

Until the Pink Unicorn gave me back both.

And now it's time to give back to it.

During the next three weeks we organize and get the word out. Eva starts up the GiveFunds campaign immediately, and thanks to the social media promotions she's had me do with Beaucoup and Ujima, we make a good chunk of our goal. But not quite enough. The live event needs to make up for the deficit. So the performers in our group—Kat and Nine Tails, Beaucoup Buko, Ujima, and me and my mom plan special numbers for the show, strategically programmed to motivate people to donate as much cash as possible.

Paolo, happy to not have to wear drag for the event, focuses on the tech aspects. He learns how to link our Give-Funds page to SYNGX and project it on the large screen behind the stage for everyone to see as they come in. During the event, we'll be able to follow along as the total amount goes up and can even see who donates and how much, as long as they allow their profile names to be seen.

And speaking of being seen, in the spirit of continuing to be open with our loved ones, Paolo and I have told everyone that we're together. Although it's not really a surprise to anyone. Almost everybody had pretty much figured it out from the *Mulan* lip-synch performance onstage together.

My mother and Eva are ecstatic, of course. As is my dad when they tell him that Paolo is Sonny Sazon's son.

"Perfect, anak!" he said, slapping me on the back and

almost making me choke on Eva's shrimp sinigang when I told them all at a family dinner. "Now it's okay if you don't make any money in drag! Paolo will be the one to support you."

"Thanks, Dad," I said, catching Eva's glance and knowing how hard we both wanted to roll our eyes.

Kat wasn't surprised, of course, since I'd told her about my feelings for Paolo at Susan's party. There's a reason Kat's my best friend. She knows me better than anyone else. She'd sensed something was going on between Paolo and me from the beginning. And she was right.

But Tito Melboy was more than happy to not have been right.

"I was wrong what I told you about men. How they can only love you one way," he said, clutching the garment he was helping me to sew together at his place—a design of my own for the event. "Most of them are closed-minded. Afraid. But not all. Not the good ones."

"It's like you said, Uncle," I say. "How people used to respect baklas because they were beyond the gender binary. We don't have to be either masculine or feminine. We can be both. And being both can be beautiful. I think people are starting to understand this. I know I finally am."

"And Paolo certainly does."

"Yes," I say, smiling. "He does."

"And so does your dad now."

"Are you guys finally talking again?" I ask.

"Yes! All thanks to your mom. She tried to convince your

dad to talk to me for years, but she gave up after a while. It was really your return as Regina Moon Dee that made her try again. You made her remember what joy we drag queens bring to the world. She wanted to make your dad understand what that means to you and me."

"My moms are amazing," I say as Tito Melboy grins, handing me my finished garment. It's exactly what I wanted. It's all exactly what I've wanted.

ON THE FRIDAY EVENING OF THE LIVE EVENT, my dad is by my mom's side as we arrive at the Pink Unicorn, wearing his nicest suit. We've all decided to get dressed up for the night, treating it like a red-carpet event.

"Ninety-five thousand dollars so far!" my mom says, looking at the large screen behind the karaoke stage. She's dressed in a black velvet halter gown with a long string of pearls. "That's wonderful, anak!"

"But not good enough yet," I say. "We need more."

"We'll get there, pamangkin," Beaucoup says, patting my hand. She's in one of her own custom-made gowns, a high-slit number that flatters her curvy figure.

Ujima, not to be outdone by Beaucoup, has on a skintight red vinyl dress that renders me and everyone else in the Pink Unicorn speechless. "Manny's told me he's already collected close to a thousand dollars in volunteer entrance fees at the door! And we haven't even come close to capacity yet," they say. "By the way, I feel like he's been eyeing me a lot lately."

"Oh, he definitely is," Eva says. "Manny's really into you."

Ujima glances at Manny at the front entrance and winks at him. He sees this and turns so red it looks as if he might faint.

"We'll make our goal," Beaucoup says. "I have faith."

"Me too!" Kat says. She's just arrived, ready to rock the house.

Eva says to me, "Just try to have fun. In a lot of ways, you've already won."

She's right about that. My dad is here, seeing me as Regina Moon Dee in public for the first time in my entire life. He even complimented me on my outfit. Though, to be honest, I don't think he quite understands it—a strapless gown that transitions from red on the bottom to orange at my chest, topped off with a green fascinator. I call it my "mango dress." Since it's a look I've done completely on my own, it's more kitsch than high-fashion. But I still love it.

My father squinted at me when I first arrived, as if my dress were too bright. "It looks . . . tasty?" he said.

"Awkward, Dad."

"Okay. Getting a drink now," he said, hurrying off to the bar.

He's there, chatting with Bryan and Aaron, who have also reached a new understanding in their own relationship. Over the past few days, checking in with them about the fundraising campaign, it definitely feels as if they've gotten closer, as committed to working on their new father-son dynamic as they've been with the financial plan for the bar.

I catch Aaron's gaze. He sees me, smiles, and gives a friendly upturn of his chin before going back to making drinks for people.

And then there's Paolo.

Paolo and his spotlight shining on me. Paolo with my smeared lipstick on his face. Paolo with his insistence that everything about me is beautiful and worthy of love. Especially his love.

I go to him onstage, to the same spot I met him that first night, lost at the KJ controls.

But he's not lost anymore. He's figured things out, found the things he was meant to find. Including me.

"Hey, you." I lean down and give him a kiss on the cheek. He smiles, pulls my face to his, and kisses me on the lips. When I pull away, I see the imprint of my bright orange lipstick on him and laugh. "Here." I pull a tissue out of my mango-shaped bag and hand it to him. "You got a little something there."

He smirks. "Oh yeah? Why don't you clean it off me?"

I roll my eyes. But I still raise the tissue to my tongue, moisten it, and wipe his lips with it. "There. All better."

"Yep," he says, his voice low. "Much better."

"Mmkay," I say, giving him a lighter, non-stain-leaving kiss on his lips. "Before you decimate my tuck, let's get ready for the top of the show, shall we?"

It's eight p.m. The place is packed. Eva's done a fantastic job getting out the word for both the GiveFunds online campaign and tonight's fundraising event. I wave for her to come closer to the front of the stage and signal to start operating the phone that she's set up on a tripod for the livestream. Paolo hits the lights and mics.

"Hello, darlings," I say to the audience in the bar and to the livestream camera. "It's me, your host, the one and only Regina Moon Dee. Now, are you all ready? Because tonight the category is 'Purse First,' hunties! Put your money where your mouth is and come together to save this historic, fabulous Oakland bar that we all know and love."

The crowd roars, and behind me, the total surges ahead several hundred dollars more.

"The rules are simple," I say. "We've connected the SYNGX app to the GiveFunds campaign. So if you want to sing, make a donation. You want one of us to sing something special? Make a donation. You like what you hear? Make a donation. No amount is too small—or too big! Now let's ka-ka-ka-karaokaayrrrt!" I say, ending with a lip trill.

Paolo organizes the queue to begin with some of the Pink Unicorn regulars. José starts with a Bruno Mars song, raising the total up a few hundred dollars. Jenny surprisingly donates a staggering five hundred dollars all by herself when she goes up to do an encore of "Anaconda." Her enthusiastic butt-slapping must get someone online named Bootylicious in a very good mood because they donate two hundred more after she's done.

The night goes on. Mom doesn't let the shock and disappointment of no one requesting her to sing get her down and donates money herself to sing "Like a Prayer," finally scratching the itch to perform it that the church choir denied her. The total reaches a hundred thousand dollars, and she attributes the entire amount to her performance. "Oh, see? I got us to one hundred thousand! You're very welcome," she sings into the mic as she walks off. I'm surprised she doesn't drop it before she goes.

After Mom, we start bringing in the big guns.

Beaucoup Buko performs a moving rendition of "I Am What I Am" from *La Cage Aux Folles*. Ujima goes up after her. They have Paolo queue up a Mary J. Blige song, but the video screen lights up behind them with a special online request. A donation of five thousand dollars from...Emmett Aoki? *The* Hollywood hunk Emmett Aoki? He wants Ujima to sing "I'm Here," from *The Color Purple*. And not only does Emmett's huge donation move up the total that much closer to our goal, so does his song request. Ujima's heartfelt performance gets everyone on their feet at the end with a standing ovation.

"Tens, tens, tens across the board!" I say into the mic when the total moves up to one hundred ten thousand dollars.

Kat goes up next. The Nine Tails gals don't follow her, though. "Where's your band?" I ask.

"There," she says, pointing. I see them in the back, drinking and having a great time. "Too much of a logistical headache to bring all our equipment, so we recorded something ahead of time." She hands Paolo a thumb drive and gives me a big kiss on the cheek. "It's karaoke, after all."

And though the song is an original and unfamiliar to the audience, the crowd eats it up. It helps that the Nine Tails gals in the back are screaming their heads off in support, but Kat doesn't need it. She kills it like always and gets the total to one hundred twenty thousand dollars.

I'm about to step in and announce the next singer when everything stops. Or at least, I do.

I see the hooded figure from the past few karaoke nights. He's here. Standing right at the foot of the stage. He takes his hood off. I can finally see who it is.

"Ivan?" The spotlight shines on me. It feels so hot I swear I can smell smoke.

Paolo gets up from the KJ desk to stand beside me. "That's Ivan?"

Kat, who's just left the stage, rushes up again, pulling back her hair. "Oh, I will fuck up this motherfucker right now!"

"Wait!" I say, waving at them to stand down. I take a deep, cleansing breath to dispel the burning sensation inside me and force myself to face Ivan. He's just standing there, not moving, barely able to meet my eyes.

He gives a weak wave. "Hi."

My cold hands clench into fists by my side, long, French-tipped nails digging into my palms.

"I've seen you here before," I say as calmly as I can. "You came a few times the past couple of weeks. Why? And why are you back now?"

Out of the corner of my eye, I notice that Eva has reposi-
tioned the phone camera to film both Ivan and me.

"I've been trying to do it," Ivan replies. "But I couldn't get
up the courage."

"To do what?"

His mouth quivers. "To apologize for what my friends did
to you."

An uncomfortable silence falls over the bar. I feel Paolo
and Kat at my side. I can see my parents, my sister, and my
uncle. Beaucoup is being held back by Ujima, ready to rush
the stage if Ujima loosens their grip for even a second.

And while I appreciate them all being there for me, I
know I won't be needing them. Ivan's not a threat to me. Not
anymore.

"Your friends?" I say.

"Not my friends. Not for a long time."

"Why did you wait until now to apologize?"

"I didn't! I went back to Dreamland the day after those
fuckups told me they'd beat you up. Your uncle told me to
keep the hell away. I came back the next week, kept trying,
but you never returned. You disappeared. Until now. That's
why I'm here. Well, and also because of one other reason."

He turns around and waves for someone at one of the
tables in the back corner to stand up. A woman who, up
until now, has been sitting in one of the room's dark spots.

"Hi, girl!" she yells out.

I cover my mouth with my hand. "Benta Box?"

Beaucoup stops struggling against Ujima when she sees our Dreamland sister.

"I don't understand," I say.

"I didn't, either, that day," Ivan says. "I didn't understand what I saw onstage at Dreamland. But it doesn't mean that I was afraid of it. Not like my friends—my former friends. It wasn't until I kept going back to Dreamland to find you and kept getting turned away by your uncle that Benta saw me and started talking to me. She helped me make sense out of so many things. Not just what was going on at Dreamland but in my life. Because of Benta, I ditched those idiots. She even encouraged me to get sober. That's what love can do, I guess. Help someone be a better version of themselves."

He turns to Benta and blows her a kiss. She wraps her arms around herself and sways, as if giving Ivan a hug in return.

Just then, a pinging sound behind me means that the donation total on the screen has gone up. By twenty dollars. Ping, another fifty. Ping, a hundred. Ping, two.

"So," Ivan says, cowering, "apology accepted?"

I could say no. Decide to kick Ivan out of the Pink Unicorn. After all, he was the one who brought a bunch of thugs to see my uncle and me perform. A gang who tried to take away a part of me and almost succeeded.

But they didn't. I'm here now. Surrounded by people who love me. Here in this room and out there in the world, watching. What I do here, now, matters. I could either resist and fight back—or show forgiveness.

The pinging of the total continues, going up and up.

I decide to forgive.

Mostly.

"I'll accept your apology," I say with a wry smile. "But only if you do something for us."

Ivan's face starts to pale.

I look straight at the camera. "Years ago, I quit being Regina Moon Dee because people Ivan knew assaulted my uncle and me in an alley for being drag queens. But I refuse to give in to fear. And hate. I choose love and forgiveness. But only if Ivan sings."

The tension in the room breaks. I feel everyone's delight in my demand.

"Uh, what?" Ivan says.

"What song, you ask?" I say. "Well, that's up to all of you out there. Whoever donates the most money in the next two minutes gets to pick the song. Now's your chance to make this guy squirm."

The donations rush in. *Ping, ping, ping, ping, ping.* With every sound, Ivan's color fades more.

After the two minutes are up, I turn around to look at the screen. Someone from New York City has donated three hundred dollars.

"Baby!" Beaucoup cries out, noticing the profile name on the screen.

I make a heart sign at the camera. "So happy you could join us this late at night, Baby Buko! And what song have you chosen for Ivan?"

Three dots blink on the screen as she types her answer.

Creep. By Radiohead.

The Pink Unicorn crowd laughs at the excellent choice Baby has made. "The donor has spoken, Ivan. Now hop on up here!"

Though I have to pull him onstage, he eventually gets up. And despite his entire body shivering from stage fright, he sings. Horribly. So badly, in fact, that it makes me wonder if he's ever heard the song before. If he's ever heard music before, period.

But it doesn't matter. The audience appreciates his attempt, and the donation total moves up even more. At the end, Benta Box leads the audience in clapping while a shell-shocked Ivan hands me back the mic.

"You're forgiven," I say, taking back the mic. "Now get your bony white ass off my stage." I slap him on the butt as he jumps off and hurries back to Benta's open arms.

We manage to get in a few more singers giving generous donations, taking us all the way to one hundred twenty-five thousand. At 10:50, it's time to start bringing an end to our streaming event. I know that it's finally time for me to sing and hope that I can carry us over to the finish line. I ask Paolo to close out the queue and program "All By Myself."

But when the screen updates, it says: "Regina Moon Dee and Paolo—Come What May." The total moves up by $1,000. A donation from him.

"Paolo?" I say.

He takes his mic off the KJ table and walks over to me, joining me in the light onstage. Everything about him glows.

"I know 'All By Myself' is your favorite song, Regina, but you're not all by yourself anymore," he says. "So how about a duet? With me?"

My eyes water. I nod silently.

He smiles. And the world around me just disappears. Everything he says to me next is to me, and me only.

"For so long I've felt lost in my life," he says. "Like everyone else around me had things figured out while I just kept stumbling along. Until you showed up one night, looking as lost as I was. And I somehow knew that I needed to make you feel like you weren't lost. That you'd been found. By me."

He takes my hand and interlaces his fingers with mine.

"And then when I saw you as Regina Moon Dee and you asked me to keep your secret, that's when I knew—you weren't lost. You were just hiding. And everything I did with you afterward was because I wanted you to see in yourself what I saw in you. Someone who was strong and beautiful.

"But you helped me to see, too. You helped me accept that I need to find my own path. So I want you and everyone else to know that I've decided to open up my own restaurant. Right here, next to the Pink Unicorn. Maybe even tear down a wall and connect the two worlds, just like we're connected now," he says, his hand gripping mine. "So thank you, Regina Moon Dee. I want to sing this song with you because everything in it is true. The world seems perfect now. Everything is so much clearer. No matter what else happens, I'll love you. Come what may."

Ordinarily, I'd attempt to wipe any tears away with the tips of my fingers to avoid messing up my makeup. But there's no point in doing that now. My face is a complete and utter mess. Mascara and eyeliner run down my face as I turn to Paolo and kiss him.

Ping.

We turn to look at the screen mid-kiss. Someone has donated...holy crap. That can't possibly be right. One hundred thousand dollars?

The entire place erupts with cheers.

We look at the donor's profile name as it scrolls up. TheSunnySeason.

The following words appear in the chat box: For the restaurant and bar together, okay, anak? I'm proud of you.

"Dad," Paolo whispers, his eyes glistening.

Everyone in the Pink Unicorn is on their feet, clapping and shouting and hugging each other, but when Paolo pulls me in again to kiss me, the cacophony around us disappears.

He smiles and turns around to start the karaoke. And we sing. Everyone else joins us, but I don't hear any of them.

All I hear is Paolo's voice joining mine. Off-key, but still sweet, lovely, and perfect.

EPILOGUE

SIX MONTHS LATER

"So, you going to be working here permanently, sis?" I ask Eva, watching her make turon. She takes thinly cut slices of saba—or what we like to call "baby"—bananas, dips them into brown sugar, and places them into a spring roll wrapper with thin ribbons of canned langka, or jackfruit, still glistening from their sweet syrup.

"I keep trying to hire her. But she keeps saying no," Paolo says. "Eva, you have what it takes to be a professional cook."

"Aww. Thanks, Paolo. I'm okay to just pop in every now and then and learn a few things from you. The real master chef."

"I wouldn't go that far. But thank you, regardless," Paolo says. "Hey, don't forget to add my little secret ingredient."

"Oh, right!" Eva says, pulling a bowl of chopped candied ginger closer to her. She sprinkles bits of it on top of the filling before rolling everything up and placing it on the sheet pan next to Paolo at the stove. The air crackles with the sound of him dropping each one into oil and turning them to cook equally on both sides. When they're golden brown, he dunks them into a pan of freshly prepared caramel and sets them on a serving platter.

I reach out to take one, but Paolo points at me with his kitchen tongs. "Not yet! They're too hot. And watch your scarf."

"Oops, thank you," I say, sweeping back my colorful jacquard pashmina wrap. I'd tied it into a festive ascot, but it had come loose and was dangling dangerously close to the hot oil. "I wouldn't want to suddenly go up in flames."

"Not any more than you usually do, at least," Paolo says.

I give him a dramatic, outraged look. He laughs and gives me a quick kiss, leaving a trace of the caramel he's been tasting on my lips.

In the past few months, I've welcomed back my childhood flair for over-the-top clothing, jettisoning my old, boring wardrobe and buying new pieces. I've added back silk shirts, sheer textiles, scarves—as well as even more genderfluid clothing like crop-tops and skirts. Today, I've paired the scarf-ascot with a pink polka-dot romper. Admittedly, not such a great outfit for a restaurant kitchen, but I feel damn cute in it.

"Well, Eva, if you ever change your mind about working

here, let me know," Paolo says. "We could really use the help. I never expected we'd be getting this much business this quickly."

He didn't. But I did. Not only because I knew how talented Paolo was, but because all the stars seemed to align.

With the GiveFunds donations we received, plus Sonny Sazon's financial assistance, we were not only able to get the Pink Unicorn financially stable, but we were also able to implement all the renovation plans my mom had helped me put together previously, and more. The interior was repainted, the furniture pieces mended, the awning cleaned, and the sculpture sign outside replaced with a shiny, new pink unicorn.

Paolo was also able to lease and fix up the abandoned space next door, turning it into SAZON, his casual, street-fare-style Filipino restaurant. As per his dad's request, a pass-through window was created in the shared wall between the two spaces, allowing Pink Unicorn patrons to order food. In the months that followed, Paolo planned the menus, cooked the meals, and stayed open late for the huge crowds that had started to regularly appear for all the ongoing Pink Unicorn events: a new open mic night, live music night (when Kat and the Nine Tails often performed), a *RuPaul's Drag Race* viewing party hosted by Benta Box, and, of course, karaoke night. Hosted by yours truly.

"Okay, you can take one already," Paolo says, handing me the tray of cooked turon. "I see you salivating."

"Only for you, honey," I say, grabbing one before he

changes his mind. I take a bite. My teeth crunch through the thin candy coating and crisp wrapper before sinking into the gooey center. I taste the sweetness of the bananas, the tenderness of the langka, and the bright punch of ginger, all in one glorious bite.

"Oh. My. God," I say, my eyelids fluttering with ecstasy. "Eva, I have to hand it to you. You've improved leaps and bounds learning how to cook from Paolo," I say. "You sure you don't want to go into the restaurant business?"

"Maybe as a backup plan," Eva says, grinning. "Because I've been meaning to tell you. I interviewed for a new job, and I just heard back. I got the position!"

"A new job?" I ask. "But I thought you were happy working at the hospital?"

"I liked it okay, but this position's way better. Say hello to the new Youth Services Manager at the LGBTQ Community Center in Oakland."

"Are you serious? That's great, Eva!" Paolo says.

"Thanks! I don't know how much of a difference I'll be able to make, but I want to try to make sure kids don't have to go through what you did, Rex."

"You're going to make a huge difference in so many people's lives," I say. "I'm so proud of you, sis."

I hug her. She smells of fried food, and it's wonderful. She smells like home.

My mom pokes her head into the kitchen. "Hoy, why don't you all come out and join us for the rest of the meal? Dito na kayo!"

"We're coming!" Eva says.

"Can you take the turon out?" Paolo asks us.

Eva and I carry out the tray as well as a huge plate of ube crinkle cookies that Paolo had baked earlier. Everyone else is at the big table in SAZON's dining room, finishing up a huge brunch. Mom and Dad, who have come right after church, Kat, starving after a late-night set with Nine Tails in Berkeley, and my uncle, still recovering from a full evening of performing at OASIS and a long night with—

"That Bryan! Susmaryosep, he kept me up all night!" Tito Melboy says, fanning himself. "I'm telling you, he's insatiable."

My mom cackles and slaps Tito Melboy's shoulder while my dad rolls his eyes. "Rex," he says, "are you sure you can't just sneak a beer in here from next door? I need a drink."

"Still working on the liquor license. For now, it's one way only," Paolo says, emerging from the kitchen with a tray filled with glasses of fresh buko juice. "These glasses of coconut juice will have to do. In honor of Tito Melboy, of course."

"I approve!" Tito Melboy says. "Maraming salamat."

"Paolo, the fried pork belly is amazing," Kat says with her mouth full. "I'll take a bucket back for the band."

"It's called lechon kawali," I say. "And Paolo's is special. He smokes it at the end."

"Something I tried out at AquaMarine," Paolo says, winking at me. "Oh, sorry, guys. Just noticed you're out of water. I'll go get more."

"I'll join you." I stick my arm in Paolo's and accompany him back to the kitchen.

We sneak to the refrigerator where he's hidden a small bottle of champagne. Not for serving, for us only. He pours us two glasses.

"You know," I say, "once you get the liquor license, you'll really be connected to the Pink Unicorn. You give them food, and they'll give you drinks in return."

"It's more of a commitment, for sure," he says, sipping his drink and eyeing me. "And speaking of commitments, have you been thinking about my offer?"

About a month ago, Paolo suggested we move in together and offered up his place for us to live. And though I do want us to be together, I'm not quite sure about the arrangement.

"It's just, everything is here in the East Bay. My family, the Pink Unicorn, your restaurant."

"Well, maybe we could look into getting a place together? Like here in Oakland?"

I smile. "I like that idea."

He puts his glass on the counter, does the same with mine, and takes me in his arms. "Good. For now, I'll just have to settle for having a stash of my things at your place."

After the big fundraising event was over, Paolo had come back to my condo. I'd gotten into my mango dress in a hurry that night, so my trunk was still open with all its contents scattered around it.

"It really is a beautiful trunk," Paolo said.

I had kneeled down on the ground and started trying to organize things. "It's a total mess, though. I'm going to have to reorganize everything."

"Or hear me out," Paolo had said, gently taking my hand. "Don't put any of it back. Keep your drag with the rest of your clothes in your closet. Where it belongs."

I'd never done that before. Never given myself the permission to put my drag next to my day-to-day clothes. I'd always kept them apart, as if they had no right to comingle.

But I liked Paolo's idea. My Regina clothes were equally as important as my Rex clothes.

"I guess I can figure out some other way to use the trunk," I had said. "Maybe as a coffee table?"

"Hmmm." Paolo stooped down and slid the trunk over until it lay at the foot of my bed. "How about here? Instead of keeping your drag in it, I'll keep a bunch of my things."

His things. Not Regina Moon Dee's. There seemed to be a bit of poetry in that. We'd turn my trunk from where I hid a part of myself to a place where a part of him could openly stay.

"And why would you want to keep a bunch of your junk in my trunk?" I asked.

"For whenever, you know, I just happen to sleep over?"

The look on his face was the same one he has now in the kitchen of his restaurant. Earnest, and excited, and slightly devilish. He leans in and kisses me deeply. So deeply that we fog up his glasses.

"Well then," I say, catching my breath. I pick up my champagne again. "Here's to SAZON. And to you, the new king of Filipino cuisine."

"And to you," Paolo says, clinking his glass against mine before kissing me one more time. "My karaoke queen."

ACKNOWLEDGMENTS

FIRST OF ALL, thank you, dear reader, for choosing to spend time with Rex and Paolo. This book is my love letter to karaoke, drag, and Filipino artistry and culture. I hope it brought you joy. If so, then I've accomplished what I set out to do.

To my incredible agent, Gina Panettieri, thank you for being the world's best agent and for taking a first look at my story. It all could've gone horribly wrong without you steering me in the right direction.

Thank you to my editor, Alex Logan, for helping me shape my novel into something so much better than I had envisioned. I can't tell you how much I appreciate your insight, guidance, and kindness. I hope our partnership continues for many, many books to come.

To Estelle Hallick and Dana Cuadrado, even if you were paid ten times your current salary, it wouldn't be enough.

ACKNOWLEDGMENTS

Thank you from the bottom of my heart for tirelessly supporting me and my queer Filipino love stories.

Thanks to Abigail Lee for the beautiful book cover. It's joyous and sassy and so, so gay (which means it is absolutely perfect).

Maraming salamat to Spens Soria for reviewing my Filipino details and, in particular, making sure the sections regarding queer life in the Philippines were on point. I'm also grateful to Eric Aviles aka Vanity Ytinav for providing her drag queen expertise.

Diane Paulus and Randy Weiner, Barry Ivan, and the Oberlin Drag Ball—thank you for giving me the opportunity to explore drag in a safe and welcoming environment (though I wish I'd had more help in the makeup department)!

Thank you to the incredible authors I've met over the past year while promoting *All the Right Notes*. I was blessed with the best debut year ever, in no small part due to the wonderful friends I made at all the conferences, book festivals, and readings I was lucky enough to be a part of.

Many thanks to my colleagues and friends in the Writers Grotto and Babylon Salon, who all continue to lift me up and inspire me. I am so enriched by being a part of these two wonderful writing communities.

Mom, thank you for filling my life with music and literature, for always embracing my love of the arts, and for never dismissing my passion for performing. It's not a surprise that all us kids are musicians in some form or another—your beautiful singing voice was the soundtrack to our lives.

ACKNOWLEDGMENTS

And to my dear husband, Peter, thank you for being there for me all last year, even during the times when I could barely be there for myself. I don't know what I would have done without you by my side. I will love you for a thousand years, until my dying day.

ABOUT THE AUTHOR

DOMINIC LIM has enjoyed a lifelong love affair with music. Dominic holds a master's from Indiana University Jacobs School of Music, is an alum of the Oberlin Conservatory of Music, and has sung with numerous professional choral ensembles. As a proud member of the Actors' Equity Association, he has performed off-Broadway and in regional productions throughout the United States. Although he probably shouldn't admit to having favorites, the thrill of singing "This Is the Hour" in the chorus of *Miss Saigon* still pops up in his dreams.

Dom supports his local writing community as a member of the Writers Grotto and as a cohost of San Francisco's Babylon Salon. He lives in Oakland with his loving and supportive husband, Peter, and their whiny cat, Phoebe.